Whisper
to the
Wind

Marianne K. Martin

2024

Bywater Books

Copyright © 2024 Marianne K. Martin

Print ISBN: 978-1-61294-305-3

Bywater Books First Edition: October 2024

Printed in the United States of America on acid-free paper.

Cover design: TreeHouse Studio

Bywater Books
PO Box 3671
Ann Arbor MI 48106-3671

www.bywaterbooks.com

The lyrics excerpted in this novel are either in the public domain or referenced as permitted under Fair Use practices and are as follows:

"At Seventeen," 1975, by Janis Ian.
"Bells Will Be Ringing," 1960, by Charles Brown and Gene Redd.
"It's Beginning to Look a Lot Like Christmas," 1951
by Meredith Wilson.
"I Found a Place in My Heart," 2019 by Dom James
and Tommy Antonio.
"Baby It's Cold Outside," 1944 by Frank Loesser.
"(Your Love Keeps Lifting Me) Higher and Higher," 1967,
by Gary Jackson, Raynard Miller, and Carl Smith.
"We Are the World," 1985, by Michael Jackson and Lionel Ritchie.

For Jo

Listen to the wind
It talks
Listen to the silence
It speaks
Listen to your heart
It knows

Native American Proverb

Author's Note

During the years that I taught in the public school system, it was common for teachers to spend an immeasurable amount of unpaid time working with and for their students. Sometimes it was their open classroom door during lunch for extra help or just to talk about what concerned them. It was attending sports events, school plays, and music programs. Sometimes it was brokering dental care for a student whose family had no health care and picking up a student in the mornings to be sure they got to school on time. Or organizing a group of parents to take a student, who was living with her mother out of a car, into their homes so that she could legally stay in school. Always, it was what needed to be done. It was, and is, what teachers do.

In this current social and political environment, public schools are facing considerable challenges. Parents, students, and teachers emerging from a pandemic have all been affected. There has always been a lot asked of our underfunded, overloaded educational systems, even more so now. Districts across the country have had to adapt and change their policies, procedures, and expectations. I am thankful to several educators for sharing those with me so that I was able to fashion a realistic fictional school system set in today's social and political environment.

They also shared personal feelings and experiences that raised my already high respect for their dedication. The struggle is real, and it is ongoing.

Teachers, we must remember, are human. They worry and cry, laugh and love. They succeed and fail, find energy where they can, and fight exhaustion. So, I have centered this story around a teacher and a parent, a school and its students because what happens in our schools affects us all. Sometimes even if, and who, you love. After all, most teachers do have a life outside of school. And as Mr. Man says, later in the story, "I just figure that if *my* personal life don't have anything to do with keepin' this school runnin', then hers shouldn't have anything to do with her teaching."

Marianne K. Martin
June, 2024

Chapter 1

SUMMER SIZZLE

Wall-to-wall women. Beautiful, talented women. They filled the large conference room while red, blue, and gold lights colored their excitement. An excitement that tempted Johanna Beals to spread her arms wide, twirl like Julie Andrews on the mountaintop and take it all in.

She moved further into the room and joined the fray to congratulate and mingle with the musicians and singers of the Great Lakes Music Festival. She gripped each hand, engaged each directly, and said the words personally, sincerely: "What a beautiful performance." Over and over, she collected their smiles and hugs as special treasures.

Toni Reynolds took both of Johanna's hands and pulled them tightly to her substantial chest. "What a blessing this festival has been," she said with a squeeze of her hands. "It fills my soul to be able to sing with my sisters again."

Minutes later she was enveloped in the thick, strong hug of Dee Wilson. With the hint of an unusually pure contralto evident even in her speaking voice, Dee said, "Thank you for all your hard work this week." She released Johanna and added,

"If it weren't for the village, the festival would not have been possible."

Hard work, Johanna considered. No, not hard at all. If they could only know how much she had enjoyed the past week. And celebrating with everyone after a flawless show was the *crème-de-la-crème*. She smiled to herself but was snatched from her thoughts by an excited voice.

"Hey, there you are," exclaimed Jenna, a rugby player who worked as hard as a volunteer as she did on the field. "Come on," she said, grabbing Johanna's arm, "let's hit the food table before they start the video of the show."

Kay, a high-energy volunteer with the frame of a teenage boy, joined them. "Oh, my God! Will you look at this spread."

"I know," Jenna replied. "I'm going to sample everything I'm not supposed to have. I figure these last twelve pounds aren't going anywhere tonight. I'll have my weight down by the time league play starts this season."

"Diets are meant to be broken," Kay added, passing by the salads and adding a plate of various desserts to a large portion of chicken marsala. "If you didn't break 'em, they wouldn't exist."

"Somehow, that makes perfect sense," Johanna said, smiling. "I figure we did enough physically all week that whatever we eat tonight won't make one bit of difference." She added a scoop of this and a bit of that to her plate. "We built sets and painted them, moved equipment on and off the stage, chased down—"

"Anything the stage manager needed," Jenna said, laughing as she claimed a tall, round table.

Yep, anything, Johanna thought. She scanned the room between bites for the object of her week-long private fantasy. *Miya. Her name is Miya. Stage manager. Fantasy.*

"We *did* work hard," Kay added.

"And I'd do it again next week," Johanna said, "if it meant putting on another show like tonight."

"The best one I've ever worked on. No miscues, no glitches,"

Jenna added. "I can't wait to see the video, to see what the audience saw."

Johanna made another glance around, looking for the shock of loose dark curls, clipped close on one side. But still no sign of Miya. Surely, she would want to celebrate tonight, too.

"Hey, everyone's moving," Kay said, picking up her dessert plate. "Come on, they're about to start the video."

They joined the others—organizers, volunteers, and performers—at the far end of the room where a huge screen occupied most of the back wall. The overhead lights dimmed to dark as a stage spot shone a light in purples and blues on the screen.

Moments later Johanna became the audience for performances that had been made all the richer by her time backstage. She knew the preparation, the essence of each performance, the soul of what she was watching. She saw each performance from the inside out.

Emma Baker's commanding figure filled the screen, a brilliant white suit contrasting with deep brown skin. Her flawless voice, Johanna knew, had been warmed by one shot of whiskey, and could now be heard coming from behind Johanna as well as from the speakers on either side of the screen. She turned and smiled as Emma sang.

When Dee Wilson took the stage under softened light and sang "Your love keeps lifting me higher and higher," Johanna visualized her kissing the silver charm hanging around her neck before she took the stage—a private dedication the audience never saw.

The lighting changed again, flooding the stage in deep reds and flashes of orange, a dramatic setting for Demi Lewis's powerful timpani and bass drum performance. Johanna watched closely, grateful that Demi had taught her early in the week what to do if she cramped. She looked now for confirmation that kneading the susceptible trapezius had loosened the muscle and relieved Demi's pain. The movements were strong, powerful, no easing up, no missed beats, as the felt-tipped mallets struck their beat, delivering a dynamic rhythm that could be felt reverberating from the floor. And with timing just as perfect, Johanna felt a hand on her back and Demi's voice close to her ear. "Couldn't have done *that* without you. Thank you," she said and continued further into the crowd.

She couldn't say exactly when, but at some point, as she watched, Johanna stopped noticing the lighting and the timing, the ways each of the performances were presented, and began simply enjoying them. Pure, each performance like a deep breath of air after a spring rain. She floated on that air through the finale, swaying with the rest of the women, joining her voice to the crescendo of notes carrying the words "We Are the World" into the rafters. We *are* the world, she thought, every color, every shape, every one—blending, harmonizing, pure and true. Lifting the whole. Stronger together.

The feeling carried her past the last lingering note, away from the screen and directly into the path of a zing of electricity. There *she* was, standing on the edge of the crowd, looking right at her. Miya. Blue-grey eyes locked intensely on her own. The corners of Miya's mouth lifted slightly into the beginning of a smile, and then a step in Johanna's direction. But before she could take a second step, someone took her arm and turned her away.

Then, just as abruptly, Jenna grabbed Johanna's arm and snatched away the chance for another glance. "Come on," she said, "let's party!"

The lights came up, a DJ called for requests, and there was no need for arm-twisting. They made their way to the bar, came away with margaritas, and claimed a tall round table. "*That*," Johanna began, raising her glass toward the big screen, "was beautiful."

The rims of their glasses met with a clink and Kay added, "Job well done."

"Oooh, this is good," Johanna said after a sip of her drink.

"Yeah," Jenna grinned over the rim of her glass, "I'm gonna want another one of these."

Johanna nodded at her. "Hey, since this *is* a party, *I* suggest we party." The alcohol warmed its path down her throat and dance music moved her hips and shoulders where she stood. It was a good feeling, a young feeling.

"Come on, you two," Jenna said, "the music is calling."

"Oh. God," Kay replied with a spark of excitement in her eyes, "I haven't danced in way too long."

"Me either," Johanna added. "That is unless YouTube dance workouts count."

Jenna laughed, set her drink down and grabbed Johanna's hand. "Okay, time to let loose."

The energy in the room kicked into high gear. The beat of the music drew women together, enjoying the freedom of movement, enjoying each other. A contagious enjoyment. Johanna was alive in the moment with no worries or responsibilities to limit it, laughing at Jenna's antics. No, the Funky Chicken did not meet the beat—it completely ignored the beat. But it was amusing and fun and made people laugh.

Kay joined with her own rendition, but before Johanna could be coaxed, someone covered her raised hand from behind and turned her, directly into paralyzing blue-grey. Johanna managed only the backend of a shallow breath. She tried a deeper breath, searching for a word, a greeting, anything. But everything seemed to have stopped: the music, the celebration, breathing. A magnetism held her tightly in the moment, unable to turn away. *She* was supposed to be a fantasy. Miya. Just a fantasy. Yet, *this*, this was no fantasy.

One dance. What's the harm? She opened her palm against Miya's and felt the warmth travel from her arm to her body.

Then, she met Miya's other hand held high in the air and mimicked the rhythm of the music. Any hesitation melted away under Miya's emerging smile. It drew her in, teased a smile in return, and altered the world.

It felt good—to be pursued, desired. To have *this* woman move in close, to feel her body moving with the music and brushing against her own. The warmth of their closeness, the feel of the hand trailing over her hip as Miya circled close behind her, took over. Nothing challenged the feeling, not the women dancing around them, not the lights, not the music—there was nothing except the sensations from Miya's hand sliding across her abdomen, and breasts pressing against her back. Johanna wanted nothing beyond that moment.

Yet, in the next moment, she realized it was no longer true. The music morphed into a slower beat, and she felt the length of Miya's body press against her. Her movement matched the sensuousness of the beat, the words sultry in her ear, "I found a place in my heart, I found a light in the dark." Now there was more than enjoying the sensations, more than the desire to stay in the moment. Now there was anticipation—for the warmth and the dance to continue, for the *next* moment.

Johanna turned into the space only a breath away from Miya and looked into her eyes long enough for the message to be clear, long enough for Miya's fingers to trace a feather touch along her cheek and down the tender skin of her neck. She pulled her eyes away and rested the side of her head against Miya's, welcoming the embrace that pulled her into the rhythm of the music, the movement of the hips and body pressed against her.

If only she could hold this feeling, stop time, Johanna thought, keep the freshness of it. If only she could save it just as it was, untainted by should or shouldn't, free of before or after. All she wanted was to enjoy the feel of this woman's body, warming her, tempting her, moving her to the sensuous beat of the music. That's all.

Reality, though, would not allow it. The touch of Miya's lips, warm against the base of her neck, made that clear. She should have pulled away. She didn't. She let the sensations sear their path, knowing what they demanded of her body. Desire, free and untethered, took over.

Miya lifted her head, brushing warm breath over Johanna's cheek. Her lips teased light touches to Johanna's soft, full lips, waiting for permission, waiting for Johanna. It wasn't a conscious decision. Johanna pressed into a kiss, tasting of alcohol and absolution, and for a moment lost all reasoning. She wanted what that kiss promised, and to lose herself in the warm wetness of this woman's lips. And she did—until the kiss deepened, and reality forced a decision.

Johanna slowly turned her head and rested her forehead against Miya's cheek.

"Where have you been?" Miya whispered.

The answer was easy and true. "Looking for the yellow brick road."

The music changed again, livelier now, and Johanna eased from Miya's embrace. She chanced one last look into the eyes that had captured her all week, dancing with multi-colored highlights. Were they highlights of Johanna's own life that she saw reflected there? Sparkles of blue, touching the loneliness. Of gold and silver, dancing sparkles of long-felt promise and hope. And red, deep and sultry, stirring desire. A life Miya could know nothing about. One held in check for a long time.

"I have to go," Johanna said. And the next moment, she made her way through the celebrating crowd toward the door.

Outside, with the music muffled in the darkness and the night air cooling the dampness from her skin, she ran down the block to her car—to her life.

Chapter 2

FRIDAY NIGHT LIGHTS

The emerald green football field gleamed brightly below the black void above the lights. Stark white uniforms and the gold helmets of the home team Falcons were easily distinguished from the bright orange of their crosstown rivals. It was the one game, the yearly event, that guaranteed packed stands and heightened emotions.

This year, the chance for a Falcon victory looked impossible. They were down four points with eighteen seconds left in the game and the ball in the possession of their rivals. All the other team had to do was run out the clock. But a backup quarterback with adrenalin surging and a chance to impress his coach threw a pass that was intercepted by the Falcon cornerback on the thirty-four-yard line with a path down the sideline to the end zone. Kayla Beals and her friends were on their feet with the rest of the fans in the home team bleachers, pumping their fists and yelling for a miracle.

But a touchdown-saving push out-of-bounds stopped both the run and the clock on the seven-yard line with eleven seconds left in the game.

"One play," Kayla said, grabbing Zack's arm. "There's still time for one play."

"Two, if they try a pass," Zack replied.

Almost everyone remained standing through the team's last timeout. And when they took the field again, it was as if Zack had read the coach's mind. The call was a quick pass to the tight end just over the line on the left side of the end zone. A quick flick, on target, with everyone holding their breath. But the defense was good, and the pass was batted down, stopping the clock once again with six seconds left.

One last play, one last chance for victory, with the call to the Falcons' star tailback, Josh Carter. It was a clean hand-off with perfectly executed blocking by the line. A momentary hole in the defense, and Josh jutted through. Just two steps from the end zone, he lunged forward, players collapsing on top of him. Kayla held her breath, along with fans from both sides, and waited for the signal. The bouncing of the metal bleachers stilled under her feet as fans stood silent, nervously watching the officials, waiting for their arms to be thrust straight up, and ready to shout and throw their own arms up in victory. But there was no signal, only the officials clearing players away to locate the ball.

And when they did, it wasn't Josh leaping to his feet. A player in bright orange jumped up from the two-yard line, holding the ball high and starting a roar of celebration from the visiting bleachers. It was over. The game lost on a last-second fumble. And in the home team bleachers, deflation, a collective exhale of disappointment and loss.

"Nooo," Kayla droned. "We were so close."

"Yeah," Zack returned, his voice stripped of its earlier excitement. "But, like my mom's boyfriend says, 'close only counts in horseshoes.'"

"It was exciting, though," Kayla added, following others down the steps of the bleachers. "It was exciting, and they never gave up."

The teams finished going through the congratulatory line, a difficult thing to do with emotions so high. The throng of students and parents, slumped shouldered and quieter than usual, made their way to the parking lot.

"Your mom's picking us up in the staff lot?" Zack asked.

"Yeah. You know my mom, always knows the quickest way to navigate any situation."

Friends and classmates peeled off down rows of cars to meet parents and rides home as shouts of celebration carried across the parking lot from the line of visiting buses.

Zack shoved his hands into the pockets of his jean jacket and began a solo version of the school fight song. "Birds of prey, talons strong, Falcons soar— "

His attempt to lighten the mood, though, was shortened by angry shouts coming from the next row of cars. They stopped and saw a bear of a man in a camouflage jacket shoving someone in front of him.

"What the fuck was that?" he yelled and shoved again. "You little pussy!" Then he raised his arm and brought it down with a loud slap that knocked someone into view. Josh Carter, cowering and backing against the car. "You fucking pussy," the man spit through a full reddish beard. "Couldn't hang onto a football for two more fucking yards. Is that what I taught you? Is it?"

That's when Josh noticed them, locking eyes as they witnessed his humiliation. "Fuck. That's his father," Zack whispered.

"Whoa," Kayla whispered back. "What should we do?" The humiliation continued as they stood paralyzed, afraid to move, afraid not to. Kayla grabbed Zack's arm; she didn't know why.

His father slapped Josh again and slammed him against the car. "Get out of this uniform," he said, grabbing a fistful of jersey. "You're an embarrassment," he shouted, only inches from his son's face. "Get your sorry ass home on your own," he added with a full-hand push to Josh's face. Dan Carter turned abruptly and stormed past his son toward his truck.

Kayla and Zack froze in place, unsure of what to do. Kayla wanted to say something, something that would help. But there wasn't time. Her search was quickly stymied when Josh squared his shoulders, stared hard back at them and snarled, "What are you looking at?" He lunged threateningly toward them and added, "Get the fuck out of here."

He didn't have to say it again. Kayla and Zack turned and ran the rest of the way to the staff parking lot, scrambling into the car, and breathlessly talking over each other to fill Johanna in on what had happened.

"Mom, what should we do?" Kayla asked.

Johanna looked out across the sparsely occupied lot and thought for a moment. "I don't know, honey. It's usually not a good idea to interfere in someone else's family business. We may not agree with how they handle things, but . . ." She started the car. "I'll drive through the big lot and around the block in case he didn't get a ride home."

She circled the block twice with no sight of Josh, then drove through the almost empty lot. "Well," Johanna said, watching as she headed for the exit, "I'm guessing that he either got a ride with friends or his dad had second thoughts."

"It doesn't seem right to be punished for making a mistake," Kayla offered.

"No," Johanna replied, "it doesn't." She pulled the car out into traffic. "I was just thinking that it might make Josh feel better if someone let him know that." When neither of them responded, Johanna asked, "Do either of you know Josh, beyond football?"

They both shook their heads. Then Kayla offered, "His girlfriend has a locker next to mine. She's not very nice, though."

"Well, everyone makes mistakes," Johanna said. "But he's a good football player, right?"

"Yeah," Zack replied. "I overheard some of the guys saying there were going to be college recruiters at the game."

"Big mistake in a big game," Johanna said, "and big hopes. It's no excuse, but it explains why his dad lost it."

"I don't see how that helps," Kayla replied with a frown.

"No, I don't either."

Chapter 3

SEE NO EVIL

Josh Carter sauntered down the hall, his arm draped heavily around the shoulders of his girlfriend. After he fist-bumped two of his teammates, he noticed Zack heading in the other direction on the other side of the hall. He pointed to get his girlfriend's attention and asked, "Who's that geek?"

Julie looked as they passed him. "Oh," she said, "Zack somebody. Remember when that woman came to school before the shutdown, drunk on her ass? That was his mother. She was stumbling down the halls carrying a lunch bag, going in and out of classrooms calling for him." She mimicked a drunken slur and added, "Zack, Zack baby, I'm so sorry. I forgot your lunch."

"So, ol' Zack's mother is a lush," he replied with a grin.

"Yeah, everyone was laughing. She could barely stand up. It took Mr. Hogan and the principal to get her down to the office. They had to call the police to take her home, and they had to have her car towed. She'd left it running in the middle of the parking lot."

"Hey," he said, releasing her from under his arm, "you go on to class." He watched as Zack exited the south-end doors leading to the football stadium. "I gotta take care of somethin'."

Zack clipped the art pass to the cover of his sketch pad and pushed open the grey metal door of the back exit. His new pass allowed him to draw wherever his assignments took him. Today, his assignment was an ink drawing of the stadium for the athletic department, something that could be used for a variety of applications.

The spot at the top of the concrete steps just outside the exit had a perfect view of the football stadium. He settled on the first step, opened his art pad and rested it on his knees. His pencil glided over the paper with free easy strokes, outlining the surrounding brick wall and the iron gate entrance. He loved that even after renovations, they had kept the unique historic character that set their stadium apart from other schools.

"You skippin' class?" The voice from close behind him startled Zack.

He turned sharply to find Josh staring down at him. "Oh," he replied, "no. Mr. Parker gave me a pass to do a drawing for the athletic department." He refocused on the sketch, but could feel Josh still looming large and close. He hadn't forgotten Kayla's mother's words about Josh needing to hear someone say what a good player he was, but this was the first chance he'd had all week, and he didn't know how to start the conversation. The silence from Josh, though, was even more uncomfortable, so Zack tried. "What colleges are you thinking about?"

"What's it to ya? It's none of your business."

The tone of Josh's response stopped any question of why skipping class was any of *his* concern. Josh was used to lining up behind his guard, counting on him to pull from the line and lead the block on the sweep. Protected, confident. But Zack had no such protection, no the-team-has-your-back confidence. Yet, he tried again. "I'm not trying to be nosey. I just think you're a really good player— "

"Yeah, nosey like last Friday night?"

Zack turned on the step, looked up, and strained to inch back a little distance from an imposing Josh. "I was just waiting for my ride home."

Josh moved a step closer, negating the little bit of distance Zack had gained. "I was thinking about inviting you to a party next weekend. Mostly football players and friends."

The words alone seemed to be a simple invitation. Josh's expression, though, despite its subtlety, sent a different message. There was something about it. "I don't really know anyone," Zack replied.

"That doesn't matter as long as you bring your mother's stash."

Zack stared at him. "What do you mean?"

The hint of a smirk that Josh had offered earlier was now full and clear. "Everyone knows your mother's a lush. Don't pretend you don't raid her hiding places when she's passed out drunk."

Even when the incident was fresh, when many had seen it firsthand, nobody had said anything like that to Zack. Responses darted back and forth in his head. He had to answer, didn't he? He couldn't just ignore it like he had the looks and rumors when it first happened, could he? Zack gathered his sketch pad and rose from the step. A step higher and a half a foot taller, Josh loomed above him. Zack backed down to a lower step. "There's nothing in the house," he replied. "My mother isn't drinking."

"Yeah?" Josh snarled with a cock of his head. "You're either lyin' or denyin'."

"I'm not doing either," Zack replied. "I couldn't deny it when my mother's struggle was right out there for everyone to see. Why would I lie when she's doing so good?"

"Well," Josh said, stepping down into Zack's personal space, "maybe you just think that that makes you better than everyone else."

"We all handle our struggles the best way we can."

"We?" He pushed Zack's chest, making him grab the railing to keep from falling. "There ain't no we."

Chapter 4

DEEP IN SCHOOL DAZE

"Is everything okay?" The question, asked by Ginny Westmoreland, co-owner of the Bright-Westmoreland Insurance Company, pulled Johanna's attention from her phone screen.

"Oh," she replied, stopping in the middle of the office. "Yes, Kayla just sent me a text letting me know that she stayed for the girls' soccer game so she can interview the coach after. And that Zack will be coming home with her." She tucked her phone back into her purse and smiled.

"You might as well claim that boy as your part-time son," Ginny said. "He spends as much time at your place as he does his own."

"Yeah, I'd claim him in a minute. He's a good kid. And it looks like tonight is a good night for pizza. I can pick it up and get home by the time they get there."

"We've designated grandson Saturdays as our pizza night," Ginny said, slipping the strap of her bag over her shoulder. "No cooking, no cleanup, just time devoted to whatever makes a six-year-old boy happy."

Johanna smiled and nodded. "I'm grateful that at fifteen and sixteen, and after quarantines and Covid shutdowns, they're still okay with spending time at home."

"Amen to that," Ginny said, following Johanna out of the office and toward the parking lot. "Enjoy that time for as long as you can. It won't be long before you become toxic, and then it's years before they want to hang out with you again."

They walked down the sidewalk and stopped in front of Ginny's car. "I'm grateful for a lot of things," she said. "Getting through a pandemic and not losing anyone I care for, a good job," she flashed a smile at Ginny. "And a daughter I'm pretty darn proud of."

Ginny leaned against the hood of her car. "And Kate," she added.

"Goes without saying, she's way up there on my grateful list."

"I learned more about you from our lunch with your Aunt Kate than I have in the five years you've worked here."

"She knows more about my life than my parents do," Johanna admitted. "My parents' solution was to withhold help and support for going through with the pregnancy and keeping Kayla without marrying her father. They said that if I was going to raise her, then I was going to do it on my own. Stepping in when I needed help would have been counterproductive. And Kate," she said with a raise of her eyebrows, "was not having *that*."

"I'm with Kate. I don't even think that qualifies as tough love. It seems more like punishment to me. Love by condition. What does that do?"

"Create resentment, feelings of inadequacy, fear of failing. Feelings I've fought for years, and feelings I don't want to affect my daughter."

"You'll get no argument from me," Ginny offered, moving around to the car door. "Maybe someday your parents will understand that love should not have boundaries."

"Don't ask me to hold my breath."

"Hey," Kayla greeted Johanna from the side door. "I smell pizza."

"Yep, thanks to your text," Johanna replied. "The timing was perfect. I was just leaving work." She greeted both Kayla and Zack with a hug as they dropped their backpacks on the mudroom bench. "Happy pizza night to us!"

Their response seemed less than enthusiastic, which usually meant that Zack was dealing with something uncomfortable at home. Kayla retrieved sodas from the refrigerator and placed them on the kitchen table while Johanna handed out paper plates and napkins and asked the usual. "Your mom knows you're here, Zack?"

He nodded, helped himself to a piece of pizza, and avoided eye contact.

Johanna looked quickly at Kayla and caught her eye in a silent message. "You sent her a text, Zack?"

"Yeah," he replied. "It's fine."

He didn't have to say anything more. The pattern had been established and clear over the years. His mother had probably relapsed again. Stopped going to meetings, stopped answering her phone, started drinking—again. Johanna knew without asking what fears he was dealing with. He'd dealt with them in varying ways all his life. His mother had been capable and there for him, and then she wasn't. She had a job, and then she didn't. She had a husband, not Zack's father, then she didn't. And now, another boyfriend, another job, and maybe another relapse. But the one thing he never had to worry about, the one thing that she knew Zack knew for sure was that he was always welcome, always safe, here.

Zack placed another piece of pizza on his plate, wiped his hands on a napkin, and fished a folded paper from his pocket.

"What do you think of these?" He directed the question to Kayla as he smoothed the paper flat on the table.

"Oh, these are great," Kayla exclaimed, surveying detailed sketches of four hobbits. "With shoes. They're Stoors."

"Yeah, I thought we have enough Harfoots, and we could make a couple of undergrounds on the banks of the stream and some boats for Stoors."

"Okay," Johanna said, "now you're talking a foreign language. I'm assuming they're some version of hobbits for Kate's Magic Forest."

"Look," Kayla slid the drawing across to Johanna. "They're so cute." She raised her hand for a high five with Zack and added, "I'll cut some more wood blocks, and we can carve next time you come over."

"They *are* cute," Johanna said between bites, "I like that you added another girl hobbit. Hey, Zack, why don't you stay over tonight, and we'll go to the mall tomorrow."

His face said exactly what she hoped it would. It brightened as he looked at Kayla and lifted his brows. "Zap Zone," he said and added the first smile since Johanna got there.

Kayla nodded. "Bumper cars, so I can practice my driving skills." She shot her mother a quick grin.

"Right," Johanna replied with a mimic of her daughter's grin. "Your defensive skills."

"Cat-like defensive skills," she said with a quick motion of her head and shoulders from side to side.

Zack reached for the last slice of pizza. "Not me," he said. "I'm going to hit as many as I can, as hard as I can."

"Well, Zack, that's a stress release I could have used a few times myself," Johanna offered as she lifted the empty pizza box and dropped it in the recycle bin.

His pale blue eyes were wide and sincere. "You should do the cars *with* us, then."

She smiled at the blessing Ginny had reminded her of. His

invitation was honest and appreciated, but "Aw, thanks, Zack, maybe next time. I have a lot of errands I want to get done. If I get them done tomorrow, I don't have to do them after work next week."

Kayla picked up the paper plates, kissed her mother on the cheek, and said, "Thanks, Mom."

For pizza, and more, Johanna suspected. Kayla was bright and compassionate, and the best thing that had come out of the confusion of her own early years. And, so far, Kayla hadn't pushed too hard against the boundaries.

She started to gather the soda bottles, but Zack took them, rinsed them out at the sink, and dropped them in the returnables bin. Johanna passed behind him and gave a quick squeeze of his shoulders. "Your clean clothes are on the shelf in the laundry room." She retrieved a blanket and pillow from the hall closet and dropped them on the couch as Kayla flopped down next to Zack.

"We're going to watch movies," Kayla said.

"Okay," Johanna replied. "I'm going to read and let Stephen King scare the crap out of me."

Kayla laughed. "We're right here if you need us."

Yes, they were. And it brought a smile as Johanna settled in her bedroom. She left the door open, something she had done ever since Kayla was old enough to sleep in her own room. It said that she was always accessible and served as reassurance that all was well. She needed it as much as Kayla did. Early on, it had made dating a bit of a personal challenge, but the rules had always been clear. Her daughter came first—and both her date and her daughter knew that. It meant Kayla spending the evening with her aunt and uncle, which usually meant a relationship cut short.

Rules for Kayla, well, they were also clear. Social time with friends in the living room. No boys in her bedroom, even Zack. Simple. Clear. And so far—respected.

Kayla kept her voice low. "What would they have done to you if Mr. Brennen hadn't stopped them?"

Zack shrugged his shoulders.

"They wouldn't let you out of the shower room?" She knew that answer, but she knew there had to be more. And patience was how to get it. She waited, let it be his timing. It almost always worked.

"They squirted shampoo all over the shower floor and kept dragging me over it and wouldn't let me get up."

"It's been a week of them harassing you on the bus and throwing shade on your mother over Twitter — "

"I told you I'm okay."

"Are you?" Kayla shook her head. "I wouldn't be if I were in your place."

"What *would* you be if it were you?"

"Afraid. *Angry*," she said, catching her rise in volume and lowering it again. "Very angry."

He kept his voice low as well. "Of course, I'm angry—and scared. What am I supposed to do?"

"Tell somebody."

He shook his head. "I'm trying to wait it out."

Her eyes fixed into a hard stare. "But it's getting worse."

Zack turned his eyes from hers.

She waited, but he didn't answer. "Do you really believe they'll get tired of it and leave you alone?"

He lifted his eyes to meet hers, let them rest there for a long moment.

"At least tell my mom," she pleaded. "Or let me."

"So, she can tell *my* mom, and she'll want to know what they're saying? And then she'll tell her boyfriend, and I'll get lectured on how I need to be a man and not let them say shit like that about Mom? No."

"Then what am *I* supposed to do?"

"Watch some movies with me."

Chapter 5

LEAVES OF RED AND GOLD

The large fenced-in backyard was already alive with barking dogs and the squeals and laughter of kids. Adults coordinated efforts to set up tables and chairs, a big screen, and a volleyball net. Johanna and Kayla greeted and hugged, added a colorfully wrapped gift to the table, and scanned the melee for the birthday girl.

Aunt Kate's characteristic laugh, a hearty, full-throated release carrying happily over the lighter tones of children's play and adult conversation, made it easy to find her. She had been stopped in her attempt to reach the steps of the deck by twin five-year-old boys wrapped around her legs.

"Need a little help here, Danny," she called to her son. "I'm being held captive by baby monsters."

It took daddy monster roaring and growling to chase the twins into hiding under the deck and free Kate to greet everyone as they arrived.

Birthday wishes, as usual, had been translated into Kate's celebration of family. Every birthday, every holiday served as a perfect reason to gather the family together and enjoy each other. There were two rules—bring your favorite dish to share with everyone, and bring only gifts that could also be shared.

Eating was top priority while the food was fresh and warm, and it was always an absolute feast. You could count on triple-cheese lasagna, smoked wings, brats, and mac and cheese, and potato cakes fried in a secret batter. Johanna's unusual "walking salad" had quickly become a favorite of kids and adults alike. She had carved out over two dozen Granny Smith apples, and Kayla stuffed them with grapes, cherries, walnuts and marshmallows mixed with Miracle Whip. They began disappearing off the tray as Johanna made her way to the food tables.

Kate rushed across the deck and grabbed both Johanna and Kayla in an embrace. "Welcome to mayhem," she said, adding a wide smile. "I'm not quite sure how all this got organized. This has been such a crazy couple of weeks. Your Uncle Brad is gone with his National Guard unit, so I ended up having to organize the boys and the kids to help Shannon and Dave move. It seemed like every time I planned to give you a call, someone needed something." She took a visibly deep breath. "Can you stay a bit after they take the kids home? I want to catch up with you."

"Sure," Johanna replied. "I knew you were busy, but that doesn't mean I didn't miss you. All that time having to rely on Zoom, and now with everyone vying for personal time, I just miss our personal face-to-face time. I've found that it only takes a couple of weeks before I start flappin' in the wind."

"Well, we can't have that," Kate said with a kiss to Johanna's cheek. "We'll get those tippy toes back flat on the ground."

And she would. It was the one thing Johanna had always been able to count on. Johanna's anchor in the wind. Kate would listen, and care, and offer what no one else had—clear understanding and acceptance of who Johanna Beals was. Meanwhile, there was a celebration at hand. Catching up would have to wait. There was food and birthday cake, and gifts to be opened and shared.

Later, the younger kids gathered on the far side of the deck to watch *Frozen II* on the outdoor screen. Older cousins began the ominous task of sorting pieces to a thousand-piece puzzle of a Michigan Winter Wonderland. And Kayla took a group of excited cousins back to Kate's magic forest to find the perfect place for two new hobbits along the cobblestone path that wound through trees and plants at the back of the property.

She looked proudly at the work she'd done with cousin Derrick to carve hobbit houses out of dead tree stumps and create others out of wood and stone and tuck them into the forest terrain. They roofed them with little wooden shingles, put lights behind plastic windows, and added working doors. At night the lights from the little windows glowed from their places tucked into the landscape along the path. It was truly a magical place.

As the last of the extended family collected serving dishes and kids and headed for home, Kate joined Johanna and Kayla at the dining table. She motioned to the partially separated puzzle pieces organized by color and shade.

"Well, this one's going to be a challenge," she directed to Kayla. "You and I have some puzzle hours ahead of us. Are you up for it?"

"Snickerdoodles and milkshakes?" Kayla asked.

"Well," Kate began with a look of befuddlement, "I don't see how anyone can focus that long without Snickerdoodles and milkshakes."

Johanna shook her head. "So predictable. I swear you two are sister spirits." She watched them grin at each other and added, "How about next Sunday?"

Both Kate and Kayla nodded.

"How is school, by the way?" Kate asked.

"It's okay. I'm going to be working on our online newspaper."

"Hey," Kate exclaimed, "that's right up your alley."

"Yeah, I get to cover girls' sports."

"And it sounds like she has some really good teachers this year," Johanna added.

"You know," Kate said, "they're the ones you're going to remember later in your life when you've forgotten so many other things. You'll be surprised how many of those teachers and what you learned from them stays with you. Of course, the bad ones can stay with you, too. Hopefully, you'll never have a Mrs. Smythe who seemed to derive some sort of pleasure from reading misspelled or horribly wrong test answers out loud to the class."

"I remember hearing stories. English, right?" Johanna asked.

Kate nodded. "Or better known as Embarrassment 101."

"Fortunately, she retired before I got there. If not, I'm afraid we would have seriously butted heads."

"What would you have done, Mom?"

"Probably told her that she was a terrible teacher and walked out of class."

"And your mother would have been called," Kate said. "And we know how that would have ended."

Kayla frowned and asked, "How?"

"I would have been told to apologize in class and in writing, and then grounded for a month."

"That's so wrong," Kayla replied. "You would never do that to me."

Johanna shook her head. "Only if I was convinced that you were at fault—that you had been rude out of spite or anger. But I would never expect that from you."

"So why wouldn't Grandma have believed *you*?"

Kate interjected. "Because your mom was, and is, too much like your Aunt Kate. She questioned traditional rules and pushed against what others expected of her. Oil and water—just like your Grandmother Karen and me growing up together. We couldn't be more different, and your mother and her mother couldn't be more different."

"She and your grandfather," Johanna added, "wanted what they thought was the perfect family, perfect kids. Your Uncle David and I were expected to get all As in school, be the star athlete and cheerleader, and marry early and well. Your uncle is living the life they approve of. I'm not."

"Because you're a lesbian?" Kayla asked.

"Partly. I wouldn't marry your biological father, and I chose to have you and raise you without him," she replied.

"I already know that," Kayla replied.

"That's pretty much it in a nutshell," Johanna said and cocked her head. "But, at the root of it all is that they value different things in life than I do. Or, at least, at a different intensity than I do. They laser focus on, well, everything. That's how they've been able to grow a local realty company into a successful statewide business. But it means spending an excessive number of hours in meetings and traveling. They are so absorbed in their own achievements that they don't enjoy things like family time, or ballgames, or an afternoon at the lake."

"They have no idea what roses smell like," Kate added.

"For them, those things are wasted time," Johanna continued. "They're even pathological about fitness. Workouts at the fitness club on a strict, unwavering schedule. And me? Well, I work for someone else, rent a house, keep a car as long as I can, and thoroughly enjoy days like this." She offered a quick smile, then added, "And then, of course, there's politics."

Kate leaned back in her chair and shook her head. "Something we're not discussing tonight. Today, we're celebrating the good in our lives. I'm concentrating on good right now."

"Yep," Johanna agreed, "that's something we all need."

Kayla's expression turned pensive. She looked briefly from

her aunt to her mother, including them both in her question. "Have you ever felt helpless, though, like the bad is stronger than the good, and you don't have the power to change it?"

"Often," Kate replied. "But we *have* come through some tough times, and it proves that we do have power to make changes. And that should prove that we should never stop trying."

Johanna nodded. "That's why I regularly call our legislators, sign petitions, march— "

"And vote," Kate interjected. "It's our loudest voice." She cocked her head. "End of political conversation."

"I don't mean just politics," Kayla said.

Johanna looked at Kate. "Do you remember the quote by L.R. Knost that you gave me when I was questioning— everything?"

"Like your place in the world, your right to happiness?"

Johanna nodded. "I keep it in a drawer next to my bed. I memorized it a long time ago." She directed her attention to Kayla. "I'll pass it on to you now: 'Do not be dismayed by the brokenness of the world. All things break. And all things can be mended. Not with time, as they say, but with intention. So, go. Love intentionally, extravagantly, unconditionally. The broken world waits in darkness for the light that is you.'"

Kayla's response was characteristically thoughtful. "What if intention isn't enough and there's no fixing it?"

"What has you so worried?" Johanna asked.

Kayla shrugged. "It just seems like hate and meanness is so powerful."

"You'd be surprised how strong love is, though," Kate replied. "Not just romantic love," she shifted her focus to Johanna, "that has its own healing properties. But the kind of love that works for peace and fights for fairness and safety for others. That's a powerful love. We just have to figure out how to use it."

This, Johanna thought, was why Kate and not her mother,

was an integral part of Kayla's life. Shielding Kayla from much of the world's nastiness had been important. But now, it was time to address her awareness and her concerns, as prudently as possible.

Kayla absently pushed pieces of the puzzle's border into place next to a completed corner. Johanna knew her well enough to know that she was listening, letting the words, the message, form a personal meaning. And she was sure that once she did, Kayla would talk with her about it. Just as *she* had talked with Kate.

"Is it okay," Kayla asked, "if I go check my phone?"

"Sure," Johanna replied, "go ahead." Her daughter had done what most her age would have acted out over, she'd gone all day without her phone—no Twitter, no messages, no Instagram.

Kate winked at Johanna as Kayla circled behind their chairs and placed kisses on both her aunt's and mother's cheeks. Once she disappeared into the living room, Kate asked, "How did you manage that?"

"Some days, it's easier than others. It comes down to her not wanting to lose the use of her phone for a full week."

Kate chuckled. "I wonder how many teens would survive a phone death."

"Or most adults, for that matter."

"That doesn't take anything away from the fact that she's a good girl and you have done a fine job of raising her."

Johanna offered a gentle smile. "*We* did a fine job," she said. "I could not have done it without you."

"Well," Kate replied, "we had good material to work with."

Another smile as Johanna hesitated before saying, "I assume that your usual invitation for the rest of the family to join us today was ignored."

"Oh, as expected, I got the obligatory birthday cards from your folks and your brother. I called and listened to the usual; this weekend they are trouble-shooting some big contract in Grand

Rapids. That sliver of hope that I had for a breakthrough seems to have vanished. You know, it took me a long time to realize that they don't have any malice toward you. They are just self-involved people who have a very narrow view of life. I think that if they were ever to get out of their own way, they would regret not being closer to you and Kayla. And you, whether consciously or not, somehow managed not to let resentment or anger affect your life. And that makes me happy."

"Confusion was a bigger problem," Johanna added. "I didn't want to be Alice falling down the rabbit hole."

"No, you're no Alice. And if I'd ever thought you were, I'd have grabbed you by the pigtails before you got too close to that rabbit hole."

Johanna smiled at the vision. "Do you remember when I pleaded with Mom to let me take karate? I was nine, and that wasn't on her list, the one that had dance classes at the top. Remember what you told me?"

"Girls can do anything boys can do, many times better."

"I wasn't confused about what I wanted. Not then. That came later when I couldn't draw the line from what I wanted and what Mom wanted me to want. I just needed someone to accept and believe in me," Johanna said. "Thank you."

"I was just there when you needed a nudge. The rest has been all you. I just want you to be happy."

Johanna tilted her head and said, "I know. But I've come to realize that happiness is relative. It must conform to immoveable perimeters." The tone of her voice matched her expression—introspective, resolute—and Kate recognized it.

"Perimeters and situations can change," she said.

"Some," Johanna replied.

"But not yours."

"Not all of them. Not right now, anyway. I'm busy and needed, and in many ways happy."

"Even late at night?"

"That's the immoveable at the top of the list. I'm not bringing someone else into our lives and taking a chance on disrupting Kayla's life again. You know what a rollercoaster Zack's life has been; I don't want that for Kayla. Once she's in college . . ."

"Then, just date, Johanna. Casual dates, no commitments or expectations. You know that I love having Kayla stay over here with us. Take a little time for yourself."

"You know how much I appreciate that, and Kayla loves spending time with you. But I'm not good at just hooking up— and it isn't fair to keep seeing someone who's looking for more than that."

Kate, though, wasn't easily dissuaded. As was her nature, she was about to probe her way through the less-than-effective smoke screen her niece threw up. Predictable, and not a deterrent. "Nobody that has even tempted you to take another chance, especially after all this time when it really hasn't been possible?"

"You really are incorrigible."

"Yes, I am," Kate replied, followed by a sly grin. "Spill it."

"Even though it has no chance of going anywhere."

"Humor me."

"I met her this summer working on the music festival. Pure chemistry. And all it proved was that temptation has nothin' on me."

Kate's face brightened with interest. "Chemistry, huh?"

"I sure hope Kayla will confide in me like I do you." She acknowledged Kate's knowing smile. "Yes, chemistry. Nothing more, nothing less. Temptation overcome. I haven't seen her since, and I'm good with that."

"And she feels the same way?"

Johanna shrugged. "I wasn't asking questions. I guess I really didn't want to know anything that would tempt me into getting to know her better."

"So, for that full week your discussions never revealed anything about her life, who she is?"

With a shake of her head, Johanna replied, "I watched. It was supposed to be my private enjoyment, my personal fantasy. A week of fantasy, away from real life and responsibility. Whatever I gleaned from watching was enough; that way, I could make of it whatever I wanted."

"And you liked what you saw."

"I did. I liked how she volunteered so many hours, how easily she smiled, how much others enjoyed working with her. I imagined that there was more about her that I would like, but I dismissed that curiosity and left it at that. Even at the after-party." Johanna leaned forward, arms folded, forearms resting on the table. "Do you remember the words from that Whitney Houston song, 'I want to dance with somebody. I want to feel the heat with somebody'? That was me, right then. I wanted to feel like that, if only for a short while. And she didn't ask any questions either, not even at the party when it was possible that we wouldn't see each other after that. It seemed that she was doing the same thing I was. It felt like we both wanted a night of heat and nothing more."

Kate offered a coy turn of her head and lifted her brows.

"No, I didn't sleep with her."

"But you wanted to."

"Chemistry should never have the last word."

Chapter 6

LISTEN TO THE WIND

The feeling of deja vu, alarming and persistent, had stayed with Miya since lunchtime. Since she had forgone the teachers' lounge and spent her lunch period in her classroom reading essays from her first hour English class.

One essay, one thoughtful and deeply personal answer to a first-semester assignment asking, "What Does Goodness Mean to You?" caused her concern.

> ". . . That's what I thought
> goodness meant. That's what my
> family taught me. I believed it. I
> thought everyone did. But I was
> wrong. Goodness doesn't bring
> safety and happiness to everyone's
> life, even if they are kind and
> smart and funny and talented. The
> truth is goodness doesn't really
> matter. And I don't know what life
> is worth without goodness."

Those words, Miya thought, *could have been mine, are too close to my own silent fears muffled with tears into my pillow at night. Does she struggle like I did, question like I did, to find any recognizable good? Is she searching, too, to find the redeeming value that my parents and their pastor and the Bible claimed that I was missing? I only knew I had to find it, had to change. How could anyone love me as I was? I was sure that I had to do whatever necessary to cast out the demon, my nemesis. And I tried, wanting to be accepted, needing to be worthy even while thinking that it wasn't possible. But it wasn't necessary, wasn't even possible. Is Kayla facing the same struggle to change what can't be changed? And if she is, someone has to help her find the strength to believe in her own goodness.*

Miya slipped the folder of essays into a worn leather bag, still holding the worrisome paper separately. Her decision to share her concerns was an easy one, and who to share them with took no thought at all. She headed down nearly empty halls to the Head Counselor's office. Dr. Chandra Reed, Miya's comrade in arms in a frustrating school environment, would still be in her office, even at the end of a long day, even on Friday.

Miya stuck her head around the half-open door. "Hey, Sister Warrior, do you have a few minutes?"

"Always," Chandra returned, offering her usual wide smile framed in dark red lipstick. The gap between her front teeth was a casual contrast to a high-end professional polish. Striking. It was the first word that came to mind the day Miya met her. Striking, with her artfully braided hair, flowing caftan perfectly disguising extra weight, and large gold hoops shining against the dark brown glow of her skin.

"Would you read something for me?" Miya asked.

"Sure," Chandra replied, moving her chair clear of the computer and accepting the paper. "What am I looking for?"

"You aren't. This is an assignment I always give out near the end of the first semester, 'What Does Goodness Mean to You?'

I just want your reaction to it."

Chandra was already reading, and Miya waited patiently, vacillating between hoping she saw the same signs and hoping that she didn't.

Chandra lowered the paper as though she was finished reading, but quickly raised it to re-read something. She read the words out loud. "'The truth is goodness doesn't really matter. And I don't know what life is worth without goodness.'"

Miya nodded and let the doctor be the first to speak. "This may or may not be the first time, the first step for her, but it sounds to me as though she is done whispering to the wind," and added, "Whether or not she's fully aware of it, I don't know."

"I don't know anyone who can explain something so worrisome and do it so beautifully."

"Uh-huh," she replied, rolling her chair back to the computer. "Keep on sprinkling sugar."

Miya didn't have to ask. Chandra noted the student's name at the top of the paper, and in a few minutes, she would have whatever information the school had on record for Kayla Beals. Miya watched the screen reflection change on Chandra's glasses as she scanned through student records. It would all be there—grades, activities, sports, social interactions of any consequence, and comments or recommendations from each of Kayla's teachers through the years. At least everything that had been visible, was noticeable to the attention of dedicated teachers.

Chandra slowly shook her head. "Nothing stands out as anything to be concerned about. Grades have always been above average, book club, nature club, not a large amount of other social interaction, but no mention of problems."

"Could have gone undetected," Miya replied. "A 'sleeper' until this year. Maybe something festering at home, or here, has changed things for her."

An agreeable nod from Chandra. "It's possible that your assignment struck a chord, and offered an opportunity for her to express what she hadn't been able to otherwise. How is she in your class?"

"Quiet, studious. No red flags until today." Then to the purpose of her visit. "Do *you* see it as a red flag?"

Chandra moved from behind the computer and settled back in her chair. "She wasn't writing in a journal; she knew it was going to be read—by you. So, it was purposeful."

"Then it warrants having her come in to talk with me?"

"I'd say so. It sounds like she wants to talk to someone, and many times it's easier for them to talk with a teacher or a counselor than a parent. Keep me in the loop. I might want to talk with her, too."

"Yes, I will feel a whole lot better when she is in your hands. I wish I had had someone like you to talk to when I was her age." Miya rose to leave but stopped at the door to add, "I did a bit of whispering myself."

Relief began to replace the concern Miya felt that she might have colored the red flag from Kayla's essay with her own experiences. What she couldn't seem to shake, though, was the concern that Kayla Beals could be living through something like her own growing-up years. Had she, like herself, found places for protection, hidden, shadowy places? Was she ducking in and out of those shadows, unnoticed—and protected? They could be safe, those shadowy places. The same ones that she had searched out when she was young—quiet places, alone places, safe places. There was the fort in a tree in the woods by the railroad tracks, the loft hiding place in the garage, her grandmother's house, and the freedom that her bike afforded her. But her no-fail place was between the covers of books, where she had traveled the pages as a witness. There, she escaped into lives unlike her own, into families and struggles and happiness, unlike her own life. The characters became friends, spilling their feelings to her, sharing their fears and their dreams, and offering her hope for better things in her life. How likely was it that Kayla was doing the same thing? And if she was, Miya wanted to know why.

Chapter 7

KNOWING

Kayla quickly deposited her history book, unneeded over the weekend, and grabbed her backpack from her locker. She found that packing up her backpack at lunch allowed her the extra couple of minutes after her last class to make it to her locker and leave before Julie Bradford and her friends gathered at the locker next to hers. Julie with her popular girlfriends and star football-playing boyfriend and their increasing nastiness would be avoided, at least for now.

She hurried down the end of the long hall, down the stairs, and out the door to the east parking lot where the faculty park. As she reached the sidewalk, her phone whistled an incoming message.

"Hey, wait 4 me, E dr." From Zack.

"Here now," she returned.

"Don't leave."

"K"

Ten minutes later, still waiting on the bottom step next to the sidewalk, Kayla snugged her jacket tighter around her and asked, "Where r u?"

Minute later. "Don't leave."

"K." He needn't worry. She wouldn't leave, but the questions were mounting. *Why is he missing his bus? Is he being threatened again?* Another ten minutes dragged by, and she was about to text him again when someone called her name from the top of the stairs. She turned to see her English teacher, Ms. James, approaching her with a smile.

"I was just thinking about you," she said, standing in front of Kayla now. "I've read your essay."

Kayla felt her cheeks flush as she rose. The one teacher, despite her good looks and popularity, that Kayla trusted. Admittedly, a blind trust. A secret hope that she was different from someone like Julie Bradford—a hope that the heart of her was as attractive as the rest of her. A hope that Kayla's trust was warranted. Kayla chanced a look into the waiting gaze and squared herself for whatever she was about to hear.

"It is so well written, Kayla," she began, "and quite thought-provoking. So much so that I read it a second time."

"Thank you," Kayla replied, sure that her relief was evident in her voice.

"I'd like to talk with you about it. Would you be able to come in and talk one day after classes?"

It wasn't her intent for it to stand out like this, for her thoughts to garner such attention, was it? It was only a need to put it into words, to give it form, give it room to breathe. She hadn't expected this, had she? "Ah, okay. I have to check with my mother, though."

"Of course. You can let me know what day works best." She offered a bright smile and added, "Have a good night, Kayla."

"Okay, thanks." Ms. James turned toward the parking lot. "I hope you have a good night, too," Kayla said, watching the slender figure close the distance to her car with long, sure strides. The worn leather bag slung over her shoulder had aged, probably long before it carried English assignments home each night. Why she noticed it, Kayla couldn't say. Maybe a piece of a puzzle that she hadn't realized she was fitting together. A puzzle piece like the absence of a wedding band or engagement ring, and the subtle signals of disinterest in Mr. Aggar. The signals she gave every time he showed up in their classroom and leaned in close with one hand on the back of Ms. James' chair and the other on the desk. At first Kayla wondered if it was an attempt by Ms. James to keep a personal relationship under the cover of a professional one—to make it look like something it wasn't to her students. But now the minimal eye contact and her moving away the few inches that his posture allowed looked like something else.

Kayla watched until the silver Subaru turned left out of the parking lot. She checked her phone for a message from Zack. Nothing. But the time made it clear that she needed to text her mother. There was a reason he didn't take the bus home, and whatever it was, he was obviously coming home with her.

The door opened behind her, and Zack poked his head out and looked around before hurrying down the stairs.

"What's going on?" she asked.

He continued toward her without answering. His 'just the usual' expression changed quickly into something Kayla didn't recognize.

"Are you okay?"

He hesitated beside her and shook his head. "Come on, let's go. Will it be okay with your mom?"

"Yeah, but what's going on?"

He looked around, behind him, across the parking lot. "Come *on*."

She didn't press further and started down the sidewalk. A few steps later, she noticed his unusually slow pace and slowed down. Something was more wrong than usual. She glanced sideways at her best friend. They'd grown up together in happier times, their families living in the same apartment building, attending elementary and junior high schools together. He became the brother she didn't have, and she the friend who accepted him unconditionally, the only person he trusted beyond question.

He would tell her, eventually. So, she let it go, put in her earbuds, and listened to music until Zack tapped her arm in front of a neighborhood park halfway home.

"Let's sit here for a few minutes," he said, dropping his backpack on the closest bench and sitting down.

Kayla joined him, feeling the November cold of the cement through her jeans, and waited for an explanation. She zipped up her jacket as a breeze sent leaves from a large maple into an orange free-fall. After too many minutes of silence, though, she lost patience. "Was it the same guys?"

He nodded.

"Did they threaten you? Hurt you?"

He stood, opened his jacket, pulled his T-shirt up and pushed his waistband down enough to show red marks and welts covering his chest and abdomen.

"What the hell, Zack? What did they do?"

He lowered his shirt and sat down. "Snapped me with towels after gym class."

"A hundred times? Where was Brennen? I thought he stopped them last time?"

"They came in early from lunch again. Brennen left to do something before their class started. I wasn't going to go into the shower room, but they grabbed me and stripped off my clothes and held my arms and legs."

The image wasn't hard to visualize. He was slight, wiry, no more than an inch taller than her, and generously rounded up to a hundred and twenty pounds. And the boys bullying him were all taller, heavier, and older—including Josh, Julie's boyfriend.

He met her eyes, then dropped his focus quickly.

She knew that look. For as long as she had known him, it

always meant the same thing. He wanted, needed to tell her something—something very personal, something that putting into words made too real. Like the time he told her about the dream he had about an older boy putting his arms around him and telling him that he would never let anyone hurt him. He needed to analyze it, needed her to analyze it. Even more, he needed her honesty. Honesty that said his dream didn't necessarily mean he was gay, that it could mean that he longed for an older brother or a father who would always be there for him—to love him and protect him. And an honesty that said even if he was gay, that it didn't matter, that it didn't change who he was.

Kayla waited through the hesitation and reminded herself of how much he counted on her.

He pinched the space between his brows into a groove before looking up again. "Josh Carter aimed right at my privates. I tried not to scream, but it hurt so bad. It just made them laugh harder."

"Oh, my God, Zack! You have to tell someone."

"I am telling someone. I'm telling you."

"So that I can tell someone?"

"No," he replied quickly. "It'll only make it worse."

"Zack, you've got to do something. *We've* got to do something. This has gone way past trashing your mother, way past trying to get liquor from you."

"They warned me. They've got embarrassing pictures."

"So, if you don't tell someone, they're going to miraculously stop? What about what they can do to you physically?"

"Promise me," he said, his eyes pleading. "Don't say anything."

Kayla hesitated. She'd never betray him. Not when he'd lie about where the bruises came from, not when he'd hide out at her house to avoid scrutiny by his mother's boyfriend. Not even when she had to keep her own mother in the dark. She'd ride the line as always.

"Kayla, promise me."

"I won't say anything," she relented. "But what are you gonna do?"

"I'm not going to gym anymore."

"Well, how long do you think it'll take before Brennen turns your name into a counselor? They'll ask you why you're not going to class."

He slipped his arms through the straps of his backpack and stood without answering her.

It was an easy assumption. He didn't answer her because he had no answer.

Chapter 8

SILENCE

"Hi, Kayla," Miya greeted her student as she entered the classroom. Per Miya's usual practice, she was sitting at a student desk with another pulled around to face her. The intent was to create a comfortable, far less intimidating arrangement to encourage trust and an honest exchange. Intended to say, "I'm right here. I see you. I hear you." And it usually did just that.

"How was your weekend?" Miya asked, adding a friendly smile.

Kayla settled at the desk. "Okay," she said with a shrug.

"Just okay?"

"I needed to get my regular homework done so I could work on my online article."

"Oh," Miya replied, "Your interview with Coach Charbonnet?"

Kayla nodded.

"The girls have a good chance at the league basketball championship this year."

Another nod from Kayla.

"You really did a nice job on that article. Do you enjoy

covering sports?"

"Uh-huh, it's fun," Kayla replied without further embellishment.

Nowhere, she was getting nowhere. Most kids start chattering by now, Miya mused. Usually, one or two questions and they were open, willing to share, happy for the interest. Usually. Miya tried again. "What do you do for fun on the weekends?"

A shrug and Kayla replied, "Hang out with friends, watch movies, or go to my aunt's." The end. Nothing more, only a look of waiting. For the reason she was there, Miya assumed. For what must be more important than what she did on the weekend. But if she wasn't going to talk about the easy stuff . . .

One more try. "I used to live for the weekend," Miya began, as memories of freedom came floating back. That "feet off the ground," "floating on the wind" freedom. Out the door at 6 a.m., not home until nine at night, with answers "what and where" as short as Kayla's. "I learned to appreciate Mondays, though," she said, "with their new possibilities and new chances. My grandmother used to sing 'Monday, Monday' by The Mamas & the Papas every Monday when I stayed with her." She acknowledged Kayla's smile. Finally, Miya thought. "I know, it made me smile, too, but it was a real group. And the song said things like, 'Monday morning couldn't guarantee that Monday evenin' you would still be here with me.'"

"She didn't want you to leave?"

"At first, I thought that she just liked singing the song because it was Monday. But, yeah, I think that was what she was saying. I wasn't brave enough then to tell her that I would stay with her permanently if she'd let me."

"Why did you want to stay with her instead of your parents?"

"Because she let me be me. She never tried to make me into something I wasn't." Kayla's eyes had not left her own— attentive, waiting. Miya continued. "She saw good in me that my parents didn't see. I think that's why your essay stood out to me. Recognizing the goodness in someone is important, and necessary. I often wonder how my life would have turned out if it hadn't been for my grandmother. She nurtured the good in me. She gave it room to breathe and grow and radiate out into the world. I believe she saved me."

Kayla's brow furrowed. "From what?"

"From believing I would never be good enough, that no matter how hard I tried, I could never be what my parents wanted me to be." She lifted the essay from her desk. "You said here that you wondered what life is worth without goodness. There were times that I wondered that, too." Oh, too much, too personal. If only she would just start talking.

"I wish what your grandmother did for you was possible for everyone, but I don't believe it is. That's why I wrote that."

Finally. "You believe that it isn't possible for *you*?"

Kayla hesitated and averted her eyes. "No, just not there for everyone."

"Of course, not everyone will have someone like my grandmother in their life," Miya replied. "That's why we have people like Dr. Reed. She is wonderful to talk with, and someone who cares deeply about her students. She's there, Kayla, for *anyone* who needs someone to talk with. Anyone who needs support and to know that they are going to be okay."

"What if someone wanted to talk with her, but they didn't want her to tell anyone else what they talked about?"

Miya thought her answer through carefully before replying. She was aware of the reporting requirements but did not want to discourage anyone from getting help. "They could talk to her about anything. The only time Dr. Reed would say anything to anyone else would be if they were being hurt. If that was happening, she would get them help."

Kayla lowered her focus to her hands, clasped and resting on the desk.

Let her think it through, Miya thought. Most likely, it was

not what Kayla had wanted to hear. Right now, fresh from whisper to word, she no doubt wanted confidentiality. Understood. But all Miya could offer was advice—honest, compassionate advice. The best that Miya could hope for was to establish a trust that allowed Kayla to take that advice.

"For you to write so passionately about this," Miya began, "it seems like it must touch you personally somehow." Kayla's eyes met hers briefly before dropping again. "You know," Miya continued, "you can come talk with *me* anytime, if you'd rather."

This time Kayla's eyes lifted and remained, wider, more hopeful. "Just you?" she asked. "I mean, you wouldn't tell anyone else what we talked about?"

Don't lie to her, trust is built on truth. Always, at every turn. So . . . "I would only say something if someone were being hurt." The eyes lost their hopefulness. "There's a law, Kayla; if we know about it, we have to report it."

"To authorities?"

Miya nodded. "To Child Protective Services. That way, we can get help to stop it from happening."

Kayla returned a nod. "Thanks, Ms. James." She picked up her backpack from beside the chair and stood. She made eye contact and said it again. "Thank you."

"Just know that we are here when you need us." Miya watched her nod again and offer a half smile, then slip her backpack over her shoulder and leave.

Miya dropped heavily onto the chair in front of Chandra's desk. She exhaled audibly. "Well, *that* was a giant fail."

"Maybe you should let me be the judge of that."

Miya covered her face with her hands and dropped her head back.

"I'm assuming this is about your talk with Kayla."

She uncovered her face and replied, "Yes."

"Okay, the doctor's in, so give it up."

"Remind me again why the truth is best."

Chandra raised her eyebrows and looked over the top of her glasses.

"I couldn't get her to engage. She'd only give me a nod or enough words not to be rude. But when one of those short answers was that she liked to stay with her aunt, I saw a way to connect with her. I stayed with my grandmother when I was her age, someone who saw the good in me. It seemed like the perfect tie to her essay. Too perfect." She raised her hands in frustration. "I overshared, made it too personal. And even that didn't give us anything definitive. So, here I am with only assumptions and frustrations."

"Not a comfortable place, but one that I am all too familiar with. Tell me your assumptions. I can get the frustrations from there."

"She would talk with either of us if we could promise confidentiality. When I told her that we would have to report it if someone is being hurt, she shut down."

"Did you offer that information, or did she ask?"

"She asked."

"Hmmm," Chandra replied with a frown.

"Yeah, I didn't expect that. Although I guess I should have. She's a smart girl."

"Typically, that means she's afraid that the situation will escalate, or of getting someone she cares about in trouble, or whatever is happening is happening to someone else."

"I went over her essay again, but it's ambiguous enough that I can't tell which it is. When we talked, she said that it wasn't her, but I don't know if I believe that."

"It doesn't come down to whether you believe her. It's whether you *suspect* that she's being neglected or abused. She's made it clear that *something* is happening, and if you know who,

Public Act 35 says we must report it."

"And if it's not her?"

"Then we need to figure out who. And whoever it is, the key word here is *suspect*. We won't have a choice at that point. I'm going to talk with each of her teachers tomorrow. I'll let you know if I find out anything that helps."

Miya rose and offered an appreciative smile.

"You said something earlier," Chandra said, "about wishing that you had had someone to talk to when you were Kayla's age."

Miya nodded. "I would have camped out in your office."

"What happened when you didn't have someone?"

"I ran."

It had felt like the right decision, the only decision back then. Miya drove through the neighborhood where she'd grown up as waves of emotions and memories swept her thoughts. Her parents had moved from the old neighborhood and its increasing diversity years ago. The house was still there, though, looking much like she remembered it. A traditional two-story house now painted a soft grey, with a screened-in porch perfect for sleeping on warm summer nights. A one-car garage sat behind it at the end of a gravel driveway.

Miya stopped the car at the mouth of the driveway. The garage door was open, and she could see the bottom framing of the loft where her father used to store storm windows and scrap lumber. It had made the perfect hideout. At first, it was a refuge needed for a few hours to avoid church meetings meant to save her wayward soul. A soul held captive by a horrible demon. The proof, the visual that verified all her parents' suspicions, was that fateful day when her mother looked out the kitchen window just as Katy Springer's lips met Miya's in a lusty full-on kiss on the back steps. A kiss that had lit her, mind and body, with excitement. Together with numerous junior high crushes on older women and, later, the diary she thought was so well hidden, it was the last bit of evidence her parents needed. As if it was a recording, she could still hear the tone of her mother's voice, the words that had seared their message into her brain. "A demon has captured your soul and will take it down in flames if we don't stop it."

So, she had hidden there in the corner of the loft, behind pieces of plywood, with a flashlight and a book. She could still smell the pungent, dusty grey wood and the motor oil staining the concrete where the car sat. But her corner of the loft felt like a steel fortress, solid and safe and undetectable. When her parents' frustration turned to a plan for intervention, she stocked her refuge with food and water and a collapsible camp toilet and hid there for a week. She'd timed things perfectly, coming down to replenish her supplies and empty her toilet when her parents and her brother and sister were gone. Since she had disappeared before, the police only reminded her parents of the three-day requirement to consider her more than a runaway. Her parents argued about whether to call the police or not, and what punishment to give when she finally came home. Her throat tightened like it did when she stifled a laugh as she listened to them trying to figure out what to do, frustrated and fearful that a horrible demon was destroying their daughter. They had stood right there in front of the garage, with no idea that she was only fifteen feet away.

Miya drew her eyes from the remnants of her past, but her body remembered the tensing, the acuteness of sounds, the need for her own silence. *Stay still, stay silent, listen carefully.* She stretched her legs and straightened her back against the tightness of the long-ago space.

No one had ever found it, not her little brother, not her Miss Kiss-ass know-it-all sister, or her parents. Before, they had always been able to track her down at friends' houses, but they had never found her hideout right there in the garage in the backyard. There was still a sense of satisfaction after all those years, and a smug smile as she continued driving slowly through the neighborhood. The loft, though, had been no match for a Michigan winter. So, as the weather turned cold, Miya turned to a new friend, one her parents knew nothing about. A year older, more truant than not, Lyn came to the rescue. With the threat of another intervention to cast out the looming demon, Lyn stowed her away for days. It was easy with a single mother working afternoons; that was until Miya made the mistake of showing up at school to take her exams. A school on notice and a phone call home was all it took to make her vulnerable again. And when she refused to even pretend that the demon had magically been cast back to hell, her parents planned their last resort. She overheard their argument, their resolution, and the words *conversion therapy*. That night she had snuck out of the house, and in the morning, taken a bus to Ashland, Ohio and her grandmother.

Chapter 9

THE YELLOW BRICK ROAD

It was true. The parents that most needed to show up for parent/ teacher conferences didn't. The ones with children who were missing classes or homework, failing tests, or acting out in class. Parents like the Roberts, whose son hadn't been turning in assignments and too often fell asleep in class.

Miya sat at her desk in her empty classroom and made good use of the Roberts' time slot to grade a few more papers. The more she got done now, the fewer she would have to take home. It was already going to be a short night, and taking *no* papers home was a pipe dream. She checked the clock over the door and made a bet to herself that the seven forty-five appointment would indeed be there. After all, Kayla Beals turned in all her assignments, consistently got A's or high Bs on tests, and paid attention in class. There was only one thing that needed discussion, and she was certain that tonight was not the best time for it. The logic was tried and true: probative questions barely disguising suspicion of neglect or abuse was not the best approach when meeting a parent for the first time. Subtlety. Listen carefully. Observe. That, Miya decided. Stay disciplined.

Comfortable with her strategy, Miya refocused the use of the last ten minutes on grading one more assignment. But a minute later a voice from the doorway interrupted her.

"Am I too — "

Miya looked up into eyes wide with surprise, mirroring her own. "Johanna," she said, doing her best to mask her shock.

"I . . . I don't . . . I had no idea."

"*You* are Kayla's mother?" Miya said, watching the woman who had haunted her thoughts for months walk hesitantly into the room. *Awkward. Oh yes, terribly awkward. And, of course, as attractive as she remembered*—wispy brown hair kissed by the sun, tasteful cleavage defined in sage green, and fluid brown eyes, bringing back flashes of a quickened heart and heated touches. The woman who had intrigued her, who had matched her movements beat by beat, and met her lips with unquestioned desire—*that* was the woman she saw approaching her desk, not a mother, not a parent. *Who is this woman?*

"Yes," Johanna replied, "Kayla's mother. It's the one thing I'm sure of right now."

Miya stayed with Johanna's eyes, searching for something beyond her words. What did she expect her to say? What *was* there to say? Words certainly hadn't been a priority the night of the party. "So, what is it you're *not* sure of?"

"What I should be thinking." The pink of Johanna's cheeks deepened. "Or feeling. Right now. Here."

Miya nodded, still refusing to break from Johanna's eyes. "Well, I'm crystal clear on what we *should* be thinking and feeling, but I admit I never expected this." She motioned to the chair beside the desk. "Will you please sit down so we can find a way around this awkwardness?"

Johanna dutifully sat and offered a half smile.

"You know," Miya began, "the elephant actually shrinks in size and weight when you talk about it."

Another half-smile from Johanna. "And it'll be easier to deal with a baby elephant?"

Miya relaxed against the back of her chair and smiled. "There's not a lot of history that we need to wade through," she said. "Just one night, one experience. We haven't had the opportunity to identify what it meant, at least not together. Maybe we should start there." Johanna seemed hesitant, or deep in thought. Miya couldn't tell which, so she started. "For me, it was a chance to let you know how attractive I thought you were. It was a chance to let you know that I was interested and to find out if you felt the same way. I was sure you did. But when you left so abruptly, I assumed I was wrong."

"You weren't wrong," Johanna admitted. "*I* was. I wasn't being fair, or honest."

Miya waited. *Give her room to find the words she's searching for. Let her find comfort in talking about it and get past awkwardness. Talking helps.*

"That whole week was an escape from my real life. Time away with no responsibilities, no worries."

"What about the night of the party?"

"It was supposed to be the end of my fantasy."

"So, you left."

Johanna nodded. "That wasn't fair to you, and I'm sorry. At least now you know why."

"I know now what you were doing when you left the yellow brick road. But *that* night you didn't know that I was a teacher, let alone that I would be Kayla's teacher."

"But you are." Her eyes seemed to plead. "So can we please talk about Kayla?"

Miya broke from the gaze that puzzled her, nodded, and consciously overrode the temptation to ask more questions. Maybe another time would be better, or maybe never. "So, Kayla, then," she said. "She's a good student and a joy to have in class." *Yes, Kayla—take my mind, my thoughts where they should be. Take us both to the place where a parent and teacher should be.*

Johanna nodded, a resolute nod, following Miya's lead. "She loves to read," she began.

Miya offered a disarming smile. Her own heart rate was a good clip beyond normal, but she hid it much better than did Johanna, who was still nervous, fidgeting with a gold and silver bracelet. *Come on, talk about Kayla. That's got to be your comfort zone.*

"I used to read to her every night when she was little. I came into her room one day when she was four and she was 'reading' the story out loud. I thought she was just retelling it, but I sat down next to her and watched. She said every word exactly as it was written and stopped precisely at the end of each page. I figured that she was either reading or she had memorized the whole book as I read it to her."

Miya watched Johanna take a deep breath, an apparent attempt to slow the pace, to settle her nerves. "Uh-huh. And then she read a book you hadn't read to her."

"Only once. I'd only read it to her one time. She *was* reading."

"I know that she's doing the reading for class," Miya added, keeping their focus where it needed to be. "I always include questions on a test about something we haven't discussed in class, and Kayla always knows those answers."

"That's my girl," Johanna said with pride and a bit of obvious relief. "She's always been a good student. But I make it a point to meet her teachers and let them know that if she is having any problems or if there are things that she can improve, to tell me so that I can help from my end."

"I wish every parent was as engaged as you are. I see the difference that makes every day."

"Is there anything she needs to improve on in your class?"

Miya's expression was pensive. She shook her head slowly. "You know, I try to avoid pushing expectations that might be contrary to a child's natural personality." The questioning look from Johanna was expected. Miya continued, "She's very quiet in class, doesn't offer answers or ask questions. But anytime I call on her, she's ready with an answer. I'd love for her to be more involved, but I don't want to make the classroom experience uncomfortable for her."

Johanna seemed relieved and more at ease. "Kayla's reserved, but she isn't shy. She has a quiet confidence that surprises people. Her first day of kindergarten, she started up the bus steps then turned and said, 'It'll be okay, Mom. I'll be back soon.'"

"Oh, that's priceless."

"It is," Johanna agreed, adding a relaxed smile. "And that memory has served to temper a punishment now and then."

Miya offered a soft laugh and replied, "As it should."

"I must admit, I'm lucky. She's a good girl. She doesn't cross the line often, and when she has, so far, it's been a soft step."

Miya raised her eyebrows. "I've found that that's often a testament to good parenting."

"A mother can't hear *that* too many times."

"Especially a single mother?"

"*Especially* a single mother." Johanna rose slowly from the chair. "And as such," she said, "I suppose I should get home." She took a quick look at her phone. "I'll be getting a text from Kayla if I don't get moving. Sometimes I think she worries more about me than I do her."

Any temptation Miya felt to pull out Kayla's essay and have Johanna read it, any temptation to take the conversation to what could be at the core of that essay, had just been squelched. Maybe she *should* have turned the conversation, taken control of it, taken the chance to take it to an uncomfortable place. But she didn't. Miya rose, moved around the corner of the desk, and extended her hand. *Take the chance now—you've already set it up.* "Thank you for letting me know a little about you and Kayla," she said, holding their handshake longer than normal. "Would you meet with me again? There is something else that I'd like to talk with you about."

Johanna offered a hesitant nod.

"Something that maybe we can help Kayla with that we haven't had time to talk about tonight."

"Yes," Johanna replied. "Kayla is my top priority, so I'd be more than happy to meet again."

"Great." Miya reached into the leather bag, retrieved a card with her number on it, and handed it to Johanna. "Give me a call and let me know what day works for you. My schedule is flexible after three thirty."

Johanna entered the house through the side door from the garage. She dropped her purse on the end of the counter as Kayla's voice reached her from the family room.

"They kick me out yet?"

Johanna leaned over the back of the couch and kissed the top of her daughter's head. "No, I talked them into keeping you for another semester."

Kayla offered a spoonful of ice cream over her shoulder.

"Mmm," she mumbled as the dessert melted in her mouth. "You're welcome."

Johanna turned back to the kitchen for her own bowl of ice cream. "You know I have to keep you in school," she directed toward the other room.

"Yep," Kayla called back. "So that I can get a good job and take care of you in your old age."

Johanna joined her on the couch, propped her feet on the coffee table next to Kayla's and added, "I won't need a lot—my own room, balanced meals—"

"Clothes allowance, transportation."

Johanna turned to face her daughter and grinned around a mouthful of ice cream.

"And don't worry," Kayla said, "I know that you'll do *anything* to stay out of a nursing home.”

Another grin from Johanna. “I love you.”

“Uh-huh. Aunt Kate calls it sweet talkin’.”

“Your teachers had good things to say about you.”

Kayla nodded and scooped up the last bite of ice cream.

“I’m really proud of you.”

She pushed against her mother’s shoulder.

“Do you like all your teachers this year?”

“Yeah, pretty much,” Kayla replied. “Mr. Harris talks while he’s facing the board, and it makes it hard to follow.”

“Seems like your history teacher could make things fun in class.”

Kayla nodded. “He calls himself a punster. We have Punday Fridays. He gives us quizzes on Thursdays, and on Fridays we write down every pun we catch, turn in the list at the end of the hour, and he adds the points to our quiz scores.”

Johanna leaned her head back in thought. “That’s clever,” she said. “Are the puns things that he wants you to remember for the test?”

“Yeah.”

“Clever,” she repeated. “Making the list, and making it count on Friday when everyone is anxious for the weekend. That makes you focus. And the puns help you remember past the weekend. I like him.”

“Me, too.” Kayla collected their empty bowls and took them to the kitchen.

“You know,” Johanna said, waiting as Kayla rejoined her on the couch, “your English teacher isn’t at all what I expected.”

“What did you expect?”

“I guess more along the lines of what the English teachers I had were like—older, grey hair, and kind of stuffy. A far cry from Ms. James. I sure can’t visualize Mrs. Perkins, in my senior year, clipping one side of her head and leaving the rest to those crazy curls.”

"I like it."

Johanna smiled to herself. Her cheeks warmed. "I do, too."

"So, your teachers were stuffy?"

"Oh, you know, teachers who are so used to their material that the excitement is gone. It's like they're talking to the room, and not the students. As if the words are put out there, they will automatically be absorbed and understood. Ms. James, on the other hand, seems quite tuned in to what students are getting out of her class."

"Yeah, definitely not stuffy."

"Then you like her?"

"Uh-huh. Tami's older sister really liked her class. She said during the second semester, Ms. James has the class act out scenes from books and then they talk about what it means. I hope she still does that. She might end up being my favorite teacher."

Another private smile. "I can see why."

A hot bath, the kind that turned her skin pink from neck to toe, was one of Johanna's favorite things. She breathed deeply the scent of warm lavender, let the tension dissolve, and leaned her head back onto the little bath pillow.

It had been a long day, but a mostly good one. She had finished her paperwork at the office, had time for a quick dinner, heard wonderful reports at the parent-teacher conferences, and then . . . Miya.

Johanna took another deep breath and closed her eyes. That was the moment she realized that sleep wasn't going to be all that easy tonight. There, behind closed lids, was the face of Miya James, blue-grey eyes sparkling their disturbing appeal. That alluring smile introducing herself once again. *Who is this woman invading my mind, distracting me, disrupting my life?*

She hadn't invited her, here in her private space, her private time. Had she? She hadn't intentionally opened that part of herself that welcomed another woman into her thoughts, into her life. She hadn't. Johanna had guarded that part of her life so tightly for so long now that she had nearly forgotten about it. Suppressed how exciting and potentially damaging another woman could be. So how did *this* one squeeze through? How had Miya James found what must have been a hairline crack? Or had she opened it herself—allowed this woman to peek into the most private part of her life? She revisited the night of the party, the desire she felt, the need unsatisfied. Maybe she had.

Johanna took another deep breath of lavender. Okay, she thought, Miya would be staying the night in her head, permission or not. She'd let her talk to her about Kayla in that smooth and confident tone and flash the smile that tumbled all defenses. Yes, tonight Miya would keep her awake longer than she should and tempt her with a dream that must remain a dream. And after tonight, she would have to go, banished into her role as teacher, and nothing more. There would not be another Lori, no other woman allowed to disrupt her life or challenge her priorities. *That* was written in stone.

Chapter 10

A F T E R S H O C K

But she didn't go. Miya James didn't cooperatively vanish from Johanna's mind. All day long she interfered with focusing on homeowner quotes and recommendations, jumping into every blank space and pushing aside attempted calculations. Instead of words and numbers, blue-grey eyes stared back at her. The sultry sound of Miya's voice still played clear and distinct over the loop of instrumental office music. Most disturbing, though, was the scent of her perfume. Here in the office. Impossible. She'd walked by Ginny's desk and her coworker's and a new hire at the receptionist's desk and found none of them to be the source. She couldn't find it, and she couldn't shake it. It wasn't on her clothes or her hands, yet it was there. Her mind playing with her and driving her to find some kind of relief.

It was all she could do to say a quick "see you tomorrow" to everyone and rush to her car. She retrieved the phone from her purse, and that's when it made sense. She hit Kate's number. "Oh my God, Kate," she began, "I'm *not* crazy."

"What?" Kate replied. "What are you talking about?"

She pulled the card that Miya had given her from her purse and breathed in the scent. The card with the phone number, of course, straight from Miya's hand. "You are not going to believe this! *I* can't believe this."

"Believe what? What's going on?"

"Make a wild, totally unbelievable guess as to who Kayla's English teacher is."

"Totally unbelievable," Kate pondered. It took a minute, then, "Nooo."

"Yes. Ms. 'feeling the heat' herself. I walked right into her classroom for the conference with no warning. I don't know which of us was more shocked. At least, I think that she was shocked. I couldn't get my senses balanced enough to be sure."

"What did she say?"

"All I can remember is that she wanted to know if I thought that night at the party was real or something like that. The rest of the time I was too busy trying not to sound like an idiot." Ginny passed by on her way to her car and mouthed, "everything okay?" Johanna gave her a thumbs-up and continued. "I was rambling on about reading to Kayla when she was little and her not being shy, and . . . I don't even want to know what she thought about me."

"Well, you called me for a reason," Kate replied. "And from experience, I'm betting you're being far too self-abasing. For all you know, she may have been just as shocked as you are."

"Don't you think a shock like that would act like a bucket of ice water on a fever? Shouldn't it have doused the sound of her voice and drowned the sight of her? But no, she was in my head all day long. I couldn't concentrate, couldn't do my job. I don't know how to shake this."

"When was the conference?"

"Yesterday."

"Yesterday," the tone of her voice sounded like Kate was smiling. "Do you think maybe you should give yourself a little time? A week? Two?"

As if she hadn't heard a word Kate said, Johanna offered, "I was fine before the conference. I'd put her out of my head, out of the realm of possibility. I'd left that night behind me without any concern about unanswered questions."

"Well, you may not want it to be, but the fact that this is bothering you so much says that it is part of your life. Now, it could end up being a part that you want to get past and not have it change things in your life, but I'm pretty sure that it won't happen by magic. You are going to have to deal with it one way or another."

"I want my quiet, uncomplicated, sometimes monotonous life back."

"And you can say that with a teenager living in your house?"

Johanna laughed and finally took a deep breath. "Oh, this has a whole new dimension of disruption."

"Give it some time."

"She wants me to meet with her again to talk about helping Kayla with something."

"Be the parent you have always been. But I would give it a week or so first before you call. Let things settle down. You'll be fine."

Chapter 11

WINGS AND WISDOM

True to her word and more efficient than school personnel have a right to be, Chandra breezed into Miya's classroom as the last student was leaving.

"Okay," she began, the indigo-blue caftan flowing around the chair as she sat, "I talked with all her teachers, checked with administration, and got nothing that would raise any concern at all."

"So now what?"

"I asked everyone to be alert for anything. Kayla seems to have different friends in each of her classes, so I'll see if *their* records raise any concerns." Chandra rose to leave. "Oh," she added, "and I asked Tee Charbonnet in P.E. to let me know if she notices any bruises or injuries on Kayla."

Miya cringed at the thought but tried not to make it apparent. Chandra's request was altogether professional and honestly naive. She couldn't know how Tee would feel about her seemingly simple request. But Miya knew.

"What are we doing," Miya asked, "waiting for something more definitive before we rattle her mother's world?"

"Yes, until we know who, we are just making accusations. It wouldn't hurt to have another go at Kayla."

She texted Tee before leaving school. "Meet me for wings and drinks at Westside?"

"Professional, social, or other?"

"Five thirty."

Miya arrived fifteen minutes early and got a table only minutes before Tee Charbonnet strolled through the door with a smile that had captured too many women's hearts. And for a while, hers among them. There had been plenty of reasons to date this woman—she was exciting, on the basketball court and off, magnetic, sexy. Together, they'd been a couple that had turned heads and attracted attention wherever they went. And privately, they teased and laughed their way through the months, and made love with passion and urgency.

She watched the tall figure make her way across the room to the bar and smiled at the twinge of—of what? Of what had attracted her in the beginning? Movements sure and smooth, skin the color of creamed coffee, light brown eyes that invited you closer, held you in, and that unmistakable hair style—the sides buzzed over her ears and a shock of loose brown curls left to their own arrangement. Just recently, Tee's hairdresser had talked Miya into a modified version for her longer dark curls.

Ms. Charbonnet certainly had her charms. But it had been four years since they'd agreed that a friendship must be paramount. Sex would no longer be allowed to delay discussions or disguise the push and pull of opinions and goals. And it hadn't been an easy transition. There was no denying the chemistry between them, the appeal that tempted the strip-down, throw-down desire that at times had consumed them. But there were things that needed resolving and facts that needed facing. Their innate competitiveness was one of them. Tee had summed it up perfectly, "I think we would have killed each other."

The twinge, the allure, had been left to settle into admiration and appreciation for a good friendship. Tee placed the drinks on the table and acknowledged Miya's smile. "Why did I know you would beat me here?" Her eyes danced with amusement as she claimed the chair across the small table.

"I don't know *where* I got *that* bad habit."

Tee tilted her head at the reference. "Acquired a few of those myself."

Miya nodded. "Like having to have the last word, the last step, the highest score, the—"

"And you were bound and determined not to allow it."

"Guilty," Miya replied. "And I don't have any idea where that came from either. It was a challenge, I guess, one that I couldn't step away from. Unhealthy—for both of us."

Tee leaned back in her chair and offered an easy smile, one that signaled a direct contradiction to her competitive nature. That smile, coupled with a tender gaze from captivating eyes, always caught Miya's breath. And Tee knew it. "There were times, though," she said, "when we were very good together."

Yes, Miya thought, *very* good. She broke eye contact when the waitress delivered barbecue wings to the table. A welcome diversion. The timing was good. They could indulge in a shared favorite meal and change the subject. She was grateful when, at times, things just fell into place.

"Okay," Tee began after dabbing sauce from her lips, "what's this all about?"

"I want to fill you in on the student that Dr. Reed and I are concerned about—and to apologize."

Tee offered a questioning look.

"For what she asked you to do. I'm sure she doesn't realize the position that puts you in."

"Watching for bruises and injury?"

"Uh-huh."

"Sadly," Tee replied, "I'm in a unique position to help, but, as you know, it takes only one untrue allegation to put my job in jeopardy. Been there once, and even though it was a different school and different administration, I'm not about to tempt fate."

"You know I would never expect you to. And I want you to know that, as much as I respect and trust Chandra, I would never tell her anything about you."

"I know you, maybe better than you think I do. More than that, I trust you. You don't have to worry about what I think. And I didn't lie to Dr. Reed. I may have misled her a tad," she said, adding a smug grin. "I told her that if I saw anything, I would certainly let her know. What she doesn't know is that I don't step foot in that locker room unless an assistant calls me in. If there is an accident, an argument, or bullying, they'll call me in. But so far, nothing has happened involving Kayla."

"Mostly, that's good news," Miya replied. "It's one more indication that Kayla was talking about someone else. But so much could be happening on social media."

"Well, we all need to keep our eyes and ears open and take our cues from the kids. Chandra told me she will be making a second round of the kids Kayla hangs around with to see if any of them have seen anything in the cyber world. Have you talked with Kayla's parents?"

"Yes and no. A single mother who, from our parent/teacher conference, seems totally dedicated to her daughter's care and education. I concentrated on listening and letting her do most of the talking. What I saw and heard was the kind of parent we all hope our students have in their corner. I didn't get any indication of abuse or neglect. And all I have right now is the discussion I had with Kayla about her essay, which raised suspicion but fell short of telling me who, or even *what's* happening. Bottom line is that I don't have enough information. If Chandra doesn't come up with who or what, it would just sound like an accusation, an unsubstantiated accusation. And if Chandra *does* come up with information, then she'll report it."

"And then it is out of your hands, no longer your quandary."

And here it is, Miya mused, the deeper reason she was sitting across from Tee. It hadn't been part of a conscious decision, but it was there under the surface—the need for the kind of honesty and insight borne of intimacy. Truths and hopes and fears shared and laid bare, the basis for their friendship.

Tee finished her last bite of chicken and took a sip of beer. When there was no rebuttal from Miya, she continued. "What happens if Dr. Reed doesn't shake anything loose?"

"It's back to me, then."

"And?"

"I don't know," Miya replied with a frown. "All I've got is an essay that triggered reactions to my own childhood and a denial from the student."

"I think you should trust your instincts."

Miya hesitated before admitting, "I'm not finding any instincts here."

"Really?" The space between Tee's brows deepened into a 'V'. "That first thought, that first reaction when you—"

"It's not that easy, Tee."

"It is if you'd stop denying your instincts. You already talked with the student. Now you need to talk with the mother. Sometimes pissing off a parent comes with the territory."

"And if I'm wrong?"

Tee shrugged. "Then you might piss off a parent. But if you're right, you're going to save some kid from more misery— or worse."

She was right, of course. Tee wouldn't hesitate. She'd act, go with her gut, trust herself. It was what made her such a tough athlete, split-second ability—assess, decide, execute. But Tee wasn't conflicted.

"There's more to it," Miya admitted. "I can't expect your best advice unless you know the full picture."

"Which is?"

"I met Johanna Beals before I knew she was Kayla's mother. Over the summer, working on the music festival."

"And you hooked up?"

Miya shook her head. "No. But I would have, in that moment, with what little I knew. She was," she stopped. Until now she hadn't had to identify it, hadn't found words that explained it. "I don't know for *sure* why neither of us took it further. We left it at first names only and knowing nothing about each other beyond the physical attraction. But after the parent/teacher conference with her, I think I can assume that it had a lot to do with Kayla."

"Yeah, kids can be a real fire stop," Tee replied. "And their mothers have a whole different set of rules."

"I'm sure they do."

Tee held her gaze, her silent emphasis. "So, you're walking on eggshells because you don't want to ruin any chance of taking things further?"

Miya tilted her head back and focused on the ceiling for a moment. When she brought her focus back to Tee, she said, "I don't know what I'm doing."

"Well, you know I'm not going to put myself in a position to say that I told you so, but I *will* tell you what I think. You have to look at the situation seriously and realistically. A relationship with her, no matter how brief, can jeopardize your job. If you've learned anything over the past few years, you know that even a law that says they can't discriminate against you at work can't be counted on. Laws can be overturned, administrations can 'find' other 'reasons' to fire you. You are Kayla's teacher. A parent will have rules you aren't used to. And kids talk."

Classic Tee. Direct, clear, right on point. Speaking truth, exactly what Miya expected. There wouldn't be criticism or judgment, only support for whatever decision she made. Something she was sure of.

Miya nodded, looking directly into Tee's eyes. "I know. *That* much at least."

"And you're going to be careful and reasonable and remember that physical attraction is only part of the equation."

A plea heard. Loud and clear. Don't put yourself in danger.

"I say that because I love you," Tee said, leaning across the table to take Miya's hand, "and because you would tell me the same thing if the situation was reversed."

"Yes, I would."

Chapter 12

WARNING

Kayla texted Zack again. Something was wrong, more wrong than usual. He wasn't answering texts or calls, hadn't gotten off the bus in the morning, and hadn't shown up in the cafeteria.

He knew that the counselors had been asking questions, and he'd been skipping gym class lately. The last text he had answered was after school yesterday, when he said that he was fine and turned down her invitation to come to her house. It made her worry even more than she usually did.

Maybe he was just sick and had stayed home and slept all day. Maybe his mother was sick or drunk, and needed him. It was probably wrong of her to hope that he was sick, but it was better than imagining him hurt or hiding out somewhere.

Kayla started down the hall toward her locker when her phone signaled a text. Zack. Her relief was immediate.

"Meet at church playground."

"U ok?"

"Yes."

"K."

He hadn't taken the bus, so he must have biked it, she

thought, as she opened her locker. She'd be asking questions and expecting answers, and he no doubt knew that.

Kayla grabbed her backpack and had barely pulled it clear of the locker when a hand came from behind her and slammed the door shut. Startled, she tried to turn around but was pinned against the locker. White leather-clad arms on either side trapped her against the grey metal. The varsity jacket made it clear who it was even before he spoke.

"Who you been talkin' to?" Josh Carter growled in heated breath an inch from the side of her face. "Huh?" he added, pushing her against the locker with the weight of his body.

"What are you talkin' about?" she replied, surely sounding less intimidated than he hoped. "Get off me." She struggled against him, trying to turn. "Get off me," she said again.

He let up enough to let her turn to face him. He kept his face so close to hers that she felt the heat of his anger. "You're gonna shut your mouth."

Kayla stared hard into his eyes, only inches away. She clenched her jaw and said nothing as she barely contained the urge to bring her knee up hard between his legs.

"You keep messin' in weeny boy's business," he warned, "and you're gonna get treated just like him." He moved back beyond the reach of her knee as if he had sensed the urge she was fighting.

Kayla looked around. The hallway was becoming busy, but she realized that how he had positioned himself around her could easily be mistaken for boyfriend/girlfriend intimacy. Easily ignored. And conveniently absent from her locker were Julie and her girlfriends.

With one last warning, "You shut your mouth," Josh shoved his finger at her face, then turned and left.

Kayla grabbed her jacket and the strap of her backpack and charged down the hall. Jangled nerves only served to amp up her already adrenalin-fueled strides, and the anger, not fear, that she was leaving with. Certainly not what Josh had intended.

The eight-block walk to the church playground served as inadequate therapy. Block by block, the harsh urgency of her steps marked time with her anger. Step by angry step made her want to yell as loud as her lungs would allow. *You have no right, no damn right to hurt people or scare people. Who gives Josh Carter the right to do that? I won't be scared,* she swore with jagged breaths. *You won't make me scared. It's not right.* Thoughts searched for resolution and failed. It frustrated her, added anxiety to her anger. She had to do *something*, didn't she? Or her mother. If only Zack would let her.

He was where she knew he would be, in the top of the playscape at the back of the playground. Kayla climbed the ladder and ducked into the canvas-covered structure. An empty McDonald's bag and soda on the floor next to him indicated he'd been there for a while.

Zack looked up from his sketch pad briefly and dropped his focus before saying, "Who did you tell?"

Kayla dropped her backpack and sat on it. Her irritation was obvious in the harsh tone of her voice. "You, too?"

His head snapped up. "What are you talking about?"

"Josh Carter just accused me of the same thing, up close and in my personal space."

"He threatened you?"

"Yeah, with the same treatment if I don't stay out of your business."

"I *told* you not to say anything." His voice rose, sounding anxious and edgy. "It's only gonna get worse, and not just for me. Now they'll go after you."

"I *didn't* say anything."

"Well, somebody did," he replied. "The counselors were all over asking questions."

"They think it's me," she said, hugging her knees. "The counselors think it's me being bullied. I wrote something in an assignment. It was about how important goodness is. It made Ms. James think it was me, and she wanted me to talk to Dr. Reed—"

"Did you?"

"*No*," she said with a frown. "Ms. James must have." She stared at him. He doubted her. She could see it in his face. And his silence—yes, he doubted her. "Zack, how many times have I lied to you?"

He hesitated. She waited.

"Never," he said, "that I know of."

She ignored the less-than-affirming answer. "How many times have I lied *for* you?"

He dropped his head back against the wall but didn't answer.

He was angry—and scared. She knew that. It kept her from being mad at him and snapping back. Instead, she felt frustration. He wanted a solution, and she had none—at least not one that he was willing to try. It left her with a tough choice: be faithful to their friendship and honor his trust in her, or expose what was happening and take a chance on it escalating.

He spoke, his head still resting against the wall, his focus on the faded blue and gold canvas covering the structure. "I told you I don't want my mom to know. What gives them the right to judge her—or me?"

"Josh Carter doesn't want anyone judging *him*. He's just a little person, taking his own fears out on someone else. The rest of them are just followers. Making others feel less-than somehow makes them feel better-than."

His focus, sharp and serious, met her eyes. "And now others think that I'm less-than, because they decided I am."

"They don't decide anything."

"Yes, they *do*," he insisted. "They decide for other people, for everyone who reads their tweets and believes what they say.

People who don't know me or my mother. And the ones who do know me? It makes them treat me like I have the plague or something."

"Not because of you, Zack. They don't want to be bullied, too. It's not because they don't like you, or don't want to be your friend. It's because they're afraid."

"Are you afraid now, too?"

"That's what you're worried about?"

"Chad and Danny won't sit with me at lunch anymore. Kids I've known since first grade stay away from me." He pushed his head hard against the wooden wall, his bottom lip quivered. "You don't know how it feels. You don't see their eyes or imagine what they're thinking." Tears formed at the corners of his eyes, and he wiped them quickly. "It doesn't matter what I do," he said, tears escaping before he could catch them. "It just doesn't matter."

He didn't want to cry; she knew that. It wasn't manly, it meant that he was weak, ultimately the perfect target. Kayla left her seat and moved across to sit next to him. "It matters, Zack, it all matters," she said. "How you feel matters."

"Only to you," he replied.

She shook her head. "They're afraid." Kayla looked closer at the graphics on the sketch pad resting loosely in Zack's lap. His hero strip—the unassuming "boy next door" with an extraordinary power. He could paralyze an aggressor with eye contact. The connection, eye to eye, dissipated anger, neutralized aggression, stopped action mid-strike. Zack liked to describe the aggressor's response as "blanked"—they couldn't remember what had made them angry or mean or violent. Stopped. Blanked. He had named his hero Peynon.

"I wish Pey was real," Kayla said. "We sure could use his power right now. I'd love to see ol' Josh's face, all confused and dumbfounded. I'd love it."

"Yeah," he replied, "but he's not."

"Hey, I have an idea," she said. "My English teacher helps

sponsor the online newspaper. Let's talk to her about including your strip each week."

But he was shaking his head.

"Why not?" she asked. "It's good, Zack. You said that your art teacher really likes it, too."

He closed the art pad and shoved it into his backpack. "It would be one more thing for them to pick on."

"I think you should think about it."

"Yeah," he said unconvincingly.

Chapter 13

HOPE AND A PRAYER

Miya sat on the little orange chair, the pages of *Thank You, Thank You, Thank You* resting high on her knees and facing the young children gathered in the corner of the family shelter. She knew the words without looking and watched the attentive little faces as they followed the story from page to page. The message was clear and simple, finding its place in the young hearts—grateful for big things and small, for the air and the seas and hugs and bees.

"What other things are we grateful for?" Miya asked.

"A nice bed," said five-year-old Kevin.

Four-year-old Alysha said, "My mom."

Jamil proudly placed his hands on his chest. "My new sweatshirt."

They all proudly voiced their thanks until a tall, slender, dark-haired man approached the group. Jamil jumped up and wrapped his arms around his waist. "I'm grateful for Michael," he said.

Michael ruffled the little boy's hair and said, "And I'm grateful that I can come and see you all every Saturday. So, is everyone ready for lunch?"

Nine little bodies jumped to their feet, and Michael added, "Okay, everyone. Thank Miya before you go."

Miya stood amid thank-you's and hugs and high-fives and smiled at her brother. "I wish I could bottle up these smiles and hand them out as medicine."

"A natural elixir," he said. "If only."

"Well, we may not be able to bottle those smiles, but we can go make more of them."

As she'd done for the past three Saturdays, Miya rode with her brother from the Family Shelter to A Hand Up, a shelter in the middle of town. Packed in the back of the truck were boxes of clothing, blankets, and books they'd collected during the week.

Michael took the boxes of clothing to the storeroom while Miya delivered the books to the day manager.

Gail Anders accepted the box with an appreciative smile. "Oh, thank you, Miya. I am so excited about our new little library, and the women just love it."

"Now that makes me happy," Miya replied. "After all, a well-loved library is our goal. I'm trying to include a variety—fiction, non-fiction, poetry, self-help. You never know what book or words will touch a need in someone."

Gail opened the box and began looking through the books. "These are wonderful."

"And if you get requests for specific books or topics, let me know, okay?"

"You and Michael are blessings. Our budget barely covers our essentials."

"Well, you should thank this guy right here," Miya said as Michael joined them. "This is all his idea."

"I didn't have to twist her arm," Michael replied. "We're

happy to help however we can." He took Gail's hand and squeezed it. "God provides the blessings."

The sun was low in the late afternoon sky, prompting Michael to pull the visor over the driver's door window. "I'm buying next week," Miya insisted as they enjoyed their favorite calzones.

"Nope," he returned between bites. "I'm going to thank you whether you want me to or not."

"Knowing that I'm helping is enough thanks." She took a sip of her drink and added, "But I'm not going to turn down a 'best in state' calzone."

Michael chuckled. "Yeah, I didn't think so."

She smiled at herself. *Predictable.* He would insist and she would concede—on the little things. It was part of how they managed an adult relationship. It wasn't always that way, though. There had been years after she'd left home when they rarely spoke. But they had learned how to stand their ground, hold strong to personal principles, and give ground to compromise when it was needed.

He grinned at her around a full bite. Blue eyes, darker than her own, seemed to twinkle with self-satisfaction. They'd come a long way from his heart-wrenching phone call to her at her grandmother's. She could hear him still during alone times, the sobbing pleas of an eleven-year-old Michael. "Just come home, Miya. Please, just come home. They're saying terrible things. It's scaring me." It tore at her heart. He only wanted everything to be okay. But it wouldn't be, it couldn't be, and she didn't know how to tell him that. "No, Michael, I can't" wasn't enough, and wouldn't be for a long time.

"Oh, and just a reminder," she said, crumbling her food bag into a ball, "Evelyn and Don don't need to know that I'm doing this with you."

"You don't have to remind me," he replied. "But I think you're missing a perfect opportunity."

"To do what? Show our parents that I'm doing God's work and that there's hope for my wayward soul?"

"Come on, Miya," he said, scrunching his brow. "Give 'em a chance. Come for Thanksgiving. Talking about the shelters would make a good conversation. That's something they can relate to. You'd be on common ground."

His voice was mature now, lower and more confident, but Miya still heard his eleven-year-old pleas. The push and pull of their relationship continued. It was unavoidable, accepted, and allowed by their love for each other.

"And what would having that conversation do? Convince them that the demon ravishing my soul had magically left and that their prayers worked?"

"Just try, Miya."

"I have. It always ends the same way—them telling me all about the beautiful life our sister is living, how successful her husband is, how precious her children are. And me choking back a reaction to scream at Evelyn that her attempt at nuancing a message is pathetic."

"They love you," he replied. "They worry about you. I saw how worried they were during the pandemic when you had to go back into the classroom." He hesitated as if he was questioning whether he should push further. "Look," he decided, "I can't explain exactly what it is, but they've been different after the pandemic, especially Mom. She called me and Sarah almost every day, and she asked about you since she couldn't call you."

"Lucky me for having an unlisted number. They're only worried about me dying before my soul can be saved. It's masochistic to keep putting myself in a situation when I already know the outcome. And I'm not going to lie to them."

"Maybe she feels bad; maybe something made her see how much this estrangement has hurt you."

"Sounds like guilt. I'm sorry, Michael, but no amount of guilt, if that's what it is, can ever erase years of rejection, years of feeling unworthy, and immoral. It can't take away the fear that gripped me in the middle of the night or the anger that threatened my chance of happiness. You'll never be able to understand that, and neither will they."

He didn't reply, only flipped the sun visor back to its position above the windshield. A typical end to their conversations involving their parents.

Miya watched his profile as he stared ahead, the dark wavy hair and strong jaw so like his father's. Still wishing he could somehow make things right. She searched for a way to help him understand, to relieve him of a futile hope.

"You said they ask you about me." She had his attention again. "Have they ever asked if I'm happy?"

His eyes held hers for a long moment before the space between his brows pressed into a hard crease. "No," he replied.

Chapter 14

BOOM

The call from Johanna shouldn't have surprised Miya. All outward indications were that Johanna Beals was committed to raising her daughter. So why wouldn't she want to know if there was something more that she could do to help her? If not surprise, then, what? Delight? A barely disguised excitement? A feeling much like opening a new book, one with the cover that drew you in with its movement of line and color, one that you knew just enough about to want to know more. *This* book, though, she reminded herself, is banned. And like any banned book, the desire to read it was irresistible.

Punctual to the minute, Johanna appeared in the classroom doorway at three forty-five, looking far too appealing. Banned, Miya reminded herself.

"I'm beginning to think that I should enroll in your class," Johanna offered, light and breezy.

Miya responded with a welcoming smile and said, "On time, loves to read, wants to be in my class." She opened her arms, palms up. "Can't ask for more than that."

"Ah, but would I be as good a student as Kayla?" Johanna

said, sliding into the chair next to Miya's desk.

"Oh, I suspect like mother, like daughter."

"My hope is that Kayla grows up to be smarter and way more accomplished than her mother."

"That doesn't surprise me about you. Not one bit." Miya leaned forward on folded arms. "Which brings me to what I wanted to talk about." The quick turn to serious concern on Johanna's face made Miya want to switch to something that would ease that concern back into the smile that had captured her just moments ago. But the paper lying on the desk urged her on. "I wanted to share an essay with you that Kayla wrote," she began. "She writes beautifully, from the heart, I think. And it really caught my attention." She slid the essay across to Johanna and watched as she read it. Her expression didn't change as she read. Lines of concern still creased between her brows. When she'd finished reading, her focus remained on the paper.

"The last paragraph was what concerned me," Miya explained. "And I talked with her about it."

"What did she say?"

"That she wasn't wondering about it for herself."

Johanna stared hard into Miya's eyes, taking time, measuring her response. Finally, she said, "And you didn't know whether to believe her."

Miya nodded. "She wouldn't talk any further with me or to a counselor if we were going to report what she would say to Child Protective Services."

"So, this is *you* investigating her home life."

Miya recognized the tone, stiff, bordering on defensive. It was to be expected. A little bit of chemistry couldn't be expected to soften it. "I need to be sure, Johanna. I'm bound by law, and she doesn't seem to have any problems at school."

"So, it must be something horrible that she's dealing with at home—is that what you're thinking?"

"Or a family member, or neighbor, or friend, or someone you

may not even know about."

"And you were, or are, willing to report what a child tells you to CPS? Is that what you let Kayla believe? Do you have any idea how frightening that could be? Why would you—"

"Because I care, Johanna. Because—"

"Do you know what a CPS investigation can do to a child, to a family—and then they find nothing? Have you thought about that?"

"Yes, I have. That's why I wanted to talk with you."

"But I don't think you see the threat, the threat to a single mother, to a single lesbian mother. I decided sixteen years ago. It wasn't an easy one, but it was the right one. From the day Kayla was born, she has been my priority."

"I don't doubt your commitment to raising your daughter, Johanna. But I'm privy to a big part of my students' lives that parents only have secondhand knowledge of. Sometimes kids don't tell their parents everything."

"I know my daughter." Her words, clipped and hard. "If there was anything wrong, she would tell me. I would know it. And I resent someone who knows *nothing* about me or my daughter insinuating that I haven't protected her and kept her safe." Johanna stood abruptly, indignation showing in the tight hold of her head and the terse tone of her voice. She turned decisively toward the door. The discussion was over. With only a turn of her head at the doorway, she said with anger tinging the words, "I know my daughter." Then she was gone.

Moments later, Miya stood, gathered her papers, then dropped them again. She started to pick them up again but didn't. Instead, she moved aimlessly around the corner of the desk toward the perimeter of the room. Thoughts jumped like aggravated nerves as she circled the room. She had said what she had to, what her responsibility demanded, partially. But there was more she needed to say, should've said. Not having your teenager come to you with everything isn't unusual, or anything that should cause guilt or embarrassment. It should be something that parents and teachers work together to solve. A team with one mission—the best education, the best support, and the best care for their children. Not always an easy partnership, but, Miya thought, one worth the effort. An effort, this time, that may have hit a solid wall.

She folded her arms across her chest and continued her aimless journey around the room. One doubt wouldn't settle. Shouldn't she have danced and nuanced her way to a better outcome? When Johanna said, "and you didn't know whether to believe her," she did not want to hear that her daughter may have lied or that someone like Miya didn't believe her. No, clearly, she should have danced.

Miya stopped at the window. The parking lot was beginning to thin out; teachers who sponsored student activities, some paid and some volunteers, were finally headed home. One of the cars winding its way to the exit was probably Johanna's. Would she talk with Kayla, take a chance on breaching the trust that she was so sure they had? Miya dropped into the last seat in the row and stretched her legs out into the aisle. She imagined herself in Johanna's place, so sure, committed. *If that trust was indeed justified, wouldn't I be just as indignant as Johanna? Or would I be able to understand the commitment of a teacher to her job and her students?* How personal would it feel—to a single mother? Not knowing what it had taken to raise a child made it hard to step into those shoes. And now, the chance to understand that, to fully understand Johanna—her strength and her weaknesses, what worried her, what she feared—was probably gone. The universe had just added a layer of protection.

The aroma of homemade stroganoff carried on warm air from the kitchen lifted Johanna's mood, a perfect diversion as she entered the house. It was funny, she thought, how she could have raised a child who, at sixteen, was a far better cook than she was. Oh, she hadn't starved, nor had her child growing up. She'd mastered the home economics basics out of a sense of necessity, a staple of survival. But Kayla, Kayla enjoyed cooking.

Johanna left her purse on the end of the counter, closed her eyes, and took a deep breath. "Ohh, that smells dangerously good." She approached Kayla at the stove and wrapped her arms around her shoulders from behind. "Have I told you lately how much I appreciate you, Martha?"

Kayla smiled and stirred the noodles into the pan on the stove. "You are so easy."

"I am, aren't I?" she replied with a kiss to her daughter's cheek.

"Set the table," Kayla said, "everything's ready." She filled the serving dish and placed the salad and main dish on the table, then added the breadbasket with warm bread wrapped in a towel.

"Uh-huh, that homemade bread that Kate sent over gave you the same hankerin' for her stroganoff."

"She gave me her recipe."

Johanna took a bite, closed her eyes, and savored it. "Mmm, perfect, Martha." She broke off a chunk of bread. "You do know that if you keep this up, I won't be able to let you leave home."

"Uh-huh," Kayla replied, reaching for the bread, "that'll work for now."

For now. Johanna looked at the young woman she had raised. Sometimes when she looked at her it didn't seem possible. All the times she had worried, laid awake nights wondering if she was making the right decisions, fearful that she was being too strict or too lenient. But despite it all, there she was—smart, kind, responsible. It had to be some kind of miracle, some force of power that placed everything in alignment. And, of course, Kate and Uncle Brad. There for advice and support, there as family. She was blessed, and tonight was a good time to be reminded of it.

Kayla began clearing the table, putting up the leftovers as Johanna drew dishwater. "My meeting was with your English teacher today."

"Another one?"

Johanna turned from the sink to face Kayla. "You'd tell me if someone was bothering you, wouldn't you?"

"*Bothering* me?"

"Harassing you, hurting you, or making you feel uncomfortable."

"No," she said with a fierce frown. "I mean, yes, I'd tell you." She placed the dish of leftovers in the refrigerator and leaned against the counter next to her mother. "I've known since I was a little girl that you would never let anyone hurt me. I know that you even broke it off with Lori because she wanted more time with you alone." There was a look of mild surprise on Johanna's face. "I was ten, Mom. It was obvious."

"So, you *would* tell me."

"I've always known that if I was afraid or there was something I couldn't handle, all I had to do was say so. Between you and Uncle Brad, I'd almost feel sorry for whoever bothered me."

"We *would* make their life miserable—that's an absolute. But you should never feel sorry for them. Bad behavior calls for tough lessons, and sometimes jail time."

Kayla nodded. "I know. But you can relax," she said with a soft smile. "I'm okay." She hugged her mother and kissed the side of her head. "Is that what the meeting was all about?"

"Ms. James was just overreacting to something that you wrote."

"My essay? Did you read it?" Kayla felt a moment of panic, of regret. It was just an essay. Or, more importantly, a lack of understanding about how it might be taken. Why did she have to say it that way?

"Uh-huh. I was pretty sure that you were talking about Zack." Kayla made no indication that she was wrong, and Johanna continued. "But she doesn't know you or your home life, and she doesn't know anything about Zack's home life. And you didn't want to tell her anything about him, did you?"

Kayla shook her head.

"He's dealt with the cycles his mother goes through all his life. And he knows to come here whenever he needs to. It's not an ideal home life, but if Child Protective Services gets involved, they'll probably put him in foster care. I doubt that they would consider placing him here with me. All they would have to hear is 'single lesbian mother.'" Johanna focused on the floor and shook her head. "Foster care would disrupt his life far more than his mother falling off the wagon. He knows how to handle that." She looked again at Kayla. "He knows that he's safe and loved here, doesn't he?"

"Yeah, he knows."

"Then we need to keep what we know to ourselves. I'm not saying that we should lie, but we don't have to give them any information that would make his life more difficult."

"That's what I thought, too," Kayla replied with relief. But almost as immediate as her relief was the wish that she could indeed tell others about the hell Zack was enduring at school. If only she could tell someone. But she knew her mother was right: no matter what, they would blame his home life and get Protective Services involved. There would be no way to solve one problem without flagging the other. "I'm glad you feel the same way," Kayla added.

Chapter 15

OPTIONS ACCORDING TO KATE

Johanna sent the text from the office parking lot. "Is reacting like an overly sensitive, overly defensive a$$hole a DNA thing? Asking for a friend."

Kate answered before Johanna could finish revising her to-do list. "Bring that overly sensitive, overly defensive friend right over."

Kate always made her smile whenever Johanna was afraid of making the wrong decision, when she was angry at things that weren't fair, at intolerance. Kate had always been able to corral the emotion, separate it neatly from the issue at hand, and whittle that issue down to size. It was time for a little perspective adjustment. So, after two weeks of self-chastisement, Johanna checked in with Kate.

She answered the door with an expression that said nothing's as bad as it seems. "Well, come on," Kate greeted her, "bring that poor conflicted friend on in. I have spirits, fresh pound cake, and two good ears."

"And my immeasurable gratitude."

"Ahh," Kate replied, waving off the compliment. "I haven't done anything yet."

"You're here." As she had always been.

"Oh, that part's easy."

Over pound cake and wine, Johanna spilled the details of a tangled mess of emotions and regret.

"You know that your reaction isn't all about Miya James, don't you," Kate said, more as a statement than a question. "You're defending against those early questions and doubts and criticism all over again."

Johanna nodded. "But I could have handled it so much better. I go right to defense mode. It's my default reaction. I reacted before I had time to sort out that Kayla was just protecting Zack."

"So how did *she* react?"

"I have no idea. I was too busy being a jackass to notice."

"Would you have handled it differently if it was one of her other teachers?"

"You mean would I have thought more clearly if my heart didn't beat out of control when she looks at me? And if I didn't want to get naked and make love with her all night?"

Kate smiled. "That," she replied, "is exactly what I meant."

"I'm a conflicted mess."

"Okay. Recognizing *that* is the first big step. Let's sort it out." Kate ran her finger around the rim of her glass. "Starting with that which will not be denied. Back in the day, we would say that you had the hots for her, but I like Whitney Houston's take on it better. So, is Miya James feeling the heat as well?"

"She did the night of the party. She made all the first moves." Johanna dropped her gaze from Kate's. "The way she touched me, the way she kissed me. If I hadn't left, I'm pretty sure we would have ended up in bed." Her gaze returned. "But that was before she realized I was Kayla's mother and before I acted like an asshole."

"I know you said chemistry would not have the last word, but there is a case for cutting to the chase."

"What are you suggesting?"

Kate's eyebrows rose as if it should be clear. "Getting past what-ifs and wasted time."

"And you're going to tell me how to do that?"

"I'm going to give you options according to Kate. The rest is up to you."

"That's why I'm here."

"And because you are, I'm assuming that muddling along like you are—letting her occupy that space in your head, making you wonder or wish, and doing nothing to shake her loose—isn't working. So, here's what I think. You can keep beating down the chemistry thing and try to get to know more about her. Invite her to lunch or something, somewhere public, apologize for over-reacting, and talk." Kate smiled and added, "Give her a chance to completely turn you off."

"Yeah, maybe she's arrogant, or constantly interrupts, or smacks her lips when she eats. Maybe she doesn't even vote."

"Definitely turnoffs."

"Or, more likely, I'll turn *her* off. Or maybe I already have, and she won't want to meet me anyway." The thought, as soon as it surfaced, seemed to be the most logical. "Problem solved," she said with resolution. "Game over."

"That's one possibility," Kate replied. "Another is that she only wants a sexual affair—meet for quickies whenever you can, no commitment, no promises." With a tilt of her head, she raised her eyebrows in question.

"You just have to go there, don't you?"

"Yes. It's logical and, frankly, quite probable. And for you to move forward, one way or another, you need to know."

"Lunch, huh?"

"Unless you think you can move on, put it behind you without really knowing."

"Maybe, if she forgives me, I'll find out she's a terrible lover, and then I could make my excuses and bow out."

"Only one way you're going to know that. You're going to have to destroy the mystery."

"And if I don't want to destroy the mystery?"

Kate leaned back in her chair. "Well, that's the safest option, isn't it? Fantasy lovers don't disappoint. They don't have warts or scars or baggage. They stay however you want them to be—for as long as you want."

"I'm pathetic."

Kate shook her head. "No. You're unsure of yourself. And wary. Could it be that the intensity you're feeling is because it's been so long since you've dated? It has been a very long time, even before Covid. Johanna, you're not a nun."

"Not officially," she said, smiling. "She made me feel . . ." Johanna hesitated, searching for the words, but nothing seemed adequate. "She made me *feel*. I was in a place that night that I had tried for years not to dream about. I felt attractive and desired. I liked how that felt. I liked it more than I should have."

"See, that's where you're wrong. You have as much right as anyone to feel like that. And you know what? At sixteen, Kayla's old enough and smart enough to accept that."

"It seems selfish, Kate. Taking a chance on bringing someone into her life, disrupting what's worked—for both of us—for what?"

"For a chance at a relationship? Happiness? You deserve that. You've committed yourself to raising a truly remarkable young woman. And I'll bet if you asked her, she'd tell you the same thing."

"I don't want another Lori in our lives, not even for a 'chance.' A child certainly wasn't high on her priority list. She had very little patience with Kayla and grudgingly spent time with her. Remember how many times I asked you to take Kayla so Lori and I could have time alone? And as much as Kayla loved being here, the truth wasn't lost on her. I had to try to answer a ten-year-old with tears in her eyes asking why Lori didn't like her.

The look on her face shredded me. In that moment, my head dropped out of the cloud, and I realized how selfish I was being. After that mess was over, I vowed I'd never do that again."

"And you haven't," Kate replied. "And you won't. Trust yourself, Johanna. You owe it to yourself to find out. And I'm going to get right to the obvious. She's a teacher, clearly cares about kids, concerned—enough despite your bit of history—to chance ruining any possible relationship to do the right thing. Who better to have around Kayla?"

Trust that reaching into a hive for a taste of honey won't get me stung. Just like that. Take the chance, never mind the risk. "Lunch," she said, more as a concession than a decision. "Just to see if Ms. James thinks I'm a complete asshole."

Chapter 16

THE MAGIC FOREST

Miya took an extra few minutes, there in her car, staring at the entrance to the little North End Grill. It was a long-standing favorite breakfast spot, a small, old restaurant crowded into the perimeter between dated residential and commercial buildings on the outskirts of the city.

Tee's warning had niggled her thoughts for days since she had agreed to meet Johanna. And rightly so, Miya conceded. *Don't put yourself in danger.* Your job, your emotions. She knew exactly what the danger was. And truly, she had never imagined having to worry about it. Attraction to a student's mother had never appeared on any "be prepared, this could happen to you" list. Nope. Never.

She finally turned off the engine and left the car before her better sense won out. It was well past the Saturday breakfast crowd and shy of the usual lunch time, so there was no wait. Miya scanned the well-worn, half-filled tables and booths and spotted Johanna, hand up and a careful half smile, sitting at a booth by the windows. Whatever that expression meant, whether it was apprehension or caution, it quickly dissolved

Miya's trepidation. Her own smile, a bright flash that said, "I really am glad to see you" elicited the one that had greeted her the night of the festival party.

"I've heard," Miya began as she slid into the booth, "that breakfast at this place has people dragging themselves out of bed at 7 a.m. even on Saturday."

Johanna nodded. "Six a.m. during the week. Food from local farms, prepared to perfection. It smells so good that my stomach does backflips before I get out of the car."

Miya smiled, ordered coffee, and picked up the menu.

"Are you a breakfast girl?" Johanna asked. "If you are, you can get breakfast here all day long."

"I am a breakfast girl, when I have time. I can brag about perfectly poached eggs and a mean spinach quiche. But today, I think I'll try something new and different." Miya pointed to a selection on the glossy menu. "Like this."

The waitress finished wiping down the table next to them and peered over Miya's shoulder. "That's my absolute favorite sandwich," she said. "And a ton of our regulars, too."

"Then I'm going to have to try it," Miya replied as the waitress produced a pad and pencil.

"I will, too," added Johanna.

"Two chicken bries coming up," the waitress said. "And coffee in ten seconds." She hustled behind the counter along the back wall, slipped the order to the cook, and returned with the coffee pot. "If I can get you anything else, just yell for Evie."

Johanna sipped her coffee, then lifted her eyes to meet Miya's.

Miya held her gaze, a silent dare for Johanna to look away. When she didn't, Miya asked, "What's this all about?"

Small talk clearly over, Johanna stayed with the unrelenting gaze. "I want to apologize," she began, "for acting like . . . for overreacting last time we spoke."

A flush colored Johanna's cheeks, her eyes diverted to the

window momentarily. It sent a physical twinge of sympathy to Miya's chest. She didn't want her to feel embarrassed or uncomfortable.

Johanna looked again directly at Miya. "I'm sorry, Miya. I realize that you were concerned and just doing your job. I never imagined that I would be one of those parents who embarrassed themselves and disrespected a teacher. It came from a personal place, and I mean this as an explanation, not an excuse. I raised Kayla under a very real threat that she could be taken from me. The fear that everything I did, everything that I said could be used to scrutinize my parenting skills and could be justification for my parents to take her or call CPS. It terrified me. It literally paralyzed my personal life. I don't know what would have happened if it weren't for the love and support of my aunt and uncle. The short version of this explanation is that my default reaction to anything remotely resembling that scrutiny is defense mode." Her posture softened. "That's exactly where I went."

It was so much more than she had expected, so personal, so sudden. Miya shook her head. Johanna deserved the same honesty. "Then you should know that Kayla's essay did more than worry me about her safety. Her words became me. The young me, too young for the fear and the anger, filling me, controlling me. Suddenly, it was tactile again, burning me, scarring me." She lowered her eyes from Johanna's gaze, hesitated while the enveloping silence buffered the memory. She raised her eyes to Johanna's again and held them. "That's why I had Dr. Reed read her essay. I was afraid *my* reaction was only personal, but the same words that had triggered *me* concerned her. So, I was left to do my job. It's a sensitive thing to ask a parent about, and I almost didn't do it. I tried to find a way around it, but then I realized that my *hesitation* was personal and not professional. So, please believe me that I did not take your reaction as disrespect."

Before Johanna could respond, Evie delivered their sandwiches and told them to enjoy, interrupting what had quickly become a personal confessional. A break perfect for deflection. There had been enough revelation, probably too much. Miya sampled her sandwich. "Oh, this is beyond delicious."

Johanna, however, did not follow suit. Her expression had changed. The stress lines between her brows softened and her face took on a look of wonderment. "Personal?"

"Eat your sandwich, it's fantastic."

"Personal, meaning that you were worried about how I would react."

Miya nodded and finished another bite. "Uh-huh," she managed, and followed with, "I generally try to avoid pissing off a parent."

"So just the usual diplomacy?"

Her persistence was unavoidable. Miya put her sandwich back on the plate, hesitated for a moment, and conceded. She leaned forward on her forearms and kept her voice low. "No, there was nothing usual about it. In eight years of teaching, I have never once laid awake wondering when I could see a student's mother again. Never once did I kiss a student's mother, or dance with her and feel the heat from her body and know that she wanted the same thing that I did. Not once—until now."

The corners of Johanna's mouth curled into a slow smile. Her eyes stayed with Miya's just long enough to send their silent message, then broke away. She picked up her sandwich, took a bite, and nodded. "Mmm." She pointed to the sandwich and offered a thumb-up.

Coy, Miya thought. She's being coy, right there, plain as day, playing the coy card. That moment said so much. She wasn't shy. She wasn't naive. Oh, no, certainly not naive. Johanna Beals knew exactly what she was doing. At least one of them knew.

Miya watched her as they ate their lunch and talked, mostly insignificant talk. Watching, listening. Learning? Was that smart? Would learning more about this woman help keep things in perspective, temper temptation, dispel unrealistic dreams? Or would it only make things distinctly worse? What she needed was a thought, a reminder, so sharp it would prick and destroy any errant daydream. *Poof.* Temptation gone. Logical ban securely in place.

So, that's it, that's the plan, Miya decided. And while she'd been fostering her defenses against spikes of enjoyment from smoldering eyes and a sexy smile, Johanna tactfully guided the conversation to Kayla. Specifically, to Kayla's creativity.

"She's always been a creative kid," Johanna said. "But even I was surprised by the Hobbit Village. She and her friend, Zack, drew it up, and her cousin, Derrick, helped them build it."

"Like the Christmas Villages?"

"Sort of," Johanna replied, "but on a much bigger scale. They're always working on something new for it."

"Where did they build it?"

"At my aunt's place. The back part of her property is partly wooded. The perfect place," she said, breaking her focus and unzipping the side pocket of her purse. "Do you have to get back to anything?" She refocused on Miya for an answer.

"Nothing that can't wait until later."

Johanna retrieved her phone and added, "I want to show you the village." She was texting as she spoke. "No amount of description from me can do it justice. You have to experience it for yourself."

"Well, I'm not going to try to visualize it, then. I love to see what students are like outside of class. That's where I learn the most about them."

Johanna nodded, her eyes still on Miya's. "Maybe like what a mother learns watching her child play with other children when they don't know they're being watched. Do they share, are they fair, do they help the younger ones, are they intimidated by older kids?"

"Uh-huh, very much like that. And knowing what things interest them helps me relate better in the classroom.

I had a student who had her hand up in class constantly. She asked questions incessantly, and I struggled to keep the other students involved. Then, I went to the school's regional debate competition and 'boom,'" Miya imitated an explosion with her fingers. "That student, as a junior, was captain of the debate team and she was phenomenal. After that, I changed how I structured discussions in her class, and it made a huge difference. Oh, and the annual talent show—wow, that's a treasure trove of talent and revelations."

Johanna was listening. Taking it all in—every word, every measure of who Miya James was. Her eyes, her attention focused tightly on Miya even after she stopped speaking. Waiting. Mesmerized. Until her phone signaled a text and broke the silence.

"Kate's not home," she announced, "but she wants me to go ahead and show you the village. Are you ready?"

Miya followed Johanna across town, south of the city, trying to justify what she was doing as she drove. It's one day, she told herself, a few hours. She could ignore daydreams and desires, yes even temptation for that long. After all, this was about learning about a student in order to make the case that all was fine. That's all.

So, the smile that greeted her as Johanna exited her car in Aunt Kate's driveway, despite the rush of pleasure it sent, wouldn't change anything.

"I'm glad you have time to see this," Johanna said, motioning for Miya to follow her to the backyard. "I know I'm a tad biased, but . . ." she continued as they crossed the yard to an area left wild and wooded, "I think this is really special."

And it was. They entered a narrow path of cobblestones and began following it between trees and around bushes. "This time of year isn't the best time to see it, but Kate and the cousins picked up most of the leaves, and it hasn't snowed yet."

Just as the path curved around the outstretched limbs of a white pine, Johanna pointed beyond a low bough and said, "I'll show you the first one and then you find the others on your own. That's part of the fun."

There, surrounded by a lawn of myrtle, was the evolution of a tree stump. Carved steps wound from the myrtle up to a house about the size of a five-gallon bucket. The interior of the stump was hollowed out, the windows were clad with clear plastic, and a working door hung on hinges. The little house was adorned with shutters and window boxes and topped with a wood-shingled roof.

Miya knelt for a closer look, peered in the windows, and opened the door. "Wow, this is incredible."

"Kayla says that everything is one-twelfth hobbit scale, whatever that is."

"My limited hobbit knowledge won't be any help," Miya returned. "It just looks like everything fits right." She stood up and added," You were right: this is not what I imagined."

"And it just gets better from here. There are eight more," Johanna said, motioning to the path.

Miya accepted the challenge with a smile. Following the path through the magical forest, she marveled at the little stone house tucked beneath cascading forsythia branches—and the sod-roofed house that was barely visible. It was nestled among the rocks that formed the bank of a narrow ravine that snaked through the woods. She moved along, scanning the terrain slowly, delighted at each discovery.

Then, as she rounded the sprawling roots of a large maple, a cluster of houses was visible in a clearing—the beginning of a village, featuring cobbled streets and carved villagers. Hobbits, carved in fine detail, chopped and carried wood and waved at neighbors. "Hobbit scale," Miya said, picking up a hobbit and holding it next to the door of a house, "whatever it is numerically, they fit through the door and in the house."

"That works for me."

Miya placed the figure back in its place and asked, "Did Kayla carve these?"

"Uh-huh. She and her friend Zack carved and painted them. They've got small glued-up blocks of wood all ready and Zack drew plans for more hobbits and houses."

"How many did you say there are?" Miya asked. "Did I find them all?"

"Nine," Johanna replied. "And, no, there's one more."

Miya continued her search to the end of the path where it opened into the manicured stretch of yard. She made a thorough search of the terrain on both sides of the path but found nothing. "So," she said, turning back on the path, "I missed it."

"No, you didn't."

Miya met her eyes and followed their focus upward to the snarled crux of an old-growth maple. Built into the space was the last house. As Miya moved closer, circling a rangy bush at the base of the tree, she saw steps winding around the trunk and leading up to a platform that bridged the distance to the door. "Wow. I can't imagine how long it must have taken just to make the stairs."

"It was tedious work, a real challenge to teenage attention and patience. They had to take turns working on it."

Miya turned and looked back down the path. "This really is remarkable, Johanna."

"I think so, too. And you should see the faces of the younger kids. It's as if they fully accept being transported into a magical world. I see the wonder in their eyes and hear excited imagination in their voices. They make up stories about what is happening in the forest. And when Kayla takes the kids through the forest, I see how pleased that imagination makes her."

"It's the sign of mission accomplished. Proof that what she

helped create did what she had hoped it would do."

"Sometimes," Johanna said pensively, "when I'm here with the kids I go back to that time in my life when I would have emerged myself in an imaginary world if I could have. A world I could make the way I wanted it."

Miya watched her, watched how her eyes traveled the distance back, and understood. "I hid and disappeared into a book. *That* became my world, at least for a little while."

"What were you hiding from?" Johanna asked, moving to close the narrow distance between them.

She was close in front of Miya, challenging her personal space, waiting for a response, and Miya hesitated. Too close, she thought, and too many warning bells ringing in her head. "I was hiding to protect who I am." Keep talking, just keep talking. "They wanted to strip it away, destroy what they couldn't understand."

"Your parents?"

Johanna's gaze seemed to draw her even closer. Miya nodded. "And the Church—trying to cast out my demons." Too much. She'd already said too much.

"You *literally* hid." It wasn't a question.

"In a way, I'm still hiding."

Johanna took the step that Miya had planned to avoid. "But not from me?"

Miya had seconds, only seconds, to stop what she knew was coming. But the feel of Johanna's hand slipping under the edge of her jacket and resting at the top of her jeans sent a message that Miya couldn't stop. Couldn't stop her heartbeat from racing, or stop the sparks of heat, or stop the need to kiss Johanna without reservation, deep and full. There was little chance she would hear the warnings now. She couldn't hear anything, see anything, or feel anything except the arms circling beneath her jacket and the length of Johanna's body pressing against her. Sultry brown eyes, intent on her own, seemed to ask permission.

And Miya gave it, meeting Johanna's lips tenderly at first, teasing the desire they promised. Brushing tenderness, though, turned quickly into firm, and open, and wet. One kiss that melted into another and another—each deeper, each more intense. The warmth of desire followed Johanna's hands as they moved over her sides and back, and the press of Johanna's lips moving slowly down her neck.

Miya tilted her head back and closed her eyes. She couldn't stop the racing of her heart, *wouldn't* stop Johanna Beals. "This is trouble," she said softly to the treetops. "You know, that don't you?"

"Is it?" Johanna whispered.

In that moment, Miya, too, questioned. She slipped her hand around the nape of Johanna's neck and pulled her into a kiss, passionate and free. No reservations. No doubts.

Their kisses ignored the risks, personal, emotional, and professional. They served one purpose, one mission—to stir the flames of desire. There was no space for thought or for reason, it was filled instead with need, growing with each breath, each touch.

Beyond the physical excitement from Johanna's hands exploring beneath tan leather, was a nostalgic excitement—so much like the early thrills years ago, stealing time for the forbidden, the kisses, the touches, the thrill of loving and being loved. Secrets. Whispers. Now in the magic forest. Now with Johanna.

Feelings like the ones capturing her here in the forest as their kisses deepened and explored and Johanna's hand slid over the front of her jeans. The heat centered quickly. The pressure and movement of her hand made it clear that there were no boundaries in the forest. And Miya made no move to claim one as she felt the snap of her jeans release and her zipper slide open. She broke from Johanna's lips, closed her eyes to the treetops again, and marveled at Johanna's boldness as she slid her hand through the opening. Fingers curled under the edge of her underwear, moving with purpose, shooting a sensation of desire through her. Taking over. Yet, Miya tried, "What are you—"

"Do you want me to stop?" Johanna whispered the words against the tender place below Miya's ear.

No, her body screamed. No. She wanted Johanna, wanted her to slip into the wetness that she had created, slip into her and take her the rest of the way. She searched for logic and reason, something, anything, but . . .

It came as a call across the yard. "Hey, Johanna," Kate's voice penetrated the sanctity of the forest. "I'm glad that you're still here." A shock that jolted them apart.

Johanna took a deep breath and said on the exhale, "My aunt."

Miya quickly straightened her shirt and fastened her jeans. But readjusting clothes was much easier than slowing a racing heart rate or cooling the heat radiating from her body, challenging the coolness of the air. "And if she hadn't announced herself?"

Johanna looked at Miya with the expression of a child snatched from the edge of a cliff and shook her head.

They exited the end of the path into the yard to be greeted by Kate's smiling face. "I hit every red light," she said, squeezing Johanna into a hug. "I was sure that I'd miss you."

"I just finished giving a tour," she replied and motioned toward Miya, who stepped closer and offered her hand. "This is my Aunt Kate, surrogate mother and best friend," she said. "And this is Miya James, Kayla's English teacher."

Kate met Miya's hand with a firm handshake and said, "Did you enjoy the magic forest?"

"It's fantastic. The creativity, the attention to detail. The doors on the houses even work. I love it, and I can see how even adults can get lost in the fantasy."

"Well," Kate began, "I had to decide whether to have it all

cleared out and made part of the yard or turn it over to the kids."

"I think you made the right decision," Miya replied. "Thank you for letting me see it. I was telling Johanna that I learn so much about my students by seeing what their interests are outside of class."

"Well," Kate followed with a chuckle, "you're welcome to watch them over here any time. As frustrating as they can be at times, they are bursting with ideas and energy."

"Which aren't always apparent in classroom discussions or homework assignments."

"I don't think any of my teachers knew who I was," Johanna offered. "But I can't blame that on them. I was all but invisible in classes."

"What would they have learned about you outside of class?" Miya asked.

"Oh, probably that I felt most comfortable being part of something bigger, and that although I wanted to learn to be good at things on my own, I struggled with the confidence to do it."

"I have a longtime friend who is retired from teaching now," Kate began. "She put in a lot of hours beyond the school day. I often wondered if that time was noticed and appreciated."

Miya smiled and caught Johanna's eyes. "I'm sure some do." And when her eyes lingered too long, Miya added, "And speaking of, I have a pile of papers that just refuse to grade themselves." She offered her hand again to Kate. "It's so nice to meet you and thank you for sharing your forest with me."

"You are welcome any time. There's always something new in hobbit land."

"I'm going to walk her out, Kate. I'll be right back."

Neither of them said anything until they reached Miya's car. "I'm sorry," Johanna said, standing at the open car door as Miya slid behind the wheel.

"Sorry for?" Miya asked. She stared into Johanna's eyes,

forcing her past the hesitation, waiting for her to sort through her thoughts. But her discomfort was obvious. "Sorry for nearly totally embarrassing your aunt? Or us?"

"Both," she replied, seeming relieved to have it said.

The response, meant to ease Johanna's discomfort, became a confession of sorts. "Hey, I could have stopped us."

"Why didn't you?"

Miya started the car, an unmistakable signal that her response would be short. "Because," she began, "when I kiss you, I forget the danger." She rolled down the window and closed the door. "Your aunt is a treasure. But you know that."

Johanna settled at the dining table, making limited eye contact with Kate. "I saw the new hobbits that the kids added," she said. "It just keeps getting better and better."

"When I turned that rough area over to them, I never imagined what they've created. Even when they showed me Zack's drawings, I thought they'd make a couple of little houses and then lose interest."

"Yeah, they've shattered *that* stereotype."

"And Miya enjoyed her visit to the imaginary kingdom?"

"She did," Johanna replied. "She found all of the houses and marveled at the perseverance it had to have taken."

Kate hesitated, emphasized her next words with solid eye contact. "Was there magic in the forest today?"

Johanna felt her face warm at the inference. "What do you mean?" It sounded even more absurd out loud.

Kate offered an amused smile. She rose from the table. "I'm going to get us a cup of cider. It's the pristine stuff from the cider mill. You know," she said from the kitchen, "I've raised three kids, got them through their teen years without catastrophe, and learned a few tricks along the way." After placing the mugs on the table, she tousled Johanna's hair and added, "I smelled her perfume on your hair when I hugged you, and your faces were way too flushed in that cool air."

Johanna rested her elbows on the table and dropped her forehead into her hand. "I lost it, Kate. I lost control, lost perspective."

Kate sipped her cider, offered a clear space of time, maybe enough for a deep breath and emotions to float gently back to pre-spike level. "Remember," she said, "everything stays right here. No one else, including your uncle, is privy to it."

"You don't have to remind me. I know that."

"And I may be your best cheerleader."

"You always have been. But there probably won't be anything to cheer. I couldn't just talk to her, tell her what I was feeling, what I feared—or find out her feelings and thoughts. No, I had to let chemistry take over, exactly what I said I wouldn't let happen."

"Well, if it's any consolation, even this old straight woman can understand *that*. She's . . . gorgeous."

Johanna tilted her head and offered a more relaxed smile. "Yeah, she is. And maybe she is just as beautiful inside. It seems like she might be, but I haven't given her the chance to show me. Instead, like today, I watched how she moved, smooth and graceful, admired how her jeans defined her legs and how the soft leather of her jacket hugged her waist. I couldn't take my eyes off her. Maybe it's just been too long."

"Maybe," Kate agreed. "And maybe it's time."

"Just because she strips away whatever protection I wrap myself in, doesn't mean I have the right to put her career in jeopardy. She doesn't have to spell it out to me. I know that she might not be protected if they know she's a lesbian, especially one involved with a parent."

"Have you talked with her about it? Do you know what *she's* thinking?"

"I intended to—today. And I blew it."

"The day isn't over, you know," Kate said. "You both need to stop duckin' and weavin' and talk to each other."

"Have I told you lately that I love you?"

"In more ways than I can count."

"Mom, can I get my hair cut tomorrow?" Kayla asked the question from the kitchen as she placed a bag of popcorn in the microwave.

Johanna stopped behind the couch, halfway between the living room and the kitchen, staring at the number on her phone and hesitating to make the call. "Hmm," she said absently, "how long has it been?"

"About a month. I want something different. I have birthday money I can use."

Still slightly detached, Johanna replied, "You just going to do a walk-in after school?"

"Yeah. Hey, I'm making popcorn."

"Don't put mine in yet. I need to make a phone call." She continued into her bedroom and sat on the edge of her bed. A phone call should be easier, she thought. No temptation to get too close, no chance of losing composure. Safer, easier. Until she heard Miya's voice on the other end. Sultrier than it should be, the sound of it sent disturbing sensations through her chest.

"Am I calling at a bad time?"

"I guess that depends on how badly I need a break from grading three sets of tests."

"And?"

"Thank you for calling."

The relief was instant. Johanna welcomed a deeper, easier breath and slid back against the pillows. "There were so many things I wanted to talk with you about today."

"So, your intent *wasn't* to seduce me in the magic forest?"

Johanna smiled to herself. "It was not. I wanted to talk with you about what you're feeling, what you're thinking."

"You *know* what I'm feeling," came a soft response. "What I'm thinking, or more appropriate, what I *should* be thinking, is another story."

"Then what's the story I need to hear?"

"And if it's not what you want to hear?"

"I think it's better that I hear it now."

"Yeah," Miya said, followed by an uncomfortable silence. "It would be if I were able to say it. And I wouldn't blame you if you lost patience with me."

She wished she could see Miya's face, search her eyes, look for something beyond the words. Just something that said the tone was true. But . . . "I'll let you know if I do."

"I get the feeling," Miya said, "that you're being more honest with yourself than I am. What happened today at your aunt's has forced me to admit that to myself, to look at why I didn't say no."

"And?"

"I like how you make me feel, how I think I make you feel."

"So," Johanna began with new confidence, "that night at the festival party—if I hadn't left when I did, would we have ended up in bed?"

"I would have taken you as far as you wanted to go."

"Even though you didn't know anything about me?"

"I knew that you'd been watching me all that week. I knew that you wouldn't make the first move."

"But you didn't know why."

"No," Miya agreed. "I only knew how much I liked the smell of your hair, and the way your eyes kept me centered, transfixed. And I liked the warm flush of your cheek and the way your body moved with me. So, I kissed you. And when you kissed me back, I knew all I wanted to know right then."

"You knew what?"

"That you wanted me as much as I wanted you."

The sensations shot through Johanna, increasing in intensity. The words, the sound of Miya's voice took her back to that night, to the want they felt, the need they never filled. Her body warmed with the thought. "And today told you that I still do."

"Yes."

"I don't want to push anything that you aren't comfortable with. I promise not to do that. But I do want to know who Miya James is. Not just what you do, but who you are. The part of you few people know, the part of you that you keep shrouded and private and safe."

"Hmm, are you sure you want to do that?"

Johanna thought for a moment. "A few weeks ago, probably not. But I'm clearly not very good at whatever it is that we've been doing."

"I guess I'm not either. Maybe we'll end up scaring each other off."

"I guess we'll have to see."

"Then we'll give up the scary parts of ourselves?"

"Why not?"

Chapter 17

REALITY

Kayla pulled the hood of her sweatshirt up over her head. "She's gonna freak," she said out loud. The closer she got to home, the surer she was of it. She sent a warning text.

"Almost home. Plz don't freak. Buzzed my hair."

It wasn't fair to her mother. No explanation, no chance for her to try to talk her out of it. Kayla had denied her that. And the why of it was about to be challenged.

The smell of fried chicken greeted her as Kayla hung her jacket on the hook just inside the door. A covered dish waited on the counter. Johanna waited in the living room. Kayla dropped onto the couch, hood still up, snuggled her arms around her mother's shoulders, and nestled her face into the crook of her neck.

"This is how you liked to be held as a baby," Johanna said, wrapping her in a warm embrace.

"Must have made me feel safe."

"And loved, too, I hope."

Kayla nodded against her. "And loved."

"You'd fall asleep like this and drool. It would tickle as it rolled down my neck, but you were so sweet I didn't want to wake you."

"I promise not to drool this time," she said lightly before adding, "I'm sorry."

Johanna rubbed her hand over the fine stubble beneath the hood. "For this?"

Kayla sat up and pushed the hood back. "No. For not talking to you about it."

"So, talk to me about it now."

Kayla kicked off her shoes, pulled her knees up, and claimed the corner of the couch.

"Was this an impulsive decision, or something you've been thinking about?"

After a moment, Kayla said, "Sometimes words aren't enough, like you can't say to everyone how you feel. Like you need a way of speaking out and saying that you're strong."

"This is your way of showing people without saying it?"

"Yeah."

"Like Brittany Spears?"

"Who?"

Johanna laughed at herself. "Your mother just realized how old she is."

Kayla wanted her mother to understand. It was important in so many ways, sharing what was in her heart with the one person who she knew held it sacred. Truths as she discovered them, as she grew, as she became who she was. Her mother had shown her the way to share her own truths. It was an undeclared promise. One that Kayla, at times lately, had not honored. She struggled now for a way to ease her own heart, to do what was right.

"Do you remember that girl from Parkland, Emma Gonzales?"

"Oh," Johanna replied, "yes."

"I keep seeing her, standing on the platform at that big

march in front of all those people—thousands of them—not saying a word for the same amount of time that the shooting took. I'll never forget that, or her. I want to be that strong."

"You *are* strong, Kayla. I'm so proud of you. You can always come to me with anything. You know that don't you?"

Kayla nodded. She did know. She had always known. It was Zack who didn't know. Zack who trusted rarely, carefully—and with good reason. His mother took care of him, the best she could. She protected and loved him, the best she could. He knew that as well. But it was rarely enough.

"There are some upper classmen who like to bully other kids," Kayla replied, not at all sure if she could balance on that tightrope and be true to them both. "Maybe if I stand up, then others might feel like they can, too."

"Who are they bullying? You?"

Kayla shook her head, threw her arms out, and balanced on the tightrope with one foot. "Anyone who they think is weak or scared. Anyone different, not like them."

"Why don't you go to the counselor and report them? The school has an anti-bullying policy. It's right in the school handbook."

"It's not just at school, Mom. It's everywhere, all over social media, outside of school. I know they try, but they can't control it. Even if they track down who is doing it, they can't erase it all. Once it's out there, it travels like a wildfire. They can expel the bullies, but they'll never get rid of the lies and hurtful stuff they put out there."

"If the school can't do anything about it, how can you stop it?"

"I don't know yet. I messaged some kids in other school districts for ideas that they think will help. And I have a call out to Tami and Amber and James. I know they feel the same way I do."

"I'm glad that you have a good group of friends."

"Yeah, we're a crew. We're small, but we're tight. I'm thinking that if *we* stand up against it then others will, too. I want kids that are getting bullied to feel like others support them."

"Can I help?" Johanna asked. "I can ask for ideas on my Facebook page. Maybe we can come up with suggestions beyond what the school policy covers."

"I can write an article about it, and I bet I could get it in the online school newspaper."

Johanna raised her hand and Kayla clasped it. "It's a plan," she said and smiled.

She hadn't said anything to Kayla, but it seemed only right that she call Miya and give her a heads-up. Johanna settled into her private time. The food was put away, dishes done, laundry drying, and Kayla was reading. Johanna turned off the bedroom overhead light and clicked on the reading light next to the bed.

She leaned comfortably into the pillows and hit Miya's number. "Hey," she greeted her at the sound of her voice, "do you need a break?" The sound of her laugh, light and unassuming, warmed her like the first swallow of smooth liquor.

"Ah, I just got back from dinner with some friends. But it's nice to hear your voice."

Friends. Of course she has friends, a life, a history, and plans. Presumptuous, Johanna thought, to think that she could fit into her world. A world that she knew so little about. "Well," she began, "I won't keep you long. I wanted to give you a bit of a heads-up for tomorrow."

"Is everything okay?"

"Actually, it is, but I didn't want you to worry."

"Me? Worry?" Miya offered another light laugh. "So, what are you saving me from?"

"Uh," weird, she thought, putting words to it, "Kayla decided to buzz her hair."

"With your permission?"

"Not exactly. But it certainly got my attention. She knows me well enough to know that I would have questioned her, challenged her to convince me, and then tried to talk her out of it."

"Would you ultimately have told her 'no'?"

A question Johanna hadn't addressed yet. "Honestly, I don't know. It did open a conversation we hadn't had before. I've tried to keep conversations about politics and other social unrest at a minimum. Living through a pandemic and a contested election is more than I ever wanted her to go through. I answer her questions, but I don't want to introduce any unnecessary anxiety or fear. I walk that thin line between wanting her to be informed and aware and wanting to protect her from things that she can't do anything about."

"That's a tough line to hold with what's available through social media. Unless you take away her phone and keep her from watching the news or talking with her friends, that's close to impossible."

"I monitor the best I can, but . . ."

"Don't beat yourself up. It's probably a losing battle. I think an old-fashioned, sit-down, honest talk is usually more effective. Get it out there and try to put everything in perspective."

"I've certainly tried my best to do that," Johanna replied. "But I didn't realize until today how much about my own daughter I didn't know, and how much control I don't have."

"That's to be expected. She's smart and aware and starting to explore her independence."

"And I thought that we've always been able to talk about anything, but . . . you know what I found out? The Parkland kids made an impact on her that I couldn't. While I was worried about the school shooting making her afraid to go to school, she was aware of so much more, especially how those kids organized afterward. She said she wants to be as strong as Emma Gonzales. And she thinks that if she sets an example, then kids who are being bullied will have the confidence to stand up against them."

"Maybe she's right. We do what we can, but with social media . . ."

"I know," Johanna said, "and so does she. That's what's been bothering her."

"Kids like Kayla give me a lot of hope for the future. They have a unique kind of optimism. Even with the threats of shootings and violence, they still seem to have a sense of indestructibility. They don't see 'why not' because they aren't jaded like we are."

"Just because they don't recognize the risks, though, doesn't mean they aren't vulnerable. It's only natural to want to warn them, to want them to learn through others' experiences."

"But what would we do without their lack of fear? We have to count on them to reach for rungs they can't see. I feel like, as adults, we too often see those rungs as obstacles."

"It scares me as a parent, though. I know we eventually have to trust that the values we raised our children with will help them make good decisions in their lives. But I didn't expect that time to be here so soon. I don't know if I'm ready to let go and let her make those decisions."

"It's not an easy thing for teachers either," Miya replied, "but necessary. In my senior year at Michigan, I found this quote by Mother Teresa that really helps: 'You will teach them to fly, but they will not fly your flight.

'You will teach them to dream, but they will not dream your dream.

'You will teach them to live, but they will not live your life.

'Nevertheless, in every flight, in every life, in every dream, the print of the way you taught them will remain.'"

"Hmm, I like that."

"I'll text it to you."

"And I like talking to you—a lot."

After a few seconds' hesitation, Miya said, "You sound like that surprises you."

"Oh, no. I—"

"Play cards with an unshakeable poker face?"

Johanna smiled privately. Yes, she was enjoying this—probably too much. The more she talked with Miya James, the more she learned about her, and the more she liked her. "It's a good thing that playing cards with you isn't my plan then."

Miya offered a soft laugh. "Yeah, I hadn't really planned on playing cards with you, either."

"What *do* you plan on?"

"Ahh." Miya's tone was low, suggestive. "I know better than to plan anything with you. I only plan things that I'm sure of—lessons, finances, holidays, birthdays. Little chance for surprises."

"And I surprise you."

"I think you surprise yourself."

"Am I really that transparent, or are you just incredibly intuitive?" The question amused Miya: Johanna could hear it in the pace of her response—a slow, teasing pace.

"Well," she began, "I'm tempted to accept the intuitive compliment. Truth is, though, you are terribly transparent."

The answer shouldn't have surprised her. Their physical attraction was clear and present, and mutual. Recognized and acknowledged. This was Miya turning the tables on her, fishing for the same deep and dark that she'd asked of *her*. The truth was that she had given Miya only a glimpse of her life, of being a mother, and a little personal glimpse of who Kayla was. In the larger scheme of things, though, it *was* merely a glimpse. And fair was fair. "So, what is it you want to know about me? Aside from the obvious."

"The obvious?"

"You *know* the obvious," Johanna said. "You just want to hear me say it, don't you?" She envisioned that smile slowly lifting the corners of Miya's mouth. Okay, Johanna thought, and lowered her voice. "I want to make love with you. To feel you against me. And for a little while, to forget about everything and everyone, except you. But you know that. We *both* know that."

"Then we've taken care of the obvious."

"Acknowledged it, not taken care of it," Johanna added. "What isn't obvious is where we go from here."

"Where do *you* want to go?"

"I want to be able to spend time with you," Johanna said, "just you. I want to find out if being with you could be more than a sexual affair."

"And if that's not possible?"

"Anything other than an affair, you mean?"

"What if nothing is possible?" Miya asked. "What if being friends under sexual tension isn't possible either?"

The thought had been skirting the edges of her mind for a while. Hearing it out loud, though, made it suddenly real. It was time to ask the question she had so far avoided. "My aunt calls them rose-tinted glasses when you don't want to see things in the harsh light. I guess it's time I take the glasses off and face reality. Do you want to leave it at parent and teacher?"

"It's not what I *want*," Miya replied.

"Then what?"

"Absent the fear of losing my job? Because that's the only way it would be possible."

Reality, Johanna decided, was about to be cruel.

Miya continued. "What I want is to be free to spend time with someone who intrigues me. I want the freedom to have mind-blowing sex with a beautiful woman. I want to hold her hand and kiss her in public. I want to know if it's possible to find the intimacy and trust I need—in you. But what I want wouldn't stand a chance against a homophobic administration or school board or parents. A law says that I can marry a woman, and a law says that they can't fire me from my job for being a lesbian. But it would take a lot for me to trust that the law won't be gone tomorrow or challenged by *finding* another reason to fire me. And, first in mind being dating a parent."

Yes, it was cruel. Even more cruel now that reality had emerged in its full height and stature. There would be no explaining it away or sugarcoating it. Not anymore. Johanna was face to face with a very real consequence of her desire.

"I may be acting and feeling like a pimple-faced teenager, Miya, but I do understand what's at stake and I will respect whatever you think we should do." It was the truth; it was what she had to do. Finally saying it felt like she had just let go of the string to a beautiful kite. The silence, as she envisioned it soaring free out of reach and eventually out of sight, tightened her chest. She struggled to stave off tears.

Finally, Miya's voice broke the silence. "Have you ever been haunted by 'what-if's'?"

Her own voice was softer now, cautious. "Sure. I imagine many people have. What are you saying?"

"That I don't want to make a decision that will haunt us."

Johanna nodded and wondered if they knew each other well enough for it to haunt them, or if they knew just enough. But it might not matter. "It's time that I start acting like an adult, isn't it? And not put this all on you. I've never hid who I am. I sell insurance in an office where I don't worry about being fired. But I will never push for you to do anything that makes you uncomfortable or risks your job. I want what's right for you, whether it haunts us or not."

"What were you like when you were sixteen?"

"Really, *that's* where your mind went." Johanna shook her head and smiled. "Are you a glutton for boredom?"

"Will you call me tomorrow?"

Johanna's heart picked up its pace. "Yes," she said, "I will."

Chapter 18

THE MISSION

Kayla strode through the hall even earlier than usual, her tennis shoes squeaking on the shiny clean floor. The full length of the hall was empty except for the occasional teacher heading to their classroom.

She visited her locker, relieved to not have to deal with Julie or her besties. They would have their shot at her without the hoodie soon enough, after the word travelled. Let them talk, let the word get around early. It would save her from some shocked looks and having to explain.

Getting to school this early had other benefits as well. She felt free, unencumbered. Her mind was clear and focused. There was nothing to impair the mission or distract her from setting everything in motion.

They met at the freight elevator at the back of the building near the loading dock. Cooler than the rest of the building and smelling of metal and oil. It was their safe place, isolated and a part of the building that few students were aware of. It was also home to The Man and his maintenance crew. Man, because it was much easier than Mangiaracino. And "The Man" because that's how his crew referred to him. But to Kayla and *her* crew, he was Mr. Man. He was somewhere north of fifty, arms covered with fire-throwing dragons, and had a look that could stop an attack dog in its tracks. Like a real-life, grown-up Pey. Someone who, if Zack got to know him, would make him feel safe. He seemed to like their little group of activists and enjoyed sporadic interaction with them. Kayla only had to let him know that they needed a safe place. He learned why on his own.

Each of them was either aware of or the victim of some form of bullying. Always possible, it seemed, raising its ugly head from time to time. Each of them handled it in their own way—by ignoring the slights and rudeness, by avoiding confrontation, or even joking off whatever they could. All were forms of insulation against something that now seemed too large to take on—alone. So, they decided to do it together.

James, Puerto Rican amateur humorist, high-fived her at the first sight of her shorn head. "I love it," he said, no doubt already planning to feature her in a drink-spewing meme.

"Oh, my God," exclaimed Amber, socially selective math geek, "your mom let you do that?"

"I sort of surprised her," Kayla replied. "I didn't want anyone to talk me out of it."

"We aren't going to have to worry about getting their attention," Tami offered. As the basketball team's most aggressive point guard, she was just waiting for the game plan.

It was a small group, but it was a start, an alert. Friends tell friends. And others who didn't know her personally would see her by noon. For many students, it would only be a passing interest, but for others, it might pique curiosity or even better, a need to be involved. And that was the goal—for others to feel empowered, to stand with her, to speak out even if they themselves were not being bullied.

"I didn't tell Zack," Kayla began. "It would probably just freak him out more. And he doesn't know that I shared what the tweets said with you. The 'fag-boy,' 'freak,' 'nobody likes you' tweets were bad enough. But you need to know why we have to do something soon. The latest tweets said, 'just kill yourself', 'do it.'"

Knowing that every tweet, every word, every picture weakened Zack's self-worth and hurt him deeply fueled Kayla's urgency. A statement had to be made, a stand taken.

"Aw, shit!" Tami said, clearly angry. "What did Zack say? Is he okay?"

Kayla answered the concern on all their faces. "I keep texting and checking on him. I think he's going to quit school."

"You don't think he'll do it, do you?" James added. "Kill himself, I mean?"

"I think he's more scared of *them* hurting him," Kayla replied. "At least I hope so. He made me promise not to tell anyone, but after that last tweet . . ."

"What if we stir things up and make it worse?" James asked. "Maybe we should tell the principal or a counselor."

"I promised him I wouldn't," Kayla said. "Besides, the school hasn't been able to do much about bullying so far. We'll get their attention today, then we need to talk with everyone who we think will join us."

The looks she received throughout the morning were expected, the barely audible comments ignored. Surprise mostly, she surmised. Totally expected since she hadn't prepared even the crew. The real challenge awaited her in the cafeteria. The temptation to skip lunch, to avoid the cafeteria had jabbed at her all morning, but bowing to it would only delay the inevitable, defeat her purpose. So, she stayed true to her plan, bought an iced tea from the vending machine, and entered the noisy throng in the cafeteria.

Her steps were sure, defiant, as Kayla crossed the width of the room and claimed a seat at the end of a lunch table. It was only a matter of minutes before Julie and her two besties stopped behind her. She saw them out of the corner of her eye, felt them close in tight, heard the words meant for all within earshot to hear.

"Oh, look, it's a lesbo."

"Might as well be. No guy wants to feel *that*."

Kayla leaned away from a hand touching her head.

Julie's unmistakable sarcastic tone added, "Careful, she might like that. *Do* you like that?"

The confrontation was expected, anticipated. "Actually, I don't," Kayla replied. "Actually," she continued, twisting to partially face Julie, "there's a lot that I don't like."

Not to be outdone, Carla, Julie's clone, rubbed her hand over Kayla's head and added, "Oooh, I bet your boyfriend will think this is really sexy."

"Oh, that's right," Julie added, "you don't have a boyfriend. What a surprise."

Before Kayla could respond, James elbowed his way between the girls and took a seat next to Kayla. "I think your GPS is off," he directed at Julie. "You're at the wrong table."

"Oh, my *God*," Julie returned, "an Island Monkey's telling *us* that *we're* lost."

That was all that Cindy the Follower needed to join in. "Why don't you go back to where you came from," she spewed toward James.

Tami and Amber set their lunch trays on the table but remained standing.

James stood up again and faced her down with, "This *is* where I came from."

When Kayla stood and faced them, too, it caught the attention of Mr. Aggar, who was leaning against the wall, talking with another teacher. He excused himself and approached the group to ask, "Everything okay here?"

Kayla's eyes remained in a hard stare with Julie.

He tried again. "What's the problem?"

Julie broke eye contact to respond. "There's no problem. We were just telling Kayla how much we like her new hair style. It's so cute," she added in that tone of barely disguised sarcasm.

It didn't take seven years of teaching, though, for Jim Aggar to recognize what most likely was going on. He looked directly at Julie, offered a disarming smile, and said, "Better get in the lunch line or you're going to miss pizza day."

She returned a less than convincing smile, then led her girls toward the other end of the cafeteria.

Mr. Aggar scanned the faces of the little group, then redirected his attention to Kayla and James. "Now, what's *really* going on?"

Kayla glanced at James before answering. "Just standing our ground. It's okay."

"Look, I know it's important to stand up and not let yourself get pushed around, but don't let things get out of hand. Your teachers and counselors are here to help. Okay?"

James nodded. Kayla replied, "Thank you, Mr. Aggar. We know you are."

With an affirming nod, Mr. Aggar returned to his post, and the group reclaimed their seats. "That felt good," James offered, "didn't it?"

"Yeah, it felt *really* good."

"Wow," Johanna called as she shut the side door behind her, "the temp must have dropped fifteen degrees since this morning." She placed the Subway bag on the counter. "You're going to want me to drive you to school next week." She peaked around the corner to the living room. "Footlong and salad okay for tonight?"

"Cheesesteak?"

"With onions and extra cheese."

"I made cookies for dessert."

"They smell great. Thank you. Hey," she said, retrieving a soda from the fridge, "how was your day?"

"Good. Julie and her besties tried intimidating me. James and I faced them down. They're laughable."

"Did you say anything to a teacher or counselor?"

"Didn't have to. Mr. Aggar was in the cafeteria and asked if everything was okay. They slithered off."

Johanna smiled to herself. "Slithered off, huh?"

"Uh-huh, *slithered.*"

Johanna leaned over the back of the couch, wrapped her arms around her daughter's shoulders and kissed the side of her face.

"Is that Zack?" she asked as Kayla finished a text.

"Yeah."

"He hasn't been over lately. Are things going better at home?"

"Yeah," Kayla replied, grateful that he stayed safely home. "Today's his mother's birthday. He stayed home from school to spend it with her. The restaurant gave her the day off and Ronnie is on a long haul. He'll be on the road for a few more days."

"Zack's afraid she'd celebrate on her own."

Kayla nodded. "She has a couple of girlfriends who would gladly take her out to celebrate."

"And tempt her to drink with them."

"Yeah, he's way ahead of her. He bought her a cake and took her to Gratzi's."

"Wow," Johanna replied, settling next to Kayla on the couch.

"He's on their joint bank account, so he withdrew enough to take her out. Gratzi's offers a free birthday dinner. He just had to pay for his."

"The roles are switched around in so many ways. He takes good care of his mom."

Kayla nodded. "I wish everyone knew what a good person he is."

"Me, too."

"So," Johanna began at the sound of Miya's voice on the other end of the phone, "at sixteen, I was madly in love with the choir director at our church. Her voice gave me goosebumps every time she sang. The first time I heard her sing, she sang Edith Piaf's 'No Regrets' in French. I sat there totally transfixed and melted—just totally melted. I was shy and withdrawn, but I would have done anything she asked. She taught me how to roll my R's and hold the note. She gave me a confidence I hadn't felt before. So, it didn't take much for her to coax me into joining the choir. In less than a year of listening and singing with her, I believed in her enough to sing a solo part in the Christmas service. She had known something about me that I didn't know. Then, she crushed me when she graduated from college and took a job in California." Johanna revisited the picture in her mind, the one with deep brown eyes and beautiful smile that she kept in her box of pictures, then asked, "Is that what you wanted to know?"

"That and so much more," Miya replied. "She had to know that you had a huge crush on her."

"I'm sure she did. But even though she was in college, and I was four years younger than she was, she still treated me as if I was older. She talked to me about a lot of things, like you would a friend. She even told me one time that she thought she was asexual, that she knew how guys reacted to her, but she just wasn't interested." Johanna hesitated to finish the memory, but it was the piece that finished the puzzle. "I spent weekends with her at her apartment near campus and dreamed that we would get an apartment together when she started teaching and I was in college."

"You were too young to realize that you were too young. But she knew."

"Years later, probably to make it easier to accept the broken dream, I rationalized that she wasn't ready to admit that she was a lesbian. Maybe it's better that I never knew for sure."

"Probably," Miya said after a pause. "And at seventeen?"

"Really? That wasn't enough?"

"Not even close."

The curiosity was good, though, Johanna admitted. They needed to get to know each other, beyond the physical, into the search for who they were. But her own words never seemed to say it as clearly as the song that had stayed with her through the years. She leaned her head back on the pillows and closed her eyes. Softly she sang.

"I learned the truth at seventeen . . . That love was meant for beauty queens . . ."

"I'm no Janis Ian, but . . ."

In an equally soft tone, Miya replied, "That was beautiful. *You're* beautiful." Neither of them breached the silence for long seconds. "How long did it take you to realize that?"

It wasn't something she had consciously thought about. "Mm, I think it was when I saw it in my aunt's eyes, and in a young Kayla's eyes."

"And in mine now?"

"Is that what I see?"

"I hope so. I've been trying to tell you that for months."

"You're quite good at speaking with your eyes. You showed me that at the festival party."

"I'm okay at math, too," Miya said, "and if I'm right, you had Kayla at about eighteen."

"Too young, too confused, trying too hard to be 'normal.' What more proof did the world need. Right?"

"What proof did *you* need?"

"The proof was there all along—needing the touch of a woman, wanting the love of a woman—I just had to accept it."

"Is that where Kate came in?"

"Uh-huh. I don't know what I would have done without her, and my uncle. They opened their home to me, gave me the time to figure out how to be a single mom."

"Your parents couldn't do that?"

"I could have stayed with them," Johanna replied. "But there were daily reminders, especially from my mother, that I was too young, too unprepared to raise a child. If I had gotten an abortion, I could have gone to college as I had planned. She could never accept my decision."

"Enter your aunt."

"With her wisdom and acceptance, and unconditional love."

"I'm liking your aunt more and more."

"Easy to do—she thinks you're gorgeous, by the way."

"Are you *trying* to make me blush?"

"I wish I could see if you are," Johanna said. "We can Zoom and then I won't have to guess."

"After so much time Zoom teaching, I kind of like wearing my Santa sweats if I want, or doing the dishes while I'm talking, or lying in a comfortable, messy bed. I like having my apartment back. I like the freedom that gives me."

"I can understand that. I was grateful that Kayla just had to keep her room neat. I had my clients' Zoom calls in the living room. Yeah, it's nice not having to share it," she said. "But now I'm envisioning you eating a late-night snack in your Santa pants in bed. You might as well go from here and tell me what sixteen-year-old Miya James was like."

"Well, I expected that," she replied, "but maybe another night. I'm helping with the school musical. One of the teachers slipped at home and broke her foot. She was part of one of the performances and I'm taking her place. It's going to mean some late-evening rehearsals. Let me see what the schedule looks like, and I will call you."

Chapter 19

MARKING TIME

They'd been keeping their distance for days, the mean girls and Zack's bullies. But looks shot across the hall or across the room said, *We're not through with you*. So, Kayla watched them, stayed aware of where they were, stayed ready. Her posse gained more confidence each day. They gathered every morning, ate together at lunch, and met again before leaving for home.

They stood at their meeting place near the freight elevator. Tami spoke first. "Anyone get harassed today?"

Everyone shook their heads.

"It looks like they have backed off," James said. "Could we be that lucky?"

Amber directed her question to Kayla. "What about Zack?"

"He's been avoiding them during school, when he's here. He hasn't been going to P.E. or eating in the cafeteria, but they're still cyberbullying him."

"Yeah, I saw the pictures they're spreading around. Pretty disgusting," James added.

Kayla nodded. "I'm betting he's going to quit school soon. He's too embarrassed."

"I would be, too. That one of him sprawled out on the shower room floor was bad enough, but that one that made it look like he was humping some other guy made me so damn mad," Amber said. "What can we do?"

"According to coach Charbonnet," Tami replied, "sometimes the best defense is an aggressive offense."

Kayla locked eyes with her. "I think she's right," she replied. "One of the messages I got back from a student in another school said something like that, too. Bullies don't expect us to stand up to them. They think we're too afraid. I think we're ready to get in their face."

"But not just physically." James directed his question to Kayla, "Do you know Elliott Dean?"

She nodded. "He's the mastermind behind the online newspaper and he manages the school website."

"I think he could help us organize a full media attack," James offered. "Hit 'em from every angle."

"Ask him if he'll help us," Kayla directed. "And we all need to stay together and be ready. I have a feeling they'll do something before winter break."

Her warning to the others had gained an urgency throughout the day. It wasn't paranoia, Kayla decided. Watching and listening hadn't identified anything that validated her concern, but just in case, she kept her vigil until the end of the day.

She pulled up her hood against the dropping temperature and tweeted Zack.

On my way home. What r u doing?

Mom double shift. Ron back tomorrow. Day to myself.

Getting your assignments?

Some.

Got lots to tell u.

Good or bad?

Good, mostly. Tell u when I get home.

Kayla smiled at the thought of telling him about the plan, about support for them, and him, growing. Maybe it would reassure him that things could get better, that he should stay in school.

The sound was unmistakable, running steps coming from behind her. Kayla turned her head for the second it took to identify the threat. Four boys in letter jackets, running right at her, told her all she needed to know,

She bolted into a full run, hindered by the pack on her back, but juiced with adrenaline. She pushed her legs hard, racing down the sidewalk, cold air stinging her nose and throat with each quickened breath.

Keep going, her brain screamed, *keep going. There's no other option. Stay ahead, keep going. Keep going.*

The steps sounded closer. She could hear breaths, expelled with sounds of determination. Too close, too close. She dared not turn to look back. She rounded the corner, across an unobstructed yard, and stayed on the route that she knew. Down the sidewalk, running hard, looking for a safe place. There was no outrunning them. She knew that and ran hard, past empty driveways, looking, desperate now. Where was it? The grey house, the Garden Lady. *Keep going—it must be close, keep going.*

There, two houses down. She'd be home. She always was. The steps were right behind her now. *No, no, no. One more house.* She pushed hard, stretched her legs to their max. Get to the porch, only a few more steps. She jumped over a low bush but wasn't close enough to grab the handrail to the porch. Out of desperation, she stopped, legs weakened and shaky, and turned, a sharp, abrupt turn, to face the threat. Only feet away, Josh regained his footing after stumbling between low-growing junipers. Face reddened by the cold, he sneered and formed a front, shoulder to shoulder with the other boys.

"What?" Kayla yelled, her hands held in tight fists at her side. "What are you gonna do?"

As he took a menacing step closer, the Garden Lady, mostly grey hair pulled loosely back, appeared quickly from around the corner of the house. Quick to assess the situation—a young, out-of-breath girl and a group of menacing boys—she grabbed the iron rake leaning against the house, raised it to her shoulder and approached.

Kayla stepped back toward her and pulled her phone from her jacket pocket.

"Keep moving," the woman demanded as the boys took a step toward the sidewalk. "You're on private property."

Josh raised his hands and smiled. "Chill out, old woman." He stuffed his hands into his jacket pockets, and the four of them walked slowly onto the sidewalk.

The woman held her post and watched as Josh defiantly pointed at Kayla and smiled. She stared hard after them until they had passed the driveway of the house next door, then asked, "Are you okay?"

"Yeah. Thank you," Kayla said. Her breathing began to slow, but her heart still beat at its marathon rate. "I couldn't outrun them any longer."

"Did they hurt you?"

Kayla shook her head.

"Come on," she said, "Let's go inside. I want to be sure they're gone."

Once inside, Kayla settled on the flowered couch, while the woman perched on the edge of an upholstered chair next to it. "I see you walking to school so often that I feel like I know you," the woman said. "What's your name?"

"Kayla," she replied. "You're always working in your garden, and I thought if I could just make it to your house, you would be home."

"Do you know those boys?"

Kayla nodded. "They're bullies from school. They're just trying to scare me."

"And did they?"

Kayla shrugged. "For a minute."

"A bit of a long minute, I'd say," the woman replied, adding a knowing grin. "Are they bullying you at school?"

"They bully who they can."

"Well, that looks like it includes you. What do you think they would have done to you?"

Again, Kayla shrugged.

The woman shook her head, concern showing in the press of her brow. "I'm sorry you're having to deal with this," she said. Then with a wave of her hand, "And I haven't even introduced myself. I'm Dorothy, and I'm so glad that you were able to make it to my house."

"They aren't going to quit on their own, I know that. But some kids are worried that if they say anything, things will only get worse."

"Look," Dorothy said, still perched on the edge of the chair, "back when I was a young girl, which at times seems like a hundred years ago, my dad gave me some good advice. I was being bullied by a girl who was bigger and a year older than I was. She'd do things like push me into my locker, trip me in the hall, throw my books down the stairs. I finally told my dad about it. And he told me that that was the only time he wanted to hear about it. He told me to take a stand, to do whatever I had to, to show that I was strong and not afraid of her."

She had Kayla's full attention. "What did you do?"

"Well, remember, it was a different time, and I was dealing with one girl, not four boys."

Kayla nodded. "I still want to know."

Dorothy smiled. "I figured you would. I waited for her to do something to me, and when she pushed me into another girl, making her drop her lunch tray, I warned her that that was the last time. She asked me what I was going to do about it, and I told her that she'd see. It was funny how just saying that gave me courage. I couldn't think about anything else for the rest of the day. I knew that she walked home and didn't live far from the school. So, I didn't take the bus home, and I left while she was talking with friends. I hurried down her street and found a place where there were bushes and a large tree a distance away from the nearest house. I hid there and waited for her, hoping that she would be alone. She was, and she never saw it coming. I jumped out, grabbed the back of her jacket and threw her on the ground. I'd never felt an adrenalin rush like that. I jumped on top of her, pinning her on the concrete with my hands and knees. I pressed down with all my might, all the time yelling just inches from her face, 'Don't you ever touch me again. You hear me? Don't *ever* touch me again!' She was crying and I kept yelling and pushing down hard, remembering all the times she had tripped me and pushed me and embarrassed me, and I just kept yelling. I was afraid to stop and get up, fearing what she'd do to me once I did. When I did get up, my whole body was shaking. And she just laid there on the ground crying. I yelled my warning one more time, and then ran back to the school to call home for a ride."

Totally not what Kayla had expected from the thin-framed woman whose hands carefully nourished the delicate blooms of her garden. "Wow," she replied. "Like my aunt says, she poked your last nerve."

Dorothy laughed, a soft, sincere sound. "She sure did. Even all this time later I can still feel how nervous, yet how empowered I was."

"Did you tell your parents? Did that girl ever try anything again? Did you get in trouble for it?"

Another laugh, and Dorothy replied, "Yes, I told my parents, especially my dad, who hugged me and promised me that she wouldn't bother me again. And he was right. She must not have told anyone, and she wouldn't even make eye contact with me from then on."

"I wish I could take care of it like that. The mean girls I can stand up to, but . . ."

"Boys pose a whole different kind of danger."

"And it's not all physical danger. There's social media where they threaten and embarrass. It's been so bad for my friend that I think he is going to quit school. They're even telling him to kill himself. I don't worry about myself as much as I do him."

"Have you told your parents and teachers?"

"My mom knows some of it, that I can stand up to the mean girls. But we have to be careful not to disrupt Zack's home life. It's really complicated. And he doesn't trust anyone except me. I've been working on getting enough kids to stand up with me, to show him that we can do it."

"I don't know how much help I can be, Kayla, but you can come talk with me anytime you want. I *can* tell you that the most important thing is for you to find your power, *your* power, and figure out how you can take that power and encourage others to find theirs. You'll have to find your own way to do it. But you know what, I'm betting on you doing it. Remember one thing, bullies are cowards."

Kayla nodded.

"They are," Dorothy emphasized.

"I'll remember," Kayla said. "But I'd better get home. I don't want Mom to worry if she beats me home." She stood and added, "Thank you so much, Dorothy."

"No," she said, "you're not walking home. I don't trust that those boys won't pull a 'Dorothy' on you. Come on, I'm driving you home."

Kayla made the decision before she left Dorothy's car. She was not going to tell her mother what had just happened, not yet.

Chapter 20

TRUTH AND DARE

The quiet of the apartment wrapped itself around Miya, the comfort of it expressed in a long sigh as she sunk into the down of her comforter. It had been an exhausting week, with only a week left before their winter break, and keeping any type of routine was difficult. Adding a holiday program, of course, increased the challenge. The thought of staying a step ahead all next week only added to the exhaustion she felt.

Right now, she just wanted to feel her body losing its weight and tension and softening into the down. And maybe just as much, she wanted to hear Johanna's voice. She'd put off calling her for days for reasons she could justify. She'd been too tired, it was too late at night, they were getting too close for comfort. Today, though, in a scurry of time between the choir's rehearsal of a holiday medley and the *December in the 50's* performance, the truth emerged bravely from the shadows. Miya didn't *want* to hear Johanna's voice, she *needed* to hear it. Beyond that, it was becoming quite clear that she needed to know more about the soul of Johanna Beals, and she needed to be ready to bare her own.

Miya dialed the number she'd been avoiding. At the sound of Johanna's voice, familiar now and disturbingly soothing, Miya's heartbeat quickened and her whole body seemed to smile.

"How are you?" Johanna asked.

"Good, except for not being able to tell where my body ends and the bed begins."

"I'm not going to say what I'm thinking."

"You don't have to."

"Well, since I can't read *your* mind, why don't you tell me what your week's been like."

"Ohhh," which sounded more like a long sigh, "I'll give you the Cliffs Notes. Let's see. Somewhere around sixteen hundred and thirty teenagers with about a two percent attention span somehow managed to handle minimal assignments and keep pranks within reason—well, except for pissing off the Grinch. They wrapped the principal's car in, like, three layers of plastic wrap. The seniors are testing the water for the end of the school year."

"So did they piss off the wrong person?"

"Oh, I'd say so. Carl Walker has seen more end-of-school years than they've been alive. He'll be ready for them," Miya replied. "That was my week. How about yours?"

"Business as usual for me, readjusting some existing policies and adding two new clients. Pretty boring in comparison. Kayla seems to have survived her new look okay. She said she and one of her friends faced down some girls in the lunchroom."

"That must have been what Jim Agger was talking about. He said he interrupted a confrontation. They're on his radar now. In many ways, the school is a microcosm of the world at large—including the good, the bad, and the ugly."

It was the perfect cue—one Johanna had waited for. "Where did Miya James fit in at that age?"

"Depends on who you ask."

"Hmm, okay. What did your teachers think of you?"

"Again," Miya replied, "it depends. Some saw me as a good girl, good student. I turned in my assignments and got decent grades. But when my attendance became spotty and not all my assignments were turned in, some lost patience with me. I wanted to pass; I wanted them to believe in me. During one of my hiding periods, I went back to school to take my tests, and they turned me in to my parents."

"Didn't the school contact your parents when you were absent so much?"

"I was pretty good at forging notes from my mother. That worked until someone started worrying about me being so sickly."

"What exactly were you running from?"

"Annihilation," Miya replied, "at least that's what my frightened, angry teenage self thought. They tried to pray away my soul, to carve me into something they thought acceptable. They would have stripped me of me if I'd have let them. Hearing the words conversion therapy from my father sent me into 'fight or flight' where there was only one option."

"Where did you run?"

"Out of state, to my grandmother. She hadn't raised my mother in the Church, but she did know how to manipulate her daughter. What my mother heard her say was that if I was there and safe, she would be able to work on saving my soul. What *I* heard was that if I was there, I was safe—who I was, was safe."

"How long did you stay with her?"

"Through college and two years of teaching. Until she passed away. I wish I had had more time to take care of *her*."

There was sadness in Miya's voice, a new dimension in the mystery of this woman. Sadness, and, at times, a hint of anger, a hardness to her words that seemed deep-seated, long held. The similarities of their early years seemed apparent at first, there, but then gone. They couldn't be more different. One was a fighter, sure of who she was, unwilling to compromise no matter how difficult it made life. The other, confused, unsure, wanting so badly to be accepted and life to be uncomplicated.

"Have you reconciled with your parents?"

"No," Miya answered, "I don't see that ever happening."

"Well, *that* I can relate to. As much as Kate tries to make it happen, I don't see that happening in my life, either. You said that your grandmother lived in another state. What made you come back here?"

The tone of Miya's voice softened into a sigh. "A woman."

"Of course it was," Johanna returned with a smile. "Must have been a special woman to lure you back here."

"She still is. Besides my grandmother, she is the one person that I believe would take on the world for me."

She chanced the question with an answer that she feared would change everything. "Are you still lovers?" Johanna held her breath, trying to ready herself for the answer.

"No, it's been over four years since we decided we could be lovers and best friends, but not at the same time."

The next breath was easier. "Do you think you made the right choice?"

"Yes," Miya said without hesitation. "Good sex is wonderful, sometimes so mind-blowing that it can take you out of this world. But there is *nothing* more important than knowing that someone would walk through fire for you."

"Do you believe there is love that gives you both?"

"At the risk of going down in flames of idealism, I do believe it's possible." And after a pause, "Do you?"

"I . . . do," Johanna replied. "But for me, it's always been more complicated than that. I learned early that anyone I have a relationship with must be willing to walk through fire for me *and* Kayla. And that won't change even when Kayla goes to college, gets a job, has relationships of her own."

"That should be a given."

"But it isn't. And I know better than to assume it is. I did that once. I won't make that mistake again."

"So have you already made your assessment of how I would handle it, or are you just looking for a sexual affair?"

"I think I know how you would relate to Kayla, but I don't know what to think about you and me."

"Neither do I," Miya admitted. "Talking is good, though, don't you think?"

"Yes, talking is wonderful."

"And as for a relationship," Miya said, "seems like there has to be a balance, or a cornerstone or something. Like a game of Jenga. There's gotta be a block that supports the weight of a relationship, *the* Jenga block that cannot be removed or the whole thing collapses."

"I hope that's what we're building, something solid," Johanna said, "something we can both trust. I wonder, though, if knowing everything I can about you—what makes you happy or sad or angry, what your goals are, what your fears are—can possibly compare with how much I want to know you physically, how much I want to feel you pressed against me, how much I want to make love with you."

It was the truth, the unabashedly naked truth, hanging between them. Put there by Johanna out of frustration, out of an increasing need for an answer. Just some idea of what to hope for.

"Yes," Miya began, "I'm blushing. Another good reason not to do video calls," she said with a light laugh. "And yes, one is not matching the strength of the other right now."

"Which leaves us where? Hoping that we will learn something about the other that will douse the fire? Or am I feeling something different than you are?"

"The short answer is that you are not. My knowing what the consequences could be firsthand has not changed at all what I feel for you. I've seen how untrue, unfair accusations forced my ex from a job that she loved. I felt her angst and her anger. We've been living through years where a law meant to protect us from discrimination is constantly challenged, our 'security' always in danger of reversal. I don't trust that security. I may never trust it. Yet, it hasn't stopped me from thinking about you day and night, dreaming about you. It hasn't lessened the heat that I feel when I'm near you, or the desire to make love to you and to take you to a place where, at least for a while, there is no worry, no distraction, only you and me and a fire out of control."

"That's what you want?"

"And for you not to give up on me."

Chapter 21

T H E   P O S S E

The last few days of school before winter vacation were always an academic disaster. It was a rare classroom that could boast of all students present. Hall passes, legitimate and otherwise, had students working on the final touches for the holiday program, joining a party in another classroom, and finishing projects in the media center or art room. Keeping track of who was where and why was a challenge not easily met. Today was no exception.

Kayla sent still another text to Zack. He hadn't answered texts or calls since yesterday afternoon. There had been short stretches of time before when she couldn't get an answer, usually when his mother relapsed. He'd been so watchful, though, checking all her hiding places for liquor and taking control of her birthday. Instinct told her that wasn't it this time. She wanted so badly for him to be part of the plan today. He could have told her "no." He could have said that he didn't trust that it would work, and that he feared the attempt would make things way worse for him and for her. She would have understood, and probably tried to reassure him that the try was worth the risk. But whether he would've agreed with the plan or not, Kayla was committed to it.

She'd met the others at their usual place by the freight elevator. They had a good plan, a simple one. She just needed them all together in the lunchroom. And she needed to hang onto the courage that Dorothy's words had given her. There would be challenges to that course—she was sure of it, and she had to be ready for them.

As always, Julie and her girls didn't miss a change to harass or intimidate. It began with a bathroom stand-off. They crowded ahead of Kayla as she started through the door. Seconds later they stood in front of each stall and refused to move.

"How embarrassing," Julie began, "you have the wrong bathroom."

Trying to push her way past them into a stall was only asking for things to escalate, so Kayla left and went up to the bathroom on the second floor. The challenge was on.

She knew to avoid her locker and hadn't participated in the holiday decorating contest. So, *someone* had decorated her locker for her. The words "Crazy Bitch," painted in red and green, covered her locker door and a fake winner's ribbon for "Worst in Class" hung above it. The teacher in the classroom closest to it had a janitor clean it off, but the point—embarrassment—was clear. An alert to the counselor's office resulted in Kayla being pulled from the math class party into Dr. Reed's office.

"Hi, Kayla," Dr. Reed greeted her with a pleasant smile. "I hate to pull you away from the festivities, but I want to talk with you about what happened with your locker. You saw what someone painted on it?"

"I saw it."

"Well, so did Mrs. Sheldon, so it's being cleaned up. Do you know who did it?"

"Maybe someone who has a problem with my haircut. I don't know." An answer that rode the line between truth and lie, and something she found increasingly useful, and too easily rationalized. School officials might be able to control what happened in school, but taking bullying off social media really wasn't possible. She was hoping that Elliott's expertise might be able to help them neutralize or counter it. The best attack, Kayla decided, was empowering themselves and others to not let hurtful comments and pictures define who they were. Bullies don't get to tell you who you are.

Dr. Reed continued. "I asked the students on either side of your locker if they'd seen anything, but they claim that they didn't. I did notice that one of the girls was part of the group that Mr. Aggar talked with me about after a confrontation in the cafeteria. Common suspicion would put her at the top of my list. Don't you think?"

"What can you do if no one saw her and she denies it?"

"We can watch her. Warn her. She's been confronted twice now," she confirmed. "Is there anything else we should know?"

Lots, Kayla thought. But nothing that will stop them from harassing kids off school grounds or increasing that harassment because they can't do it at school, especially with winter vacation coming up. No, nothing yet. Maybe after lunch today. Maybe enough to show them why. So, she walked the line. "Nothing that would help," she replied.

Dr. Reed nodded, but her eyes, locked on Kayla's, said that she was looking way past the moment and the obvious avoidance. She'd dealt with enough kids over the years to know exactly what Kayla Beals was doing. It was the "why" that she needed more on.

"Kayla, I want you to come in and talk with me if other students harass or bully you. We're here to make sure that coming to school is safe and enjoyable. This should be a place where you can learn and socialize with friends, and we want to know about anything that jeopardizes that for you. I'm personally here to help you. Okay?"

Kayla offered a nod. "I know," she said. "Thank you."

She had to admit, as she left Dr. Reed's office, that being able to hand everything off to the counselor would be nice. There was a moment of temptation when she was locked onto the counselor's dark, caring eyes when she almost gave in and gave up the weight. But it was too complicated for such a simple solution. The doctor would have her chance after lunch. And whether she knew it or not, the doctor was going to need a lot of help.

As anticipated, the cafeteria was packed for a special holiday lunch of fried chicken, green beans, and fries. Kayla's little group of resisters claimed a table and allowed enough time to eat lunch. The time had to be right if they were going to get the attention they wanted.

Kayla ate despite the unsettled sensation she felt in her gut. She talked with the group, kept their confidence up, and watched the other tables. As it became apparent that most students were finishing their lunch, the unsettling feeling bubbled up and threatened to bring up her lunch. She took a couple of deep, slow breaths and looked at each of the faces ready to stand with her. Each student was solid and committed. And they said they'd been talking and tweeting and spreading the message of solidarity. But her solid four were all she could count on. There was a chance it wouldn't be enough, that their little group would be laughed at, ineffective. And there was only one way to find out.

"Okay," she said, making eye contact with each of them, "let's do it."

They rose together, James and Amber unfolding the banner they'd made, Tami coming through with the megaphone she had promised. Kayla took the megaphone and stood up on the table.

"Bullies," she shouted, "are cowards." The noise in the room began to quiet and Kayla turned to face the other end of the room and shouted again, "Bullies are cowards."

James and Amber held the banner with the same message high above their heads. They had the attention they wanted now, especially, and most importantly, Julie and her girls and Josh and the letter boys.

"How many of you have been bullied?" The strength of her own voice surprised Kayla. It filled the room and bounced from wall to wall. "Do you have a friend who's been bullied? How many of you *know* a bully?"

"Name them," Tami shouted in her gymnasium voice. "Shame them."

Kayla watched Mr. Aggar out of the corner of her eye. No movement. She continued. "Julie Bradford is a bully. Julie Bradford is a coward."

Josh and his boys rose at the mention of his girlfriend's name. Mr. Aggar moved toward their table. More importantly, though, two other students nearby moved to stand next to the banner.

And Kayla, her confidence fueled, continued. "Josh Carter is a bully," she blasted from her makeshift pulpit. "Josh Carter is a coward."

"Shut up, you sorry bitch," Josh yelled across the room.

Two more students moved to stand with the banner.

And Kayla continued. "Carla Lowe and Cindy Smith are bullies and cowards." The crowd of students surrounding Kayla continued to grow and Kayla added the rest of the names. It was too much for the bullies who stood to leave.

"We've taken your power," Kayla added. "You have no power."

Mr. Aggar followed the bullies across the room as Tami started the chant that ushered them out. "Name their shame," she shouted, now with the megaphone. "Name their shame," she continued. This time she was joined by a throng of students, raising their fists and their voices, chanting the bullies out of the room.

It sounded like music, like an anthem, a testimony to their mission. The feelings Kayla had—relief, still unused energy needing release—created a strange kind of excitement. And she wasn't alone. She could feel the same in the hugs from James and Amber and Tami and countless others. They had done something important. Her only regret was that Zack wasn't there to see it. She had no doubt that Mr. Aggar would be on his way to Dr. Reed and the principal. There would be questions and warnings and meetings with parents. But Zack needed to feel the support and find some relief. Today was only a beginning.

It was no surprise that Kayla was once again called into Dr. Reed's office. She sat across from her more nervously than the first time.

"Kayla," Dr. Reed began, "you weren't totally honest with me, were you?"

"No," she said with a shake of her head. "I'm sorry."

"I'm not convinced that you are sorry, but I think I understand why. This is what you were talking about in your essay, isn't it? Kids being bullied."

"Yes," Kayla confirmed with a nod.

"And it sounds like you have developed a strong student coalition against bullying right under my nose. That makes me wonder if you *had* come to me first whether I could have helped make it even more effective."

"If I had told you, would you have tried to stop me?"

Dr. Reed leaned back in her chair and assessed the young woman in front of her. "I probably would have discouraged you and tried to convince you to let us take care of it. I wouldn't support something that put students in further danger."

"What would *you* have done?"

Dr. Reed slid her chair closer to the desk and clasped her hands on top of it. "The same things we'll be doing now. The students suspected of bullying would be brought in one at a time to talk with counselors, parents would be called in, and warnings or suspensions given. Teachers would be alerted to watch for further problems."

"But how does that stop them from threatening us on the way home from school or on the weekends or during the summer? Sometimes parents can't or won't stop them. Do we call the police every time we're threatened? And what is anyone going to do about the hurtful things they put on social media?" Her nervousness was gone. She saw what Ms. James had told her about Dr. Reed—she did care. It was apparent in her posture, leaning into her words, and her eyes framed with creases of sincerity. So, Kayla added the rest, the core of it. "What has the school done to encourage students to stand up for themselves and not be afraid? When we're afraid, the bullies win." She watched as Dr. Reed hesitated to reply immediately and lowered her eyes.

It was too much, Kayla worried. She'd said more than she should and overstepped the bounds.

Then Dr. Reed's eyes came up, her expression contemplative and serious. "I have a proposition for you," she said. "First, though, was your mother aware of what you were planning to do today?"

"Not everything. I didn't want her to be afraid for me and try to talk me out of it. When I cut my hair, I told her that I wanted to take a stand and show strength. But that's all she knew."

"And you made yourself a target on purpose."

Kayla nodded.

The doctor's expression softened into what looked like the beginning of a smile, followed with a slow, gentle shake of her head. She replied, "I honestly have never had another student do that. I admire you for that. And I want us to work together to see if we can do a better job of dealing with bullying. But you need to be completely honest with me, and with your mother. Will you do that?"

Completely honest. She'd carefully balanced between not lying and being completely honest for so long that she'd lost track of how complete honesty felt. It wasn't what she had wanted to do, and it wasn't how she'd been raised. It was for Zack, she'd rationalized, for the bond they had. Wasn't that how she had gotten to this place, caring about his fears and his well-being as any "big sister" should do? Wasn't it justified? But now, honesty, and a push for it that she hadn't planned on. "I know you want to help, and I want you to," Kayla replied. "I have to talk with someone first, though."

"And you'll talk with your mother?"

"Yes, I will," she replied quickly.

There were two people she needed to talk to. Zack was first on her mind, and she had been trying all day. Another text and still no answer. Worry began to set in.

Second on her mind was Elliott, the social media guru. She met him as planned by the freight elevator. "Thanks for helping us," she began. Before she could say anything more, though, he pulled her into a strong hug and lifted her right off the floor.

"Man, you were great today," he said as he released her. With a bend at his waist he added, "I bow to your courage. I work my magic quietly, anonymously, safely behind an electronic device. *You*, though, you are out there."

She liked him, this senior, this Pooh bear with knowledge beyond his years, beyond most people's comprehension. And she was sure that he was going to be a very important part of their effort. "I just got things started," she said. "We're counting on you to throw whatever wrenches you have into their cyberattacks. And there's a bigger picture that I wanted to ask you about. The school doesn't have a good plan and Dr. Reed wants to work together with us to develop one."

"They should have a whole cyber team," he said. "Do you think they will trust me to build one?"

"She asked for help. There might even be teachers who would want to be part of it if they were asked."

"Yeah, I'll do it," he said. "I've already done some easy stuff to rock their little bully world. This is going to be fun."

"That makes me feel better already. I just wish Zack would answer me. He's making me nervous. He's never gone this long without answering me."

"Yeah, he needs to know how many people have his back."

It was past worry now for Kayla. The whole time she stood inside the north door, watching for her mother's car, she continued trying to contact Zack. Calls went to voice mail; messages meant to inform and reassure went unanswered.

Johanna sensed the tension the moment Kayla slid into the front seat. No smile, no greeting, only eyes wide with a look that she hadn't seen before, and a request. "Can we go to Zack's? Right now?"

"Yes, of course," Johanna replied. She maneuvered the car quickly through the parking lot and onto the street with urgency and questions. "What is it, Kayla? What's going on?"

"He hasn't answered me—since yesterday morning."

"Did you get into an argument?" she asked, whizzing through the front end of a yellow light.

"No."

She glanced a look at her daughter, leaning forward in the seat, eyes trained ahead. Unwilling, it seemed, to tell her what was happening. She gave her the time, the distance of block after block, and tried to trust.

They followed the street winding through the sprawling apartment complex, where there was little to distinguish one apartment, one door, from another except familiarity. Johanna stopped the car in the empty parking space outside the apartment she knew as well as she'd known her own in this same complex only a few years ago.

The car had hardly settled to a stop when Kayla jumped out and ran to the door. Johanna joined her as she banged on the door. Kayla moved to the window and peered through half-closed blinds into the dark apartment. When no one answered, Kayla pleaded with her mother, "Use your key, Mom, please."

With urgency felt but not yet explained, Johanna singled out the key on her ring and opened the door.

"Zack," she called, charging through the door. "Zack." She flipped on the overhead light and made a quick search of the small apartment. No Zack. Nothing to indicate when he'd been there last or where he was. "We have to find him," Kayla said, rushing back to the car. "Maybe he's at our house."

Johanna slid back behind the wheel and backed out of the parking space, but added, "We're going, but you start talking—now."

"They've been bullying him," Kayla replied, answering her mother's tone quickly. "He's not coming to school."

Things were starting to make sense. Johanna handed her phone to Kayla. "Dial his mother, then give it back." They emerged from the complex and headed toward home. One hand on the wheel and one on the phone, Johanna tried not to sound an alarm. "Hi, Linda. Hey, I'm sorry to bother you at work, but Kayla's been trying to get ahold of Zack . . . Yes, we checked the apartment . . . Maybe someone he might have skipped school with . . . could he be somewhere with Ron? . . . Okay, yes, keep trying to call him, and we'll check our house . . . Yes, I'll call you."

But the house was also empty, with no sign that he had been there. Johanna looked directly at Kayla, still obviously stressed, and demanded, "You need to tell me everything—right now."

"He wouldn't let me tell anyone, even you."

"Well, you're going to now."

Kayla lowered her eyes and nodded. "The bullies have been threatening him and embarrassing him." Then she unloaded the rest, ending with what she knew would get her mother back into the car and refresh the need to hurry. "He said that he was just trying not to be another Matthew Shepard . . . then, he really scared me. He showed me the tweets—they told him to kill himself."

Johanna's faced blanched. Shards of fear jangled her thoughts and charged her voice. "And you didn't find that scary enough to tell me? You thought that you could handle something that serious on your own?" She clasped her forehead and tried to think as she walked a tight circle. She stopped at a frightening possibility, forced intense eye contact with her daughter. "Does Ron have a gun?"

"Yeah," she replied, her eyes wide with the realization, "he carries it in his truck."

"Linda said that he's not home yet. He's been on a three-day run, so Zack would have had to take it before Ron left." She quickly retrieved her phone and called Linda again. It took every ounce of control to contain the tone of her voice so that she didn't scare the bejesus out of her. Johanna explained that Kayla had told her about the bullying and then, "Hey, Linda, just a precaution, but could you call Ron and have him check to be sure he has his gun with him? Just in case," she tempered, "Zack might have thought he needed to have it for protection from the bullies. Just to eliminate one possibility."

Johanna waited, paced around the kitchen and into the living room. Kayla was unusually quiet, slumped on a kitchen chair, staring at the napkin holder in the center of the table. She jumped at the ring of her mother's phone.

"Let's go. Ron's got his gun," Johanna said. "Tell me where Zack might go. But we are not through talking about this."

With temperatures falling, it seemed unlikely that he'd be at any of the outside places that Zack commonly hung out at, so they began their search with his longtime friends. The same friends he had known since elementary school, the ones who now wouldn't sit with him at lunch. But they didn't have much else.

Johanna watched as Kayla jumped from the car and raced to Danny's door. The quickness of her movements, of her exchange of words showed her concern, but the look on her daughter's face when she returned to the car said that she was scared.

The quiver in her voice confirmed it. "He hasn't heard from him for three days."

"Okay," Johanna said, taking Kayla's hand. "Where does Chad live?"

When Chad hadn't heard from him, either, Johanna's concern heightened. Her thoughts raced ahead, past possible suicide, crossing the line between runaway and possible hate crime. She tried hard to focus on runaway, that much she could handle. "You be thinking about where else he might go while I call Linda again."

Linda, who all along she had assumed was the reason for Zack's behavior, his frequent need for refuge. Because it fit the pattern. Because he wouldn't tell. So, Linda needed to know. Everyone needed to know.

Linda had gone home early from work. No Zack there and still no response from him. Johanna concentrated on keeping a level tone to reassure her that they were looking for him, to make her feel part of the solution, to tell her to call wherever he might have gone, but to stay home in case he came back. It had to be hard for Linda to bear, without Ron, but it wasn't her fault. Not this time. Johanna reassured her the best she could, talking calmly, promising to call her after they checked a few more possibilities. But the doubts she felt when she hung up took a hard grip.

Kayla was staring straight ahead, hands tightly gripping the front of the seat. She was blaming herself, Johanna thought, of course she was. "Let's look anywhere Zack could be. Maybe he just needed to go somewhere to think, and he didn't want anyone to bother him."

"He's gone to the library branch before."

But the branch was nearly empty, and no Zack.

"Cold or no cold," Johanna said, "take me anywhere you can think of."

They were chasing darkness now. Streetlights began to flicker on, and the temperature had dropped quickly as Johanna made a call to Kate for a look in the magic forest, then followed Kayla's direction to the band shell in Evergreen Park.

"We could be chasing him. He might have been moving around to different places and we keep missing him."

"Go to the Community Church, the playground behind it. If he did go there, he wouldn't have stayed once school was out, though, because he knows that I would look there. But I can't think of anywhere else."

Johanna had already made the decision, but saying it out loud right now would only frighten Kayla. With nothing left except waiting, she would call the hospitals and the police if he wasn't at the playground. She tried Linda one more time before pulling into the church parking lot. Still no word from Zack and with Ron not home until later, Linda sounded too close to finding a drink if she couldn't find her son.

Kayla ran to the back of the church and headed for the play structure. This time Johanna followed her. Why, she wasn't sure. Maybe a feeble hope that she could help reassure Zack if he was there.

Large parking lot lights together with a light over the back door of the church lit up the playground area. Kayla climbed the ladder of the structure, then turned with a look of defeat and shook her head. Johanna met her at the bottom and wrapped her arms around her. "I'm sorry," she said, trying to decide how to tell her what she knew should be done next. Her arm still around Kayla, they turned to return to the car when Johanna noticed an option she hadn't imagined. There, scuffed in the dusting of snow, were footprints. She released Kayla and pointed. "Come on," she said, rushing to the back door of the church. She tried the handle. Locked. Footsteps continued around the building. "Try the other doors, Kayla."

She returned, breathless. "All locked," she said, "He was here, Mom, checking the doors just like we did."

Or a janitor, Johanna thought, making his rounds, securing the building. It was an impulse, pounding on the door. No logical reason for it, but she did it anyway, then turned her attention to what they had to do next. "We should go home. He could finally have decided to go there. Then if—"

The door opened, startling her. "Oh," she said, turning quickly to find a fiftyish man in jeans and a sweatshirt standing in the open doorway.

"Hello," he greeted her, adding a pleasant smile. "I'm Pastor Doug. How can I help you?"

"I'm not sure," she replied. "I'm Johanna Beals and this is my daughter Kayla." His expression seemed open, receptive. His eyes stayed on hers, encouraging her to continue. "We're worried about a young friend—"

"He's being bullied at school," Kayla interjected.

Johanna put her arm around Kayla's shoulders and added, "He hasn't been in school and won't answer his phone."

"I've met him here many times," Kayla said, motioning to the play structure. "He feels safe up there."

The pastor nodded. "This *is* a safe place, and I understand your concern."

Kayla impatiently asked, "His name is Zack. Have you seen him?"

"I have," he replied with a nod.

"Where is he?" Kayla asked. "Is he okay?"

"Yes, yes," he replied and motioned them in. "He's here and he's safe."

The relief that Johanna felt she knew must be magnified in Kayla. They entered a hallway and followed the pastor into a small room, its walls lined with bookshelves. He sat with them around an old wooden library table.

"I always come in during the week for some alone time to work on my sermon. I'd known he'd been missing school several times when he was here, but I wanted him to trust me, so I didn't push him. Today he came here to ask if I knew a good Community Church in another city that would let him stay there temporarily. He wanted to go to school there and start over. He was ready to buy a bus ticket to wherever I said. I'll talk with him, to basically reassure him that we are all supporting him. And I'll have to talk with his mother. Legally—"

"I know," Johanna said. "I've had a good relationship with her for years. She trusts me and he's spent a lot of time at our house. I'll let Linda know that he's okay."

"And that I'll be calling her," he said as he rose. "I'll go talk with Zack."

As he left, Johanna took and released a long, deep breath and dropped against the back of her chair. She waited for Kayla's eyes and said softly, "It's going to be okay."

"Do you think the pastor will convince *Zack* that it'll be okay?"

"I hope so. Since he's not eighteen, he doesn't have a lot of choices."

"Find out if Ron will be home tonight."

"I already know that he will," Johanna said. "What else haven't you told me?"

"He doesn't tell Ron anything because he'll just put pressure on him to act like a man. He calls him a sissy because he likes to draw."

"Well, I'll have to tell Linda. How can we expect her to do what's right for Zack if she doesn't know what he's afraid of?"

"He knew that you would tell her—that's why he didn't want me to tell you."

"He was right," she said, calling Linda's number. A lot more was making sense now—Kayla's loyalty, how assumptions had been allowed, and how two teenagers had kept too much from so many—and it was time that it made sense to Linda, too.

Hearing the relief in Linda's voice when she knew Zack was safe sent a twinge of guilt through Johanna. It wasn't Linda who had failed him. It was an assumption. One that Johanna regretted. She hadn't taken the necessary time to *know* that Linda was doing well, hadn't taken an afternoon or an evening to spend with her in too long. And frustration with her pattern of relapses was no excuse. Being there for her, for Zack, during the tough times wasn't enough. She would do better, Johanna promised as the door to the little room opened.

Kayla sprang from her seat and wrapped Zack in a tight hug, and Johanna followed.

"I'm sorry," he said. "I didn't mean for you—"

"No, don't be sorry," Johanna replied as she released him. "We're just glad that you're okay."

"Here," the pastor said, "let's all sit down for a minute. Zack and I have talked things over. And I'm going to talk with his mother to see if she and Ron will meet with me. I know that school is heading into winter break for two weeks, and I think that will help some to ease the stress that Zack's dealing with. I've also offered an idea that may help until the threats have been dealt with. We were very successful during the Covid crisis in providing a safe learning space here for students who didn't have internet access at home. It would be no problem to set up

Zoom time for Zack if the school approved. That way he won't miss any school, and I'll be here so that it won't disrupt anyone's work schedule." He turned his focus to Zack. "After I talk with your mom, Zack, I think the next step will be for you and your mom to meet with the counselor and see if the school will agree to it."

"What if Ron won't agree to it?" Zack asked.

"Let's not worry about that yet," the pastor replied. "I want to talk with them both and let them know that I am not trying to interfere, just trying to offer some options." His focus returned to Johanna. "You said that his mom is alright with him staying with you. But legally, and Zack understands this, it is his mother's decision where he stays tonight."

Johanna nodded. "Of course. Linda and I both want what's best for Zack. I called her so she knows he's okay. So, Zack, you know you're welcome at our house tonight."

"Yeah," he replied. "I don't want to talk to Ron tonight." He looked at the pastor. "Will you tell her that?"

"Sure," he said as he stood. "I'll go call her and we'll get it figured out."

There was excitement and a bit of pride in the sound of Kayla's voice as she leaned in toward Zack and filled him in on what had happened at school. Johanna watched them, grateful that today, somehow, the goodness that Kayla wrote about won out. Yet, as grateful as she was, as good as that felt, the fact that she had known so little about what was happening bothered her. What made Kayla keep the secrets of an emotionally and physically harassed fifteen-year-old from her mother, or aunt, or a counselor? Or had Kayla told Johanna in ways less obvious, and she hadn't heard her?

The pastor interrupted her thoughts to announce, "Okay, I'm going to meet with your mom tomorrow, Zack. She will work on getting Ron to join us. I told her that I would also go with them to talk with the school personnel about the Zoom classes."

"Can I stay at Kayla's tonight?"

"Yes, she's fine with that." He held his hand out to shake Zack's hand and added, "You're not fighting this alone. Remember that."

Johanna handed Kayla the keys. "Can you get the car warmed up? I'll be there in a minute."

She offered her own hand to the pastor. "Thank you for all that you're doing to help Zack. It seems that Linda and I were the last to know what's been going on."

"Sometimes," he said, releasing her hand, "I think they just need space—and someone who listens harder to hear over that space."

Chapter 22

WHISPERS

The ride home began with a palatable sense of relief; Kayla twisted in her seat and talked excitedly to Zack in the back, while Johanna finally breathed a little easier. The "all cards on the table" talk that she had planned would wait. They all needed a bit of time to reboot.

She let the two of them chatter on, realizing how important Kayla's reassurance was to him. Realizing, too, that once again she was the last to know much of what had happened—and it prompted her warning at the next break in their conversation.

"I want you both to know," she said, making eye contact with Zack in the rearview mirror, "that we are going to have a talk. Not tonight. We've all been through enough angst for one day. But keep this in mind until then: secrets often do more harm than good." She glanced a look at Kayla, who lowered her focus, and Zack, whose eyes flitted from Kayla to the mirror. "But for right now," Johanna continued, "I am relieved everyone is okay." She reached for her phone and added, "Exactly what I need to let Aunt Kate know."

Kayla took the phone, hit Kate's number, and handed it back

to her mother. It was a quick call, an "all is well, don't worry" reassurance and a promise to call her later. Tying up the ends, Johanna thought, as she started to place the phone in the cup holder. But before she could let go of it, the phone rang.

The name surprised her until she remembered how late it was. "Hey," she answered, her voice light, her face softening into a smile. "I'm on my way home. Can I call you back? Okay, about thirty minutes."

Kayla watched as Johanna slid the phone into her jacket pocket. "Who was— "

"Hey, Zack, have you had anything to eat today?" Johanna quickly said.

"No," he replied.

"Okay, we're close to Little Caesars, so chicken wings or pepperoni pizza?"

"Pizza," he replied.

"Yeah, pizza," Kayla agreed.

The whole time she gathered the bedding for the couch and Zack's clean clothes and towel, Johanna tried not to rush. She tried to make it a normal end to a most abnormal day. Kayla caught her eye a couple of times, and it didn't take a genius to know that she was curious. Right now, though, avoidance was the only answer. Johanna ate a piece of pizza, then asked, "You two all set for the night?"

They nodded, and Zack offered his "thank you" around a bite of pizza. Kayla's eyes stayed with her until Johanna turned and left the kitchen. Kayla knew something was up.

Even Johanna knew avoidance wasn't going to work for long. There was a strong temptation to close her bedroom door, but Johanna left it open and settled on the bed. Privacy was relative, at least for now.

"Hey," she greeted Miya at the sound of her voice, "I'm sorry I couldn't talk when you called. I only now took a deep breath. It's been a hell of a day."

"I'm listening."

She kept her voice low, out of range of Kayla and Zack, and rushed with increasing angst to describe what they'd been through. As Johanna talked, she realized that ordinarily this call would have gone to Kate. It would have been Kate she turned to for advice or reassurance or just to unload. But tonight . . .

"My mind's been screaming all the possibilities, all the frightening scenarios that could have been," Johanna continued. "And the things that Kayla has known all along, the dangers she and Zack were skirting. I got enough out of her that it scared the shit out of me. That he didn't trust anyone, even me, with his fears. Fears of what could have meant serious injury, or worse. Fears about his sexuality, about his worth. I am torn between anger and tears, jockeying between them even as I'm talking to you."

"But you know it now. Go from here, Johanna."

"But I made wrong assumptions all along; instead of noticing clues, I let easy answers take the place of listening, looking, asking. My head was somewhere else, thinking about myself."

"Yes, and what if there wasn't anything there you could have seen? They're kids, but if they don't want you to know something, they can be awfully good at hiding it. Hey, I know it's bothering you," Miya said, "and I'm sure it's no consolation for me to tell you it's not unusual. And it's also not unusual to be distracted. No one can be spot-on every minute, every day. Take responsibility for what you could realistically control, but don't blame yourself for what you can't."

"It seems more appropriate than blaming Kayla," Johanna replied quickly. "And I'm not just bothered by it—I'm hurt. I always thought, or maybe was hoping, I'd never have to worry about her keeping things from me. That we would always be honest with each other and trust that there was nothing we couldn't handle together. I thought she knew there wasn't anything she could tell me to make me love her less."

"You know," Miya said, "it could be as simple as she didn't want you to worry about her and that she didn't want Zack to lose faith in her."

"I did tell you that, didn't I?"

"Yes, that sometimes it seemed like she worried more about you than you did about her? Yes, you did."

And that was partly true. There were many times when she had every confidence that Kayla was fine, making good decisions, nothing that made her worry. But she also knew that Kayla felt things, worried about the rift in her family and her mother's loneliness. That's what she had seen tonight in Kayla's expression when her question about who called was cut off, and in her eyes, wondering, questioning—about the calls at night, about what her mother wasn't telling her.

Miya broke the unusually long silence. "That's not all you're worried about, is it?"

Johanna released a sigh. "I'm doing the same thing I've admonished her for," she admitted. "Not telling her about you, evading a curiosity that I know is there. But what's worse is that she knows it. I haven't lied to her, but I ignored her when she asked who called on our way home."

"No, please don't lie to her, certainly not because of me. The last thing I want is to have a negative effect on your relationship with Kayla. You can just tell her I wanted to encourage you to meet with Dr. Reed about developing a better anti-bullying plan. I am absolutely encouraging you to do that. By the way, did Kayla tell you about meeting with Dr. Reed?"

"She said Dr. Reed wants to make a team to fight bullying and wants to talk with me about it."

"She's impressed with how Kayla organized the other students, but she wants to be sure you're aware of what Kayla's doing and that you support it. And, personally, I think you should be taking a bit of credit for raising her with the skills it took, not just to take a stand herself, but to empower other kids to do it as well."

Johanna laid her head back and focused on the fingers of light casting shadows across the ceiling. "I shouldn't have dumped all this on you. I really didn't intend to."

"Actually, I feel honored that you did. I don't think I would have been your first choice for this call a week ago."

"You're right. And it surprises me that I didn't hesitate or overthink it, I just started unloading. I can't remember the last time I did that to anyone other than Kate."

"Well, I am no Aunt Kate," Miya admitted. "I can only hope that someday I will be as important in someone's life as she is in yours."

"I have no doubt you will be," Johanna said. "You listen and you care."

"I wish I knew how to ease your mind. I can't promise that everything will be okay, but now you know what Zack has been going through, and you can be a part of finding solutions. And now *Zack* knows that there are people in place to help him. He's not alone, and Kayla doesn't have to feel like she needs to shoulder his trust all herself. Try to focus on how grateful you are that he's safe. Don't let your mind go to how wrong things could have gone."

"Certainly good advice if I can do it. It may help to meet with Dr. Reed. I really want to be a part of making things better. I think it would be good for Linda, Zack's mom, too, to be part of finding ways to help."

"I'm sure it will," Miya agreed. "And make plans to do something together, something fun to lift everyone's spirits. Come to the upcoming school musical; it'll be filled with seasonal joy. It might feel good to get out, away from the stress, watch some very talented kids, and tune the world out for a little while."

"I'd already planned on coming. Now I'm going to see if Zack and his mother would like to come with us."

Chapter 23

ON NOTICE

Chandra Reed tapped lightly on the Assistant Principal's open door, announcing her arrival. "You ready to compare notes?"

"Ready." Richard Davis removed his suit jacket and loosened his tie. "And thank you for taking the meetings with the girls and their parents. I wasn't looking forward to having to arrange six separate meetings."

Chandra agreed as she claimed the chair next to his desk. And at six-three and a few extra pounds past his college football years, he was naturally suited to take on Josh Carter and his teammates.

"How'd it go with the 'mean girls'?" he asked with a grin.

"Not at all like *they* thought it would go. I'm sure they counted on being there together, supporting each other, stories all in sync. I'm sure there was a good deal of anxiety when they realized they would be separated and answering to me in front of a parent."

"Yep," he nodded, "the look in the boys' eyes was really close to that of a quarterback's eyes when his line fails and he's lookin' at a couple of 280-pound defensive linemen bearing down on him."

Chandra smiled. "Yeah, *that* look," she said, opening a folder on the corner of the desk. "They were nervous, but for the most part, I heard the usual from each of them, 'we were only joking,' 'we weren't hurting anyone.' From the parents I got, 'she was just being a teenager,' 'just part of growing up,' 'I'm sure she won't do it again.'

"The three girls fit the classic trio of a strong, controlling leader and her followers. The leader, Julie, and her mother, of course, presented the biggest challenge. The attitude may very well eventually lead to expulsion. The daughter tried to say the right words but with a tone of arrogance making them totally unbelievable. And her mother proved that her daughter was pure fruit of the tree. She was condescending and tiptoed rather precariously on the edge of a threat."

"To you?"

"To us," Chandra replied, "the school authority. Let me see if I can quote her. 'I would really hate to call my attorney over some silly teasing, but . . .'"

He offered a hint of a grin and shook his head. "Not bad for a poorly veiled threat, but Dan Carter just came right out with it. 'You keep harassin' my boy for just joking around like all teenagers do, I'm gonna make sure you answer to the school board. You ain't messin' with my boy's future.'"

Chandra's expression eased into realization. "Ah, Doug Carter. I forgot that the boy's uncle is on the board."

"Yep, his brother. He's a cleaned-up version of Dan, and I still can't figure out how he got elected to the school board."

"No doubt he gathered supporters from organizing the protests against the mask mandate when we opened the schools back up. He saw his chance to raise havoc from the inside. He has a whole list of books he wants banned."

"I know," Richard replied, "he's already got a couple of other board members stirred up over a list of books, one in the elementary library on Harriet Tubman. I'm sure you know where he's going with that. And another book about a boy with same-sex parents."

"I'm aware. He has a whole group trying to dictate what our curriculum includes and how it's taught."

"Yep, he's a real gem. But my biggest concern is his influence over other board members. We can deal with one nutcase, but . . ."

"I don't imagine that anyone on the school board, though, wants any more out-of-control meetings, dealing with parents and crazed protesters who don't even have kids in school, all that screaming in their faces and threatening their families. I hope reasonable minds can keep the cap on things. The best we can do is to be prepared to defend our actions—probably at this next board meeting."

"Yeah, I'm not confident that my encouragement for Josh to use his star power to be a team leader on *and* off the field will be enough. The 'do what's best for Josh' attitude is well imprinted. The only plus we have is that the one thing Dan Carter wants more than anything is for his son to play college football. Let's hope it's enough for him to put the hammer down and convince Josh that he doesn't want to do anything to jeopardize his chances. Remember, not wanting him to miss another year of football was the thing that finally forced Dan to get Josh vaccinated and wear a mask at school."

"You couldn't have convinced me of that the day he was spewing obscenities, unmasked, in your face outside the office. Carl had already radioed security and called the police. We were sure it was going to be a physical fight that none of us could have broken up."

"Unless he had a gun," Richard replied, "he wasn't going to win that one. That event wasn't far from my mind when I was confronting Josh today. I'm convinced his dad would have gone full ballistic if it weren't for that dream of his."

"How realistic is that dream?"

"It's hard to know. He's good, but there are a lot of good players out there. Coach Parker and I made a lot of contacts for him, and he's gotten some looks. But the college signing schedules are all off, too. Normally, if there was interest, he would have known in his junior year, but Covid threw everything off. He could still be signed to an unfilled roster, even into the summer. Coach had him join the NCSA Network, which works with colleges with roster availabilities. And there is always a remote chance that he could walk on. Both Coach and I have done our best to encourage him to keep his grades up, and to keep the dream in front of him. After all, he's the kind of kid who could cause trouble . . ."

"I'm sure."

"Yeah, I've worried more than once whether this is a kid who will show up at school with a gun. The thought stops my heart cold."

Chandra hoped that football, along with Richard leaning into Josh's attention with a rush of energy and potential, would be enough to prevent tragedy. But Josh Carter went home after school, after practice, after games, to a father with his own agenda.

"I've had those thoughts, too," she admitted. "But Josh isn't a loner. He has a crew; he has a leadership role. That used to keep me leaning toward someone like him *not* being that kid. That we should worry more about the kid who is the brunt of the bullying. That kid needs our extra support. But in the last couple of years, I've adjusted my thinking. I've widened my scope. We can't go by the established statistics anymore. So, I guess the bottom line for today is that we know who's involved, who the leader couple is, and they've been put on notice."

"As have we," he added. "Got any better news?"

She looked him in the eyes and grinned. "Actually, yes. We have commitments from three teachers and three parents to join the team of students that Kayla Beals put together. And the students aren't wasting any time. Elliott Dean is phenomenal. He already has a cyber team wreaking havoc with the bullies' social media accounts. I don't pretend to understand how they do it, but Elliott claims that the bullies never knew how apologetic they could be; even some of the horrible pictures of Zack Sawyer have magically disappeared. And the core group that Kayla put together is already working to get the word out that they are there for support."

"I saw their column in the online newspaper. They'll need to keep that from getting stale," he said. "And I'm seeing more and more of the blue arm bands and that's getting attention."

"They chose blue because they said that it stands for support, peace, and being sensitive to the needs of others."

"How's Zack doing? Do you think all this will help get him back in school?" asked Richard.

"I'm working with him and his mother. I think he's going to be fine on Zoom. It'll keep him from falling too far behind. He had every reason to be afraid, so now we need to show him this can work and that he'll be safe."

"You're pretty optimistic about this, aren't you?"

"Uh-huh, I have to say I am," Chandra replied. "I know other schools have tried methods like a hotline and a parent-teacher committee without much success, but this is coming at the problem from so many different angles. I think it has a good chance."

"So, is your husband thinking about putting together the same plan at Shepherd?"

"He's watching us closely. If we get good results, I'm sure he will."

Richard leaned back in his chair and clapped his hands behind his head. "Well," he said, "we'll have to be ready to hand out some suspensions if they push back."

"That's a point I hope I made strongly enough to the Blue Crew students—they are to support and encourage. They need to protect each other and report confrontations to us, and we'll take it from there."

"Yes," he agreed, "as much as it's possible, we need to take the heat."

Chapter 24

DECEMBER IN TIME

"Thank you for picking us up, Johanna." Linda Sawyer slid into the front seat of the car on a whoosh of crisp air, as Zack joined Kayla in the back. "It's been too long since we've gotten together."

"It has, Linda. This'll be a fun night, something we can all use about now," Johanna said to a wide smile she hadn't seen in a while. Linda was well put together tonight—hair cut neatly in a dark blond bob, makeup fresh and appropriate. No visible signs of her personal struggle, but Johanna knew Linda's struggle was day to day, one at a time. It was nice to see her putting together a string of wins.

"Ron's exhausted," Linda offered. "He's appreciating being able to sleep as long as he wants after a long haul. And I don't mind. He'd just be tired and bored. I don't know what we would have done without him during Covid. The restaurant was closed for so long, and his paycheck was all we had. I don't know what I've done to deserve him."

"Oh, he sees the good in you that you can't see yourself," Johanna replied, as she met Kayla's eyes in the rearview mirror.

"We should all be so blessed."

The auditorium was filling up fast. Parents and students, teachers and staff, and the were public grateful for being able to gather and enjoy live performances. The center section was more than half filled, so Johanna chose a row of seats on the aisle of the right-hand section. "Almost as good as being in the middle," she said, settling in a seat between Linda and Kayla. Perfect for sharing the evening with Linda. They huddled over the program while the lights were up, pointing out names of students and staff they recognized. The list of performances covered December music from the '50s through the '90s.

"They all contributed," Johanna said. "It's wonderful. Look." She ran her finger down the list on the back page. "The choir, the orchestra and band, and the drama department. And everyone who worked on the sets and lights and all the technical stuff."

"Yeah," Linda agreed, "there's a lot of talent in those kids, *and* in the teachers. One of Zack's friends is in the choir. Did you know that Mrs. Alexander, Mrs. A, has never had a choir take home anything except a first-place rating in state competition? In all the years she's taught here," she added.

"Wow," Johanna replied.

"And the marching band gets invited to perform in the Thanksgiving parade every year."

"The blessings just keep on coming," Johanna said, smiling

"Jackie, one of the waitresses I work with, has a daughter who plays the clarinet in the band. She was so excited to be able to go this year."

Yes, Johanna thought, her focus stopping at Miya's name, so much talent—teachers pulling the best from their students, and students reaching for their potential. "Oh, here we go," she said as the auditorium lights dimmed and the stage lit up.

It was no surprise that the show did not disappoint. Each performance was meticulously planned with scenery and props and costumes of the decade, from the '50s "Sleigh Ride" and the '60s "Rockin' Around the Christmas Tree," to "Let It Snow" in the '70s. Johanna marveled between each performance as the stage was reset. She laughed with Linda at the styles that began to look all too familiar in the "Winter Wonderland" of the '80s.

"Oh, my God," Johanna remarked, "my aunt had that coat with the geometrical designs."

"Between the '70s and the '80s, how did fashion survive?" Linda asked.

"Don't forget what we thought was cool growing up."

"Yeah," Linda agreed, "my favorite dress was a loud floral scoop neck. I thought I was the tits."

Johanna laughed. "Well, if my mother hadn't thrown them out, I'd probably still be wearing those acid-washed jeans with all the holes in them."

When the stage curtain opened for the next to last performance of the night, Johanna's mind jumped quickly to Miya. Throughout the evening, she had watched and waited, wondering which performance she had offered to help with. With two to go, she would know soon. Even sooner than she thought.

"Mom," Kayla whispered, "this is the one the teachers do. They do one every year, It's tradition."

Johanna's heart picked up its pace as she scanned the stage. One by one, the singing teachers entered the living room set, accompanied by unseen musicians, and assembled on the left side of the room.

"Bells will be ringin'," they sang, "the sad, sad news . . ."

Kayla whispered again, "That's Mr. Aggar," as a man entered from the right side of the stage. Then she rattled off the names of the teachers singing, but Johanna barely listened. She watched Jim Aggar, clad in black jeans and a leather vest over a black

T-shirt. The picture was coming together now. He sat in a chair by the fireplace and dropped his head in his hands.

"Oh, what a Christmas," they sang, "to have the blues."

He was sad, as the well-known song said. His baby was gone. His plea was for her to come home for Christmas.

Bright white light got his and everyone's attention as it backlit an oversized translucent door in the back wall. The silhouette appearing behind it was unmistakable. The movements were slow and deliberate, a seductive approach. Jim rose from his chair and moved slowly to the door.

Silhouetted hands placed their palms against the door. He reached to place his hands against them, but in an instant, they were gone. The silhouette turned away. He remained, hoping, his hands waiting, pressing his forehead against the door as the words to the song pleaded again, "Please come home . . ."

Johanna wondered if that was the extent of Miya's role in the performance—appear as a hope, then vanish to leave him sad and alone for Christmas. It seemed to fit the song's story.

But it didn't. A moment later, Jim's head snapped up, the silhouette returned and reached to place her palms against his. As she did, the door slid from between them. He took her hands, Miya's hands, and twirled her into the room as Johanna's breath caught short of exhale. And hers was not the only response. A portion of the audience broke into applause and cheers. Was it for the story, cheers that she came home? Or was it for the woman dressed in black form-fitting, high-waisted pants and short tuxedo blouse that hugged her waist? Or, Johanna questioned, were they cheering for a coupling they hoped was real?

She didn't know, couldn't know. But it didn't matter. Nothing was going to cool the flush she felt or stop her heart from trying to escape its bounds. She couldn't pull her eyes from them, from the dance, from the bodies turning and teasing and moving to the music. Synchronized. Beautiful. And for Johanna, painfully sensual.

Shouldn't it be her hands holding Miya's, her arms circling, her hips moving so close? Shouldn't it be her? But it wasn't, not this time, and that made it too hard to watch. And yet, she did watch, a strange kind of torture while the song pleaded "... tell me you'll roam no more ..." She endured it to the end when the music stopped and the dance ended with Jim's forehead pressed against Miya's.

The whistles and applause took the air from the room as the curtain closed. Linda's words sounded far away. "That was really beautiful," she said. Kayla seemed to whisper, "Wow, Ms. James can really dance."

"Yes," Johanna heard herself say. "Yes, beautiful." But her mind was detached, watching and listening to the final medley of holiday songs from a distance.

She wasn't fully engaged again until the cold December air chilled her lungs and splashed relief over her heated skin. She needed to clear her head and think. A relief that had to wait through the excited chatter and the ride home. It had been a good night for Linda and the kids. A nice contrast to their drama and angst. There was hope in the sound of their voices that life was going to be better now.

The comfort of that happy chatter was gone, though, once they dropped off Linda and Zack and headed home. Kayla was more quiet than usual, and Johanna was privately wishing for time alone in her room to sort out her thoughts.

Back home, she tried to bring back a bit of comfortable chatter by asking, "Are you feeling better about Zack?"

Kayla retrieved a bottle of cold water from the fridge to take to her room. "Yeah. I think he feels better. He'll feel a lot better if Elliott can do more about the social media stuff."

"He sounds like a good one to have in your corner."

"Yeah, he's scary smart. I'm glad he's a friend. If anyone can help, he can." She kissed her mother on the cheek and started toward her room.

"I hope everyone sleeps better tonight," Johanna offered.

Kayla stopped in the hallway and turned. She made eye contact, but hesitated before asking, "Does Ms. James know?"

"About Zack?"

"No," Kayla replied, "about how you feel about her."

The question caught her short of her next breath. She froze. Yet Kayla waited, her eyes direct, unwavering. "I . . ." Johanna started. Then, with a relenting nod, "Yes, she knows."

The affirmation softened the questioning lines of Kayla's expression into a hint of a smile. She'd been right. "That's who you talk to at night, isn't it?"

Johanna nodded. She almost smiled but stopped herself. "You're not supposed to be this smart at sixteen."

Kayla rolled her eyes. "It doesn't take a genius, Mom."

As hard as she had tried to, Johanna admitted, there was no denying what Miya had pointed out—she was obvious, even to a teenager.

But Kayla wasn't finished. "You can't help it. Every time you talk about her, your face flushes. And tonight, when she was dancing—"

"It was dark."

"Not *that* dark. And you weren't smiling, like maybe you didn't like her dancing with Mr. Aggar."

Johanna closed her eyes with an exasperated sigh. "It's a good thing I don't play poker." She shook her head. "I've been trying to think this through. I didn't want to say anything to you until I figured this out."

"Will you tell me when you do?"

Johanna pulled Kayla into a hug. She kissed the side of her face and said, "I will. And you need to talk to me, too. Okay? We'll figure things out together."

"Deal," Kayla said, released from their hug. "Are you going to call her tonight?"

"No, I have some thinking to do."

Chapter 25

JUST SAY IT

Sleep wasn't possible, not tonight. The words of the song repeated themselves, hijacked the notes and earwormed them into her mind. Over and over, "What a Christmas to have the blues," forcing her to hear the chorus from beginning to end each time. Johanna tossed from side to side, pulled the pillow around her head, but nothing stopped it. Frustrated, she flopped onto her back and stared at the flat grey of the ceiling. A movie screen that, despite her best efforts to block it, played the dance in a never-ending loop. Every sway of Miya's body, the reach of her arm beckoning freedom, the lean of her body back to his, the movements smooth and sensuous. It was more than she could take, but she couldn't shut it off.

And she had so many questions. There was the Miya James she knew—physically beautiful, dedicated to her job and her students, kind and well-liked, and smart. On the other side, the Miya James she feared she didn't know. Was she still the fighter of her childhood? Could she be a committed lover? Would a career take precedence over a relationship? Would she accept a relationship with a man to give her both? Was there anything, anyone she'd walk through fire for?

Too many questions. Too much doubt. She turned over, burrowed under the covers and buried her head beneath the pillow.

The ringing phone woke her. At first she thought it was a dream, but the sound was right beside the bed. The clock read 9:15. The last time she remembered glaring at the blue digital numbers was at 6:33.

Fumbling to pick up the phone, she blinked the blur from her eyes. Kate. Johanna cleared her throat and answered. "Is it a good morning?"

"Well, I don't know," Kate replied. "You're not up yet, are you?"

Johanna groaned. "I had every intention of getting Kayla to your place at nine. I will get her there as soon as I get a shower."

"Late night?"

"Sort of. I couldn't sleep. Well, until six thirty, apparently. I finally made a decision, you know, like an adult."

"About Miya?"

"I need to set her free—let her be whoever she is. I have no right to try to mold her into something that *I* want or need."

"Do you want to talk about it later?"

"Maybe," Johanna replied. "Yes. Maybe tomorrow after work. But right now, this is taking time from your shopping day. Kayla's been looking forward to it. She had her bag packed yesterday."

"Well, today's our special day, but you are welcome to join us tomorrow for wrapping day. We'll wrap yours early so you won't be spoiling any surprises."

"No, that's your time together. And honestly, I don't feel much like socializing."

"Okay, I'll see you when you get here."

The feeling shrouding Johanna as she dropped onto the couch alone was eerily familiar. The impending sadness. Emotions she thought she had left behind so many years ago about to take her captive again. Without willing it, she was back in her childhood bedroom, staring at the ceiling, unable to escape the sadness. Alone then, as she was now, staring into the stillness. At thirteen, she'd had no reference for loss. She couldn't have known that her best friend, along with their plans for the summer, their secrets, their pledge for a forever friendship, would be gone. A divorce splitting that family apart and sending her best friend to California. So far away, with nothing that she could do to change it. She'd found herself sucked into the silence of her absence, leaving a void she hadn't been prepared for.

Now, she'd prepare herself for an adult loss, this time with the psychological tools she didn't have then. But painful still, especially with her knowing more about loss now, different kinds of loss. The emotional loss of her parents, their support, their belief in her. She trusted now that support could come from somewhere else, someone else. And that was okay.

Lovers and friends could come and go without taking her dreams and plans with them. Raising Kayla had taught her that. The key was knowing the difference between *their* hopes and dreams and her own. Doing what she must do now, though, would not be easy.

Startling her, the ringing of the phone pulled her from the stillness. Johanna reached for it thinking it was probably Kate or Kayla, but hesitated when she saw it was Miya. She waited through two more rings and decided to get it over with.

"Hey," she answered, having to override the expected reaction, the zing that always shot through her, at the sound of Miya's voice.

"Did I call at a bad time?"

"No," she replied, trying to correct the less than enthusiastic tone Miya obviously picked up on. "I dropped Kayla off at Kate's for their holiday shopping spree, so I was just lying here thinking."

"I've been doing some thinking, too," her voice soft and reserved. "Can we talk—in person?"

The pang of realization, that Miya had come to the same conclusion, hit hard. It shouldn't have; the signs had been there all along. And as hard as they had tried to ignore them, it didn't change anything. "Yeah, I don't really want to talk on the phone. Do you want to meet for lunch?" Not that she had any appetite to eat, but it seemed less intimate, more easily managed.

"Would you come here?"

"To your place?"

"Yes."

Before today, before program night, Johanna's heart would have tried to leap from her chest at the invitation. But not today. "What time?"

"Your call," Miya replied. "I don't plan on going anywhere."

Waiting, delaying the inevitable, gave way to a strong need to get to the other side of one of the hardest things she'd ever had to do. Johanna read Miya's address into the GPS and steeled herself for what she was about to do.

All the way across town, she searched for the right words. How do you separate what's in your head from what's in your heart? Words, regardless of how she arranged them, were wholly inadequate. She was left with the selfish hope that Miya would take the lead and say what had to be said.

The knock sounded final, the last note of a finished song. But when the door did open, the challenge Johanna faced became flesh-and-blood real. A barefoot Miya, dressed in an over-sized white shirt and a pair of jeans, invited her in.

Johanna, not even looking at Miya in the doorway, walked in and busied herself removing her shoes and jacket. "I won't stay long," she said before turning to face Miya again. *Say it*, she told herself. *Don't wait. Do it now.*

"I need to—" they began at the same time.

"Sorry," Johanna said, "go ahead." *Please* go ahead.

Miya extended her hand, took Johanna's, and turned to move them further into the front room. When she stopped, she faced Johanna and took her other hand. The space between her brows pressed into a "V" and she looked directly into Johanna's eyes.

It's okay, Johanna thought. *Say it, Miya. Just go ahead and say it.*

Miya tilted her head ever so slightly and softened her brows. "I'm in love with you."

She heard the words, felt the electricity shoot through her chest, but still it wasn't real. It couldn't be real. Not until Miya pulled her close and slipped her hand around the back of Johanna's neck.

She dared the words. "Are you —"

Miya pulled her in, her lips brushing over Johanna's, and breathed the words, "I'm sure." She didn't wait for permission: none was needed. Her kiss was firm and full, answering, promising, parting Johanna's lips. There was no denying now, no more waiting. They wanted each other, needed each other. Would chance being together. Finally. Now.

This was their time, their beginning. Their sanctuary, bathing them in a soft glow, welcoming them to a bed of down. Their space with no worry, no doubt, no outside world—time, with its boundaries and demands—it didn't exist. Here, nothing and everything mattered. Here, where there was nothing beyond Miya, and the feel of her skin, the touch of her hands, the scent of perfume that took her back to that first night.

Johanna let go, let unspoken wishes become real, as Miya's heart challenged her own, as murmurs captured her breath and took her to a height she hadn't imagined. Control slipped away and brilliance held her forever and not long enough.

She caught her breath, still lost in the grey-blue eyes, and said the words out loud, "I love you. I love you, Miya James."

Miya smiled as she brushed the hair from Johanna's forehead. "Maybe as much as I love you."

"Maybe," she said, pulling the comforter over bare shoulders. She slid against Miya's smooth, now cooling skin, and nestled into the crook of her neck. "When did you know?"

"When I knew that *you* knew. When you called me instead of Kate."

"That *was* it, wasn't it? When I knew. When it was more than physical. Is there any other feeling this incredible?"

Miya drew her hand down the slope of Johanna's back and over the curve of her hip. "Love that touches every cell in your body and gives your soul a home? No," she said, "there's nothing as incredible."

"Then tell me this is real. Tell me I'm not imagining it."

"It's as real as we make it," Miya said, pressing her lips to Johanna's forehead.

"It scares me how much I want that to be true."

"As long as we want the same thing, we're going to be okay. Let's make this 'growing old together' real." She punctuated her words with light kisses to Johanna's face, "Lazy Saturdays and manic Mondays and nights of passion real."

Johanna pushed up onto her elbow and looked down into Miya's eyes. "I want to share it all with you."

"Dreams *and* nightmares?"

She caressed the outline of Miya's face and laced her fingers through soft, dark curls. "Everything," she whispered.

Chapter 26

FAMILY

It wasn't going to matter what words she chose, Johanna reassured herself. There were two people who she knew for sure would see beyond them, who would understand her struggle, her decision, and her hope. The future started here, it started with Kayla and Kate.

"Hey," she called, letting herself in the door, "I'm looking for my favorite aunt and my favorite daughter."

"That would be your *only* daughter," Kayla called back.

"We're in the kitchen," Kate answered.

Johanna breathed in the aroma filling the house. "Yes," she replied, "I already have a sugar high."

Kate smiled brightly at the sight of her. "Christmas cookies. Peanut butter cups, pretzel hugs, and your favorite, turtle thumbprints."

Johanna wrapped her arms around Kayla's shoulders, kissed the side of her head, and snatched one of her favorites from the tray on the island. "Mmm, still warm," she said after a bite. "I'm starting to get into the holiday mood."

Kayla picked up another cookie and handed it to her mother.

"Do you think another will get you the rest of the way there?"

"Maybe," she said with an even tighter hug. She released Kayla and made eye contact with Kate.

It was an open, locked-in invitation, and Kate needed nothing more. With a slight lift of her brows and an almost smile, she said, "Kayla. will you take some cookies to your uncle? I'm not allowed in the garage; he's working on a Christmas surprise for me."

"Sure," Kayla replied, "but you're not getting the surprise out of me."

"Wouldn't think of it," she said with a wink to Johanna. As soon as Kayla was out of the kitchen, Kate added, "I can see it in your face and how hard you hugged Kayla, but I still want you to tell me."

"Of course you do." She rounded the end of the island and wrapped Kate in a tight, long-held embrace. "I'm almost afraid to say it," she said softly. "I am so happy right now. And so much in love."

"And so is she?" Kate returned against Johanna's ear.

"And so is she."

Kate squeezed her hard before releasing her embrace and added, "It's about time."

Something Johanna was only now beginning to appreciate. Now, after she'd felt time stand so still, now when she understood how much she needed it. And Kayla, she thought, as she breezed into the kitchen, just may need Miya in her life as well.

"No," Kayla said, her face stern, her hand warding off a question from Kate. "I'm not telling you anything about what he's making . . . except that he can't wrap it, just put a large bow on it. And you can't look under the blue tarp . . . Oh, and you've been wanting it forever."

Kate returned a wide smile.

"You *do* realize," Johanna said, "that you are almost as incorrigible as your aunt, don't you?"

"She has learned from the best," Kate replied.

"Uh-huh. I see your handiwork more often than you know."

Kate raised her brows. "Does it make you smile?"

"See how you are?"

"Hey," Kayla interjected, "I'm right here—listening."

"Yes," Johanna said. "And as long as you are, I have something I want to talk with you about."

"Do you want me to get some more wrapping done so that you two can talk?" Kate asked.

"No, this is about family. I want it to be about family. Let's take these," Johanna picked up a plate of cookies, "and sit in the dining room."

"Did I do something?" Kayla asked as she claimed her favorite chair at the table.

Johanna's tone was light, teasing. "I don't know. Did you?"

Kayla switched her eye contact from her mother to Kate and back again and waited.

Johanna leaned forward. Her tone soft, more personal. "Remember when you asked me to tell you when I figured things out about Miya?"

Kayla nodded. "Have you?"

"Yes," she replied. "I have—*we* have. We want to be together, to be part of each other's lives. That is, if it'll be okay with you."

Kayla's eyes widened with a spark of excitement. "Did she kiss you? Did she say she loves you?"

With a quick glance and smile at Kate, Johanna settled comfortably in Kayla's anticipation. "Yes," she said, "and yes. She told me that she loves me."

"Because I'm not going to be okay with it unless you're sure."

Johanna's peripheral vision caught Kate's sly smile. "I was sure I wanted her in our lives before she was sure. This was a much harder decision for her than it was for me, but not because she wasn't sure she loved me, Kayla. I could tell how much she cares about her students, and how she cares about you. She's honest, brutally so sometimes, and I find that I need that." This time, she met Kate's eyes straight on. "I want the same honesty and insight that you've given me all these years. You've shown me that anything less is unacceptable."

"I knew that I was going to like her," Kate returned. "I'm glad that you've been patient and gave her time to work through things."

"I almost wasn't."

"Why?" Kayla asked.

"Because I was afraid it wouldn't be the right thing for her. What made her decision more difficult is that her personal life and her relationships could be a problem for some people. It could jeopardize her job."

"Who?"

"There's always a possibility that someone—a parent, a board member, or another teacher—could have a problem with her personal life and try to have her fired."

"But why would they fire a good teacher?"

"Because of people who believe homosexuality is wrong," Kate explained. "Maybe they think that way because of their faith, or because they were raised to fear or dislike anyone who is different or thinks differently than they do. Things like race or religion, or—"

"Bigots can threaten her job," Kayla said.

Kate cocked her head and grinned at Johanna.

"In a perfect little nutshell," Johanna replied. "Or it could be because she has a personal relationship with a parent. We're just going to have to be ready for whatever might happen."

"So, what do we do?"

How *did* she get so strong, Johanna wondered, so full of personal resolve? Certainly not from a mother who way too often lost the battle against self-doubt. Or, maybe because of it. Because she didn't carry her mother's baggage, the worry and fear that eat away confidence. Or it could be the strength of Kate's influence. She'd put money on that being an important part of it. But whatever it is, she thought, as she looked into her daughter's waiting eyes, she loved who Kayla was becoming.

"You're saying yes?" Johanna asked. "This works for you?"

"You love her, don't you?" Kayla replied. "And she's willing to take on homophobes for you." She shrugged her shoulders. "That's all I need to know—except what I should do to help."

"We need to keep it among family, so don't say anything to other students."

"Even Zack?"

"Zack is family. I'll talk with him. With how good you both are at keeping secrets," she said, "I'm not worried about that. The rest we will have to take Miya's advice on. And there is one thing she's already explained to me. You'll have to be transferred to another teacher's English class. Will you be okay with that?"

"I wish I didn't have to," she said with a frown. "But if it helps."

"It will. The school administration will know, and we don't want anyone to think that you would be getting special attention or consideration."

"I don't think she would. She treats everyone the same, even the jerks in class. But I understand."

Kate rose, grasped the back of Kayla's neck, and planted a kiss on the top of her head. "We've had dessert, so I guess it's time we have some dinner," she said, starting toward the kitchen.

"Stay out of the garage," Kayla called after her.

"Who made you boss?" Kate replied.

"Uncle Brad." She turned back to her mother's steady gaze. "What?" she asked.

Johanna held their connection. "You're kinda special. You know that?"

Another shrug. "As long as she's good to you, and you're happy. Otherwise, she'll have to deal with me and Aunt Kate."

Her laugh was a gentle, appreciative sound. And Johanna added, "I love you."

Chapter 27

FESTIVAL OF LIGHTS

Plans. Together, they made plans. For tonight, for tomorrow, for as long as they could dream. Johanna hugged the thought, the feeling of it, tightly as she snugged her jacket around her. She followed Kayla and slid into the backseat of Miya's Subaru with anticipation and a bright smile.

Both Miya and Michael turned to greet them with smiles that gleamed in the dark interior of the car. "Johanna, Kayla," Miya began, "meet my baby brother, Michael."

Michael reached his hand between the seats and squeezed each of their hands. "Just so you know," he said, "even when I'm sixty-five, she will still refer to me as her baby brother."

"Well, it's nice to meet you, little brother," Johanna replied.

"Hey, Kayla," Miya said, "I think you, especially, are going to enjoy tonight."

"Where are we going?" Kayla asked as Miya backed out of the driveway.

"It's a surprise, a la Michael. Tonight is his idea."

"You're going to see my favorite holiday event," he said. "I've gone every year since they first hired me to do an ad for them."

"Is that what you do for a living?" Johanna asked.

"Yes. I started as a graphic artist and morphed into commercial art so that I could make a living."

Kayla grabbed her mother's arm and her attention.

Johanna read the wide-eyed expression perfectly. She nodded at Kayla and said, "I hope I'm not out of line, since I just met you, Michael, but there is someone I would love to have meet you."

"Oh, no," he replied, "no worries there."

"Are you talking about Zack?" Miya asked.

"Yes. I might be biased, but I think he has a lot of talent."

"Biased or not," Miya said, "you aren't the only one who recognizes his talent. Ms. Arnold, his art teacher, is presenting a display at the national convention and is including a few of Zack's pieces."

"What medium?" Michael asked.

Kayla answered quickly, "Pencil, ink, and charcoal."

"And he helped design and build the Magic Forest," Johanna added.

Miya glanced at Michael. "The village I told you about."

"Oh, right," he replied. "Maybe we can pick a day during break and I can meet him."

"He might be a little shy at first," Johanna explained. "But I know he'll have questions and absorb any information and advice you can give him."

"Have him bring some of his favorite stuff," he added.

"Let's meet at our house," Johanna offered, "and we'll make lunch for everyone."

Miya held up her hand for Michael to clasp. "Done," she said.

Johanna met her eyes in the rearview mirror and mouthed the words, "I love you."

The surprise destination began to reveal itself first as a glow pushing up against the darkness of the sky. As they drew closer, the light grew wider and brighter until it totally enveloped them.

"Wow," Kayla exclaimed, leaning forward for a better view.

Miya pulled the car into a line of others entering a canopy of sparkling lights stretching as far as they could see. Christmas music serenaded them as they moved slowly under the canopy. Animated displays of deer and carolers and skaters interspersed with beautifully lighted evergreens drew their attention from one side of the road to the other.

"Oh, Miya, this is beautiful," Johanna remarked.

"Every year we come here," Michael said, "there's always something new, like the train there." He pointed to a lighted engine pulling three cars and winding around the evergreens.

"I had no idea this was here," Johanna said. "Thank you for sharing it with us."

"There's more," Miya replied, slowly approaching a curve. "My favorite is just ahead on the right."

And it was easy to see why as they rounded the curve to a spectacular sight. Cascading from a large natural rock formation was a crystal waterfall. Lights illuminated water frozen in mid-splash over the rocks; its natural flow stopped in time and space.

"Wow," seemed to be the most appropriate response Kayla could offer.

"I'll agree with that," Johanna said. "I can see why this is a favorite. I've never seen anything like it."

Kayla never took her eyes from the waterfall, taking in every visible angle as she spoke. "Is it real, Ms. James?"

"It is," she replied, looking closely as the car crept slowly past. "It's never the same; it changes with the temperatures and freezing and thawing. Once we have a good hard freeze, it changes day to day." They were beyond the best view now and Miya added, "As beautiful as the man-made displays are, they are no match for Mother Nature."

Exactly, Johanna thought, turning from the last view of the waterfall to the profile that intrigued her even more. Filtered light from headlights behind them outlined the gentle slope of Miya's nose and highlighted the curve of her cheekbone above the shadowed jawline. She wanted to trace the shape with her fingertips, touch the fullness of her lips as the corners lifted into a subtle invitation.

"Kayla," Miya began, interrupting the vision, "I know it will probably take a while before you are comfortable with it," she said, meeting her eyes in the mirror, "but when you are, I'd like it if you would call me Miya when we aren't in school."

Kayla looked to her mother, who understood the questioning look. "No, I didn't ask her," she said. "That's part of what I said would be up to her."

"It's something that would make *me* feel more comfortable— if and when you're okay with it, Kayla."

"Okay," Kayla replied with a nod.

"Hey," Michael said, turning to face Kayla, "I've got something special to show you next."

The inside of the events center was like walking into a miniature city coated with snow. Ribbons of streets and sidewalks defined the hub of the city and its surrounding neighborhoods. Kayla walked ahead with Michael along the aisle circling the city. Both were completely engrossed, pointing out surprising details of working streetlights and people and miniature vehicles busily moving about.

"This really is incredible," Johanna said as the man-made landscape became farmland and forests and frozen lakes. "And that," she added with a nod toward Kayla and Michael, "makes me happy."

"I thought it might," Miya replied. She took Johanna's hand and laced their fingers together. "And this makes me happy."

Happy. The word needed a new definition. Beyond the glint in Kayla's eyes, Johanna thought. Beyond the sure touch of Miya's hand and the thrill her love provided. Now it included mornings brilliant with anticipation, days ripe with promise.

And nights wrapped in a sureness she never imagined possible.

They followed Kayla and Michael, excitedly pointing and talking, around the room, marveling at the full view of the city and the ski slope on the north side. It was a working slope with miniature skiers cutting their paths down the hill and a lift carrying them back to the top.

"Thank you," Johanna said, squeezing Miya's hand, "for introducing us to Michael, for tonight." She stepped back and allowed others to continue past them. Looking into Miya's eyes, she added, "Thank you for being you."

"If I was fully me," Miya returned, leaning in close to brush her lips over the tender skin before Johanna's ear to whisper, "I'd kiss you right here, right now."

Chapter 28

FINDING NORMAL

Johanna parked the car behind the others lining the street in front of Kate's house. Icicle lights draped from the porch roof lit the front of the house, while lights on the large pine at the corner of the drive slowly changed colors from red to gold to green to blue. "I don't know that you're ready for this," she said with a half-smile directed at Miya. "Like I said, Christmas Eve is another Kate tradition. A night for the adults in the family to find babysitters and spend the evening together." A night she cherished even more this time because she was sharing it with Miya. "There will be a lot of chatter, and questions and teasing, and family nuances."

"I'll admit it's not something I'm used to," Miya replied, a soft gold light washing over her face. "Christmas brunch with Michael isn't much preparation, nor a full teacher's lounge just before vacation, but don't worry. I'll be fine. In fact," she said, leaning across the armrest to whisper against Johanna's lips, "I'm looking forward to it."

Johanna met Miya's lips with a full kiss, and breathy warning, "Careful, or we won't make it to the party at all."

"Hey, there you are," Kate greeted them at the door. "Come on in here," she said, taking Miya's arm. "I was beginning to think that Johanna had scared you away."

"Remember," Johanna replied, "she teaches teenagers, Kate. She doesn't scare easily."

"And, no," Miya added with a gleaming smile, "even if she had tried, I wouldn't turn down such a gracious invitation."

"I don't know about gracious," Kate said, with a careful hug around Johanna and her arm full of gifts, "it's just what we do here." With a hug for Miya she added, "Food dishes go to Shannon in the kitchen and gifts go to Brad. He's in charge of the game."

Johanna closed her eyes and breathed in deeply. "Oh, I love the smell of Christmas."

"Mmm, I love it, too," Kate said. "A bit of simmering cinnamon, and Brad always gets me a Fraser fir. It makes the entire house smell so good right up to New Year's. We moved it into the dining room because for Christmas this year Brad made me a window seat for the bay window where it usually is."

Johanna peeked into the living room on their way down the hall. "Ahh, was that the gift under the tarp in the garage?"

"Yes. I made Brad give it to me early so we can use it when we have people over."

"It's beautiful. I know you have wanted that for so long," Johanna said. "But what's with all the colored string all over everything?"

"A Bradley brainstorm. You'll find out later."

It didn't take long for any concern Johanna had about Miya feeling comfortable to be relieved. She watched and smiled at her own lack of faith. There was an ease to Miya's movements, breezing from one introduction to the next with a smile that seemed to pull each into her personal space. *Yes, they like her already.*

And just as easily, the normal progression of a Kate event moved to the kitchen, to the filling of plates, to claiming dining room seats crowded around the table, and to chatter. Eating, complimenting, catching up, and just chatter. The whole thing was seamless, normal, and inclusive—everything Johanna loved about her family, everything she hoped for Miya.

"Hey Johanna," Danny said from his perch on a kitchen stool behind the table, "Sara and I want to know what it will take to keep Kayla from going off to college and leaving us without a babysitter."

"Ha!" she replied, "Not happening," and motioned to Miya sitting next to her. "But I know just the person to find you a fine replacement."

"Okay," he directed at Miya, "we'll be looking for someone to sit for twin six-year-old boys, someone who can entertain them by doing things like build a medieval castle in our living room out of cardboard boxes, magic markers, duct tape, and a hole saw. They didn't even know we left. I'll bet they sleep in there tonight."

"Well, I'll do my best," Miya replied, "short of a top hat and rabbit. But I don't come cheap."

The look on Johanna's face seemed to be a mix of surprise and amusement. Yes, she was already quite comfortable with this funky, irreverent, and lovable family. And it was even more evident during this year's game, Uncle Brad's mystery plan for family fun. For the better part of an hour, nine adults called on the agility and nimbleness of children on a jungle gym to follow their colored string, around furniture, ducking under and over other strings, and each other on their way to claim their gift in the guest room.

Through all the giggling and the laughter, Johanna watched Miya. Watched as this Christmas brightened with new laughter, new sparkle, new blessings. Blessings that she cherished in her own life.

As everyone opened the gifts they'd claimed at the end of the game, Johanna caught Miya's gaze and marveled at how it filled her, how it brightened every part of her. And the smile that followed she knew was hers, meant for her alone, a private sign in a room full of people. She stayed with it until she couldn't, then tucked it safely way.

Their traditional holiday evening always ended in song, with Kate at the baby grand. Johanna crossed the room, took Miya's hand and joined her family around the piano. Such a normal thing to do, to take your lover's hand, in front of family, and to answer the surprise on her face with a loving look. So normal to feel embraced and included in a family, this family. This is what she wanted for Miya, what she so hoped to be able to give her. A new normal. A place where she would never have to stand alone, where her back would never be exposed. Decisions fairly weighed, respected, and supported. In this place, this family, Miya would be safe, her relationship safe.

The sound of voices lifted in song, celebrating the season, pulled her from her thoughts. Johanna joined the harmony, blending and warming the notes from the piano. They sang the words "It's beginning to look a lot like Christmas," joy shining on their faces and ringing in their voices. A karaoke microphone made its way around the piano as they sang each well-known verse. The timing was perfect when the mic reached Miya as they sang, "And Mom and Dad can hardly wait for school to start again." A message bringing a squeeze from Johanna and a kiss to Johanna's cheek.

"Merry Christmas, my love," Johanna offered, entering the car in a rush of winter air. She started the engine, then reached for Miya's hand.

"It *is* a Merry Christmas," she replied. "In fact, it is the most unusual and fun one I've ever had. Most Christmases I don't know where I am going to be or who I'll be spending it with." She raised Johanna's hand and pressed it to her lips. "You do this every year?"

"In good weather and bad, through engagements and breakups and marriages and pregnancies; I can count on it, and so can you."

"That means more than you know," Miya replied. "Thank you—for everything."

Johanna pulled Miya close, kissed her, and added, "There's one more thing you need to know. I have never had to ask them to circle the wagons, and neither will you."

Chapter 29

LIFE IN LINES

Large, heavy flakes of snow covered the windshield of Linda's car by the time Johanna grabbed her jacket and approached the driver's side door. "Oh, wow, it's really coming down," she said as Linda rolled down the window.

"We're supposed to get six to eight inches," Linda replied. "I hope I don't end up sleeping on the cot in the supply room at the restaurant tonight."

"Oh," Johanna said, "I sure hope not. But don't worry about Zack. He's fine to stay here tonight."

"Thanks again. Ron is back on the road. He was lucky to have Christmas off this year. And it was a good one." Linda put her hand on top of Johanna's, "A really good one." She waited until Zack retrieved some things from the backseat and closed the door. "Especially," she said, her eyes locked onto Johanna's, "for Zack."

Johanna smiled. "And for you, too, I hope."

"It's been such a good week," Linda said, then added, "Hey, get inside before you turn into a snowman."

Johanna brushed a thick icing of snow from her hair and

said, "Drive carefully. And tell your boss he should close early tonight."

"If only," she replied as the wipers cleared the windshield. "Get inside."

With a wave, she turned and followed Zack into the house. "Here," she said, shaking the snow from their jackets and picking up a covered dish, "I'll take this in. Is it what I think it is?"

"Yeah, Mom made chocolate pavlova. She sent one on the road with Ron, too."

"Mmm, she knows this is my favorite. Good thing no one's counting calories until the new year."

"Yeah," he added, "Mom calls it decadent."

"Well, Miya's picking up dinner and Michael later, so this is perfect." She motioned to the large portfolio Zack carried through the kitchen. "Oh, that's nice."

"Christmas gift."

He was happy today, happy enough for it to show. His movements were sure and confident, his smile an outwardly subtle sign of an inward pleasure. The kind of happiness Johanna saw when he worked on the magic forest. It seemed that a heaviness had lifted, so it didn't surprise her when he greeted Kayla with, "Hey, I have a new idea for the forest." She had a sense, though, that it was more than that today.

"Mom, come on," Kayla called as Zack lifted the flap of the portfolio. "You've got to see the pictures that Ms. Arnold is going to display at the convention."

"First," Zack said, pulling a picture from the portfolio, "this is for you. I'll have to have it back just for the convention, though."

The drawing, unexpected and rendered in such beautiful detail, was a more intimate portrait than any photograph ever taken of the two of them. He'd captured a singular moment when Johanna leaned over the back of the couch, wrapped her arms around Kayla's shoulders and pressed her forehead against Kayla's temple. The prelude to a goodnight kiss to her cheek, such a simple thing.

"How did you do this, Zack?" Kayla asked.

"I've seen it so many times, I did it from memory."

Johanna looked at him, his eyes wide, waiting. "I love it." She wrapped him in a tight hug. "It's . . . absolutely perfect."

"I thought so, too," he said and offered a wide smile.

While Kayla scanned the room for the right wall for its eventual home, Zack moved the pillows and proudly stood a series of pictures on the couch. A range of talent displayed in pencil and ink, charcoal and pastel, the pieces were even more impressive together. It wasn't hard to imagine a display on a national stage nudging shoulders with the best from across the country. Those rays of pride now peering carefully over the edge of a stubborn shadow had been long in coming.

"Wow, Zack," Johanna exclaimed. "These are fantastic. No wonder Ms. Arnold wants to show them off, or maybe I should say, show *you* off." Her eyes lingered on the finished ink of the stadium, and a fired-up Barack Obama in pastel, and then a pencil rendering of Zack's mother greeting customers with a captivating smile. "I'll bet your mom is very proud of you."

"Yeah," he said with a nod, "she cried. I even think . . ." He shrugged one shoulder. "I don't know . . . I gave this to Ron," he added, pulling another picture from the portfolio. It was clearly Ron, waving as he climbed into the cab of his semi. A miniature Christmas tree was visible in the narrow window behind the cab. Printed at the bottom were the words "Covid Hero." "He looked at it, but he didn't say anything. He just turned his head and went into the bedroom. I thought he hated it, that I should have gotten him a better gift."

Johanna looked again at the picture with its careful detail and unmistakable message and waited. This was the most she had heard Zack talk in a long time.

"Mom changed the subject," he continued. "She wanted to know what Ms. Arnold said about the convention. I knew what she was doing. But a little while later, Ron came back out and gave me this," he said, laying his hand on the portfolio. "Then he *hugged* me—hard—and said, 'I didn't realize.'"

"What do you think he meant?" Johanna asked.

"I didn't know. But then he said, 'I know that I'm gone a lot. Your mom and I didn't realize what all you were trying to handle on your own.' He looked right into my eyes; it was the same look I saw when he made Mom promise to see the doctor."

"During Covid," Johanna said, "I remember."

Zack nodded. Then he said, "I want you to know you can tell me, and I'll be there for you. Even if I'm on the road, I've got friends who will watch out for my boy. No one has the right to hurt you. I won't let them hurt you. He said, 'my boy.' He's never said that before."

Johanna put her arm around his shoulders and hugged him. "Yeah, that's pretty special." She motioned toward the portfolio and added, "And so is that. What a perfect gift."

"This has been the best Christmas. He got Mom a birthstone necklace, a blue topaz. It made her cry."

"He did some serious shopping."

Zack raised his eyebrows and offered an affirmative nod as Kayla headed for the door. "Hey, they made it," she said, peering through the sidelight. "Wow, it's a good thing they drove Michael's truck. The snow's up over the porch step already."

"Well, we may all be camping out here tonight," Johanna added.

Miya and Michael burst through the door, laughing and brushing large white flakes from their hair. As she handed the takeout box to Kayla, Miya said, "The absolute best lasagna, brought to you by Raptor 4x4 and Mad Michael's driving skills."

"You're in for a treat, Zack," Kayla called from the kitchen.

"So are you, Michael," Johanna said. "Come and meet Zack."

Michael shed his jacket and crossed the room to a beaming Zack, and introduced himself. "Oh, wow," he said, turning to see the display on the couch. "Are these what Miya said are going to the convention?"

"Uh-huh," Zack replied without hesitation.

"You," Michael said with a hand on Zack's shoulder, "are one talented young man. These are so good." He began at one end of the couch. "Tell me about each one."

Johanna took Miya's hand and directed her into the kitchen. "Thank you," she said. "Zack's been looking forward to this. I know it means a lot to him."

Miya watched her brother. "He's in his element, talking about art and working with young people. I think he would have made a good teacher—look at Zack's face."

"Completely enthralled. It makes me so happy to see *Zack* happy. You know?"

That happiness was more than clear. Miya saw it, in a twinkle of delight in her eyes, in the ease of an almost smile. "Oh," she replied, "I do know."

Chapter 30

SISTER WARRIOR

The scent of burning cherrywood greeted them the moment they entered through the thick old oak door. With two inches of fresh snow on top of the earlier six inches, and temps dipping into the teens, the fire in the fieldstone fireplace offered welcome heat and cast a golden glow over the interior of Thayer's Pub.

"Ahhh," Chandra sighed as she shed her coat and settled across from Miya at the old wooden table scarred by the years. "That's warming these bones already."

"It feels wonderful," Miya agreed. "And add a hot toddy for you and an old-fashioned for me, and we're going to be toasty inside *and* out."

"I'm so glad this place was able to reopen. It has to take some kind of special to keep a family-owned business open for seventy-five years."

"Absolutely," Miya replied, surveying the thick hand-hewn oak mantle above the fireplace. "I've missed our getaways here. To say nothing of the beauty in getting far enough away to avoid running into parents and kids."

"Charles insisted on finding a place out of town where we

could drink whatever we want, dress however we want, and talk about anything we want." Chandra smiled and chuckled. "Before we found this place, we hadn't had one day that we didn't run into someone from his school or mine, or both."

"How's Charles doing? I really miss that corny sense of humor."

"Well, it's still there. Who'da thought I'd be so grateful to hear another of those silly jokes? But that's when I knew he was turning around, and I dared to take a full breath. I couldn't let my mind go to that place where I would no longer have his love in my life. I still watch him like a newborn, paying close attention to his breathing and his temperature. He keeps saying not to worry so much, but we're learning about the long-term effects of Covid as we go along, and I know that if the situation were reversed, he'd be doing the same thing."

"You worry because he's back to work full-time?"

Chandra nodded and sipped her drink. "He's exhausted when he gets home and goes right to bed. He's not a principal who sits in his office all day, never has been. So, winter break couldn't be more welcome at my house."

"Amen to that," Miya said. "We need this break as much as the kids do."

"Which reminds me. I haven't had a chance to tell you how much I enjoyed the program. I know you put in a lot of time on it. It turned out beautifully."

"The real credit goes to a whole lot of talented kids and staff. When I saw all that talent coming together, I knew it was going to be a fantastic show."

Chandra raised her glass and Miya met it with a click. "Job well done," she toasted and added, "It was a lift our community and school really needed. I've heard more compliments than I've ever heard about a show, and," she tilted her head with a hint of a smile, "a bit of a rumor."

"Oh?" Miya said, watching flickers of orange and gold from

the fire dancing in her dark brown eyes.

"I didn't realize that you are such a good dancer. Your performance with Jim has the rumor mill all stirred up." She signaled the waiter for second drinks and ordered potato skins. "You're sharing these with me," she directed Miya. "A baby step toward me losing some pounds."

"You know you're not going to have to twist my arm. I've never had better skins anywhere. I'll be happy to help."

"I thought you might," Chandra replied with a wide smile. "So, the rumor."

Miya lowered her eyes to the swirls of light and color reflected in her glass. She'd planned to wait for the right moment, a good segue, after they'd had a few drinks and relaxed into their friendship. Yet, here it was, the perfect moment, and with a look back into the searching eyes, she froze. Maybe if she gave it a little more time it would be easier. Maybe she could just slow it down.

She offered a slight smile. "I've heard a little bit, people wondering if there's more than a dance between us. There isn't, and he's fine with that." She tried to read Chandra's reaction, but nothing emerged beyond that non-committal, professionally effective expression meant to garner trust. "Are you disappointed?"

Chandra seemed to press forward into a more personal space, although she hadn't moved. "You know," she began, "I've always been a good judge of character, something I think I must have inherited from my father. So, I'm going to go out on a thick, sturdy limb here and say that I don't believe you can do anything that will disappoint me."

She could still back out, thank her for being such a good friend, talk about the Jim rumor and let it go at that. But there were questions only she could answer, advice only she could give. Knowing what to expect from her and from the school was essential.

Miya sipped her drink slowly, stretching the hesitation to its limit. "I'm afraid," she began, "I'm about to challenge that." She waited, but there was no response from Chandra, only that familiar "whenever you're ready" look. "Do you remember when I told you that I'd done my own bit of whispering to the wind when I was young?"

"I do."

No turning back now. "I wanted desperately for someone to know who I was. I wanted who I was, who I *am* to be okay. I fought to be who I am as if my life depended on whether I succeeded." Miya took a slow breath. Chandra's expression changed, a subtle lift around her eyes, a smoothing of the lines of her forehead—an *ah ha* maybe. A needed signal. Miya continued. "I don't have any doubt that my dating a woman would have any effect on our friendship or how we work together, but before now I never felt the need to confirm it."

"You've also never mentioned a boyfriend or an ex or a man you were interested in."

Miya finally offered an easy smile. "Chandra Reed, your doctorate is showing."

Chandra's smile began with her eyes. "Sometimes," she said, "you don't *have* to say it. I know who you are. I see it every day in your commitment to the kids, in your kindness, in your unselfishness. That you are pretty and smart as well are just dribbles of chocolate on top of the sundae. So, no, don't ever worry about disappointing me—or anyone."

"From you I trust that's true, but from experience I know not to trust that from others." She took a long, slow breath and rested folded arms on the table. "What if Jim were dating a parent? How would the school handle that?"

Chandra's eyes shifted to the flames dancing around the logs in the fireplace. Her expression remained unchanged. "Hypothetically, I assume." She brought her eyes back to Miya's. "Any student involved wouldn't be scheduled in his class."

"There's no policy against it?"

"Officially, no. It's 'frowned upon,' but I imagine if there was action to fire an employee because of it, there would be a legal challenge since it's not illegal and it wouldn't be a breach of policy." Chandra waited patiently, respecting Miya's hesitation.

And then, "What if it were me?"

Chandra nodded with only a slight bob of her head. A knowing nod. The lead-up had been necessary only for Miya. "I want you to trust me enough just to tell me," Chandra said, visibly leaning forward now.

Miya nodded in return. "You know why I needed to whisper when I was young, but you don't know why I had to run. My parents are deep in the Church. From a young age, I knew the threat of exorcism and conversion therapy. I did what I had to protect myself. And now I am face to face with the realization that the future happiness, the life I've always wanted, will be challenged again. And as much as I thought that I was prepared, life has a way of surprising the hell out of me."

"I wish I could tell you that there is nothing to worry about, but of course I can't. Call it a double standard, or prejudice—"

"Homophobia."

"Yes," Chandra agreed. "Whatever anyone wants to call it, it's there. And you've had an option that I've never had, to hide from that prejudice. But what you hide, even successfully, is in your bones. It's in your DNA. It's who you are, obvious or not, acknowledged or not. And I suspect that the battle you fought, starting so early in your life, has taught you that. I know it's not easy or safe to live your truth or to deal with prejudice, but I also know that the alternative is not healthy either. The toll that it takes, mentally and emotionally. You know that don't you?" She noted Miya's nod. "So, it sounds as though you have fought that battle with yourself and won. Are you afraid of what winning that battle means?"

"Yes," she confirmed. "I know there is nothing wrong with

who I am and what I need in my life to be happy. Since I was young, I've chosen when to stand and fight, and I've weighed the consequences each time partly because hiding something makes it *look* as if it's wrong." Miya tilted her head and added, "I'm asking you, this time what you think I'll face, and if I can expect any support."

"You will never have to worry about my support. And I suspect that you'll have the support of our principal. Carl Walker's grandson is gay, and Carl talks a lot about how proud he is of him. And you're well-liked by the other teachers and the students, that's a big plus. But I'd never venture a guess about parents, and the school board is more of a crap shoot than usual right now."

"So, pretty much what I thought I'd be facing."

"Then you must be sure about this woman."

"I'm sure about being in love. Beyond that, I have no idea. How did you know that Charles was the one?"

"You're taking me back a few years, you know. Hmm." She thought for a moment as a gentle smile brightened her face. "I first noticed him in my college psych class. That voice. I swear the professor called on him so much just so she could hear him talk. The girls in the class nicknamed him James Earl. Anyway, we ended up in the same study group and I liked that he asked my opinion a lot. Then I started liking how I felt around him. We started seeing each other and he always made me feel special—and sexy," she said, suggestively lifting her brows. "He still does. But, past the physical, we talked, a lot. I wanted to know everything about him, especially what was in his heart."

"And you liked or loved what you found out."

"Yes, but mostly I loved that he wanted to know the same about me. It wasn't superficial, you know? Guys follow the program of questions that are supposed to make you think they really want to know what *you* want out of life."

"Yeah, no, I don't know much about that program. My

experience dating guys is limited to ice skating and movies with Terry in sixth grade."

Chandra laughed, a comfortable, happy sound. "You are just full of surprises tonight."

"Not disappointed?"

"Not at all."

"So, tell me when you knew that you wanted to spend the rest of your life with Charles."

"I think it sort of snuck up on me," Chandra replied. "We had been talking about plans and goals, and I realized that I didn't want to do any of it without him. I'll never forget the look on his face when I told him. He didn't have to tell me that he felt the same way, it was all on his face."

"I saw that look on her face when I told her that I loved her. She didn't expect it. She had decided it was best for me if she let me go."

"I think it's time that you tell me who she is."

Miya didn't hesitate. "Johanna," she said. "Johanna Beals." This time, Chandra's expression was a definite *ah-ha*. "Someone like her was never in my life plan. Not in my wildest fantasies."

"When you sat in my office struggling over what was going on with Kayla—"

"I had no idea who she was until the parent-teacher conference. Before that, I didn't know her last name. I didn't know about Kayla." Miya circled the base of her glass with her fingers and leaned forward. "Chandra, I never would have kept that from you if I had had any idea where this was heading."

"So, you did know when you met with her about the essay. And I'm going to scoot out on that limb again and assume that caused a bit of an internal dialogue that tried to find a way for you not to have that talk. It's a sensitive subject to talk with any parent about. Yet," she said with a tip of her head, "you did."

"Honestly, my internal dialogue was worse *after* I met with her. She was . . . she didn't take it as well as I had hoped. And I questioned myself for days—should I have asked it differently; did I sound accusatory? Words, usually my strong point, had failed me. I was sure of it. To make it worse, the only thing I learned for my effort was how to make a parent angry."

"Yet, you got there eventually, so something worked."

"Only because, for some insane reason, she was interested in me personally and felt compelled to apologize."

"*She* apologized? For what?"

"She calls it her defense mode, a default. A single lesbian mother raising a child and worried about her being taken away from her."

"She understands why you had to talk with her?"

"She understands," Miya replied. "But that's not going to stop me from questioning my approach if I have to have that talk with another parent."

"Don't overanalyze it, Miya. And don't second guess yourself."

Miya smiled at the advice. "Trust my instincts. I've been told that before."

"It does get tricky, though, when it comes to love. Sometimes instincts get overridden by emotion, and—"

"Lust."

Chandra offered a wide smile. "I was going to say hormones, but *lust* adds a certain excitement. *Hormone* is too academic. Not a word that adequately describes the sizzle and spark of it. Right?"

"Is that doctorate-speak for 'I hope you're basing your decisions on more than lust'?"

"No," Chandra replied with a shake of her head. "Just a friend trying to get her concerns satisfied."

"And I thought I was the one with concerns."

"Without being concerned, I would not be a good friend."

"Touché." Miya offered an apologetic frown. "And I'm sorry. I've found myself feeling my way down this tunnel alone, and it's scary at times. I trust you. I trust our friendship. You have every right to be concerned."

"Just tell me that at least part of your decision was made with careful thought and getting to know who Johanna is."

"I wish you hadn't felt like you had to ask me that." A moment later, though, with the look in Chandra's eyes, Miya knew. "The answer isn't for you, is it?" Chandra's lips curled slightly at the corners. "What happened to I should trust my instincts? Don't answer that. My instinct was to go slow, to overthink how many ways this could go wrong. I did that. We talked with each other a lot, on the phone, avoiding temptation. Until I was sure, until I was afraid that I'd lose her."

"Then you've answered both our concerns," Chandra said, this time easing into a gentle smile. "Now you just need to tell me what this friend can do to help."

"Give me advice, even when I don't ask for it," Miya said, lifting her glass. "And have my back if they come for me."

Chandra lifted her glass and touched its rim to Miya's. "You've got it."

Chapter 31

ALL THAT GLITTERS

Johanna, the last to leave the office today, pulled the car back into the parking space that she'd just backed out of. The feel of the thump, thump, thump of a flat tire was unmistakable.

She circled the car to find the rear passenger side tire nearly resting on the rim. Her first call was to AAA. The second was to Kayla to let her know that she would be late picking her up. Strange, she thought, as she leaned against the car, no angst. No "shit," "damn," or worse. Instead, in its place was a sense of calm and reason. It happened in the parking lot, not in traffic. And coverage meant that she didn't have to try to loosen machine-tightened lug nuts by hand. Positives indeed. Negatives, it seemed, had turned themselves ass-end-up. Even the air, biting cold on inhale and crystal fog on exhale, felt oddly invigorating and, over the past month, the world had burst into full color when she wasn't looking. It was brilliant in ways that she hadn't noticed before, like softly falling snow filtering the harshness of the parking lot lights and their glow glistening across a fresh covering of the cars and pavement. And when was it that patience had taken such a deep, full breath?

She smiled as she slid into the seat of her car to wait and called Miya. "I love the sound of your voice," she began.

"Yeah?"

"That makes you smile, doesn't it?"

Miya offered a quiet laugh. "And you called just to make me smile?"

"Can't think of a better reason," Johanna said, leaning her head back against the headrest. "Or a better way to wait for AAA."

"What? Are you okay?"

"Yes, yes. Just a flat tire. I didn't mean to alarm you. I worked late and came out to a flat. Kayla went to Tami's after school. She knows that I'll be picking her up late."

"Okay. Call me when you get home. I'm bringing dinner."

"Okay," Johanna began as she cleared the dishes from the table, "give it up. Where *did* you get it? We'll concede that you do know the best place for lasagna, but you need to share it."

Miya snapped the CorningWare top on the leftovers and cocked her head at Johanna. "You're expecting me to give up all my secrets?"

"Only the ones *I* can hear," Kayla said as she loaded the dishwasher.

Miya locked eyes with Johanna and offered an amused smile. "Thank you, Kayla," she said.

"Where you get the lasagna would be one of them," Kayla added.

"Fair enough. Frankie G's. It's his mother's family recipe— and that *is* a secret. I know, I've tried." She watched as Kayla high-fived her mother and added, "What *have* I gotten myself into?"

Johanna just smiled and asked, "Can you stay for a while?"

"Sure, but I'm not giving up any more secrets."

"Good." Kayla replied, "because I'm dishing up ice cream. It's the all-season dessert."

There was no argument. They settled in the living room and Kayla served bowls of pistachio, her favorite ice cream. It was nothing exceptional, nothing special, just ice cream and conversation and the sparkle of newness, of family. A creation Johanna marveled at.

"How do you like Mr. Aggar's class, Kayla?" Miya asked.

"It's fine," she replied. "We're finishing *The Adventures of Huckleberry Finn* this week."

Miya nodded. "We follow the same syllabus, so I wasn't worried about you missing anything. I was hoping that you had some friends in that class."

"Uh-huh. Tami and James. They both helped start the group against bullying."

Miya nodded with a smile. "And Mr. Aggar's a good teacher. I'm glad that switching classes wasn't a problem."

"I wish he had us act out scenes like you do. He has us write an essay instead. I have to start working on one tonight. We're supposed to pick out our favorite scene in the book and write about whether we think it would be written the same way today. And if not, how we would change it."

"What scene did you pick?"

"The one where Huck dresses like a girl to get information from Mrs. Loftus. She suspects that he's a boy and surprises him by tossing a ball of yarn in his lap."

"Oh, I remember that part, even after all these years," Johanna interjected. "He clamps his legs together to catch it instead of keeping them apart and catching it in the dress."

Kayla nodded. "That's how she knew he was a boy."

"Do you think it would have the same effect today?" Miya asked.

Kayla shook her head. "No, it's a way different world. How we react wouldn't depend on how we dress. And the whole threading a needle thing—a lot of girls probably can't easily thread a needle."

"If you think it is important to the story, how *would* she find out?"

After a thoughtful pause, Kayla replied, "I think it would take longer. She wouldn't be able to depend on dress or mannerisms so much. She'd have to make him talk more, ask a lot of questions."

"Like what kind of questions?" Johanna asked.

Another pause. "I don't know yet. But Huck is, like, fourteen in the story, so if she makes him talk enough, his voice will probably crack. Remember when Zack's voice started to change? No matter how hard he tried, he couldn't control when it happened."

"I do," Johanna replied. "Good thinking."

Miya smiled in agreement. "Keep thinking on it," she said. "And remember, in the end, the writer gets to decide what works. If it's feasible that his voice would crack, then his voice cracks. The writer figures out how to get there."

Kayla's expression turned pensive. "Mr. Aggar said that this is a book that's been banned a lot, like in schools and libraries. Why would they ban it?"

Miya shook her head before answering. "There have been different groups and different reasons over the years. Some objected to the author's use of the n-word. It was banned many times for being obscene, and disrespectful of authority. Others are uncomfortable with the way slavery is portrayed, the way the story acknowledges its place in our history." She looked at Johanna and continued. "Actually, poor Huck is on a list of books that a group here is trying to get banned from *our* school system."

"What group?" Johanna asked.

"The same one that has caused so many problems for the

school board for a couple of years now. And the book list is on the agenda for this next board meeting." She offered an exasperated sigh, and a tinge of sarcasm. "I can't wait. The whole English department will be there en masse. I am so not looking forward to it."

"But," Johanna began, "I'm glad that you're fighting the good fight. I wouldn't want them deciding what the students read any more than I would want a plumber operating on me. There are so many important lessons in those books. Things that need thought and discussion and analysis—and good teachers."

"You want to make that case to the school board?"

"No, no," she replied. "I'm leaving that to the experts, too."

"You know what?" Kayla interjected. "I think I'm going to write about a different scene."

"Why?" Johanna asked. "It sounded like you had the scene very well thought out."

"The scene where Huck tears up the letter to Mrs. Watson to turn Jim in is a more important scene."

Miya nodded in agreement. "Why do you think it's so important?"

"That's when Huck decides that he will be loyal and keep his promise to Jim and go against society's rules. It's his moral dilemma. He's sure that if he helped Jim, society would shun him, and he would live in hell. I love the part where he says, 'All right, then, I'll *go* to hell.'"

"How was that decision important to the story as the author wrote it?"

"It makes the reader wonder if he can keep his promise. And then, later in the book, you find out that he goes along with Tom and doesn't honor his promise to Jim."

"Would you write it the same way today? Is it still relevant?"

"Yes," Kayla replied. "We have the same decisions to make. Do we decide to do what is right even if we know there will be consequences?"

"You know," Miya said, "you've chosen the most important part of the book. And there are plenty of examples today that you can use that are as significant as Huck's struggle."

Kayla returned a smile. "Okay, that's the one I'm using," she said, collecting the bowls and taking them to the kitchen. "I'll go work on it after I call Zack."

Johanna called after her, "Tell him I'll pick him up tomorrow. He's eating with us since his mother is working late."

"Yep," she returned with a lift in her voice, "left over Frankie G's."

"Perfect," Johanna said, moving closer to Miya on the couch. "Like tonight."

"Even with the flat tire?"

"Even with a flat tire," she whispered, leaning into Miya's embrace and a kiss she'd looked forward to all evening.

The warmth from the kiss filled her, teased her, tempted her. It felt right. A natural part of her day, of her life now. Not an accent, but an integral part that had been missing for so long. Her lips parted, welcoming Miya deeper, enjoying the sensations of desire that it created. And knowing the natural course of them, she eased from their kiss, a whisper's distance, to ask, "Stay tonight?"

Miya answered softly, "For a little while longer."

"Kayla will be fine with it. You can stay."

"I know, and I'd really like to stay, but I have so much to get ready for tomorrow."

Johanna retrieved the remote from the coffee table and turned on the music. "I will take what I can get. But you can't kiss me like that and then leave."

At the first notes, Miya tipped her head back and met Johanna's eyes. "Ah, Emma Smith."

"Lost and Found," she replied, "now my all-time favorite song."

"And why is *that*?" Miya rose and held out her hand. The

words of the song, "I found a place in my heart," surrounded them.

"Why?" Johanna asked, as Miya took her hand and pulled her close. "Because many months ago, a woman—a crazy, sexy woman—held me in her arms and sang those words to me."

"Like this?" Miya whispered against her ear. "'I found a light in the dark.'"

"Yes," she replied softly, "exactly like that."

The truck, bright red under the streetlights, rounded the corner of Johanna's block on oversized tires. It rolled slowly down the street, an American flag decal visible across the back window.

Josh Carter brought the truck almost to a stop and peered from the driver's side window at the addresses on the houses. "There it is," he said. "That's where that little freak lives."

"Keep movin', keep movin'," Brett urged from the passenger's seat. "We don't want 'em to see the truck."

"You sound like a girl," Josh countered, but accelerated down the street. He pulled around the corner of the block and parked. "I'm gonna scare the piss outta that little bitch." He grabbed a can of spray paint from under the seat and jumped from the truck.

They sprinted down the street until they were a house away, then slowed to a walk as they surveyed the house. It was a small, almond-colored, one-story house with an attached garage and a car in the driveway. They stopped beside an evergreen at the corner of the neighbor's yard.

"Watch the front door," Josh said with a slap to Brett's arm. He stooped low and made his way along the side of the car to the garage door. He listened for a moment, then looked around before quickly spraying the words "Fuck U Bitch" in red paint.

At the last spray stroke, Brett appeared at the front of the car and motioned for Josh to follow him. In a high, excited whisper, he said, "You gotta see this."

Josh followed him around the corner of the house to a window where the curtains weren't pulled tightly together. Brett could barely control a laugh as Josh peered through the gap. "You see 'em, you see 'em?" he asked excitedly and nudged Josh's shoulder.

Josh stared, grabbed Brett's arm, and shook it. "Oh, my God." His own voice pushed dangerously close to a detectable squeal. He couldn't tear himself away from the vision of the women dancing slowly in the living room. "It's the freak's mother and—"

"Ms. James," Brett said, barely controlling his excitement. "They're queer."

"Fuckin' *queers*," Josh said with a hint of glee. He remained unmoved from the sight of the women now locked in an intimate kiss. "Wait'll my ole' man hears *this*. Ooooh," he uttered tightly in his high range, "this is gettin' good."

Brett tried to push Josh aside. "Come on, let me see."

"You better grip your junk then." He moved aside to give Brett room.

Brett grinned as he watched, then grabbed his phone from his jacket and pointed it through the gap. "In case no one believes us. Yeah, this is gettin' so good," he whispered. Then he turned away quickly and grasped Josh's arm. "Get outta here. She's gettin' ready to leave."

"Shit. No, not that way," Josh directed, heading away from the driveway and sprinting hard down the block.

Johanna flipped on the porch light, but stopped Miya before she opened the storm door. "You're sure?"

Miya met the temptation head on. "I really can't stay."

With a tilt of her head, Johanna sang, "'But, Baby, it's cold outside.'"

"Mmm, you know this is tempting. What about this weekend?"

"I think I can make that happen."

"I'll call you when I get home. Meantime, don't forget that I love you."

"Never."

Johanna watched from behind the glass door as Miya slipped into the car and turned the lights on. Loved and happy. So much to be thankful for that sometimes it seemed like it had to be a dream, or someone else's life. Reality, though, snapped her from her thoughts. Miya exited the car and motioned for her to come out. Her expression was concerning.

Johanna stepped from the porch. "What's—" she began, following Miya's arm motion toward the garage door.

"Call the police."

Johanna went for her phone while Miya walked around the car to check for damage. She looked around the corner of the garage and listened for voices or movement. Nothing except the distant barking of a dog. After a look down the empty street, Miya went back into the house and locked the door behind her.

"Police are on their way," Johanna reported.

"We'd better let Kayla know. We don't want to scare her."

Johanna nodded and called for Kayla to join them.

"Someone spray-painted graffiti on the garage door," Johanna explained. "We called the police so we can make a report."

"Can I see it?" Kayla asked.

"We should stay in and let the police check around first."

Kayla persisted. "What does it say?" When a response was delayed, she added, "I'll see it anyway."

Johanna relented. "It just says, 'F' you Bitch.'" Kayla's expression hadn't changed, and she seemed unaffected. "Look," Johanna continued, "it could be kids hitting houses in the neighborhood. We won't know, though, until the police take a look and talk to others."

Miya stood by the front window, lifting the end of one blind so that she could watch the street. Minutes later a patrol car cruised slowly past the house. No lights, no siren, only a spotlight sweeping across the house and yard, then moving on to the neighbors. "They're checking the neighborhood," Miya reported.

Curious, Kayla joined her at the window.

"I'll talk with them," Johanna said, retrieving her jacket. "Sorry, I guess that's a given." Her hand wasn't shaking as she reached to unlock the door, yet she felt an unusual quiver through her body. She took a deep breath. *Graffiti. Probably nothing personal. Maybe even the wrong house. Asshole kids on a graffiti run. That's all.* She waited, leaning against the frame of the door.

No one said anything for long minutes until Miya announced, "They're here."

Johanna met them on the porch and explained what little she knew. One officer circled the house and yard while the other continued with his report.

"This has really upset Mom," Kayla said softly.

Miya turned from the window to the obvious concern in Kayla's eyes. "It *is* upsetting. You should feel safe in your home. And no one has the right to take that away from you, even if it's only a prank."

"We need to make her feel better."

"We need to make you both feel better." Miya checked the window again. The officers were leaving. "Let's see what the police had to say."

Johanna shut and locked the door behind her.

"What did they say?" Kayla asked, watching her mother shed her jacket and drop onto the couch.

"No other houses in the neighborhood were hit and no reports called in tonight from anywhere else. There were footprints around the house, but no other damage."

Kayla joined her on the couch. "So, it's just us."

"Looks like it. But, why? I didn't have any answers for them."

"What did they ask?" Miya asked.

"If I've had any harassing phone calls, trouble with clients or people at work, problems with neighbors. But I told them that there is nothing that I am aware of."

As her mother spoke, Kayla sat quietly, her focus fixed somewhere over the coffee table. It caught Miya's attention. "What, Kayla?"

She looked up abruptly into Miya's eyes. "It's me," she said. "The message is for me."

Johanna looked from Miya to Kayla. "The bullies at school?"

Kayla nodded.

"So, I've been naive to think that things have gotten better," Johanna replied. "And that the problem could be contained to school."

"Not naive," Kayla relented. "I haven't told you everything."

Johanna's reaction, in a look shot hard at Kayla, was a mixture of alarm and anger. "We've already *had* this conversation. What do I have to do to get you to tell me what's going on?" Kayla dropped her focus, but Johanna pulled her chin back up. She tempered the edge of anger in her voice and said, "I can't help unless you tell me—everything. I can't and won't tolerate threats, so tell me now."

"I'm sorry. I didn't want to worry you."

Miya listened respectfully while Kayla gave up the events that she'd kept from her mother, all of them this time, including the Garden Lady. "But things have calmed down lately," Kayla added, "a few looks now and then, but mostly they're ignoring us."

Johanna shifted her focus to Miya. "Did you know about this?"

"I knew about the locker incident and the lunchroom, but I didn't know what she hadn't told you."

"So, now what?" Johanna asked.

"Call and add your suspicion to the police report. And it looks like I'm staying tonight."

Chapter 32

THE HAMMER

"Where the fuck you been with my truck?" Dan Carter emerged from the barn door, his words searing single-digit air with orange-red anger.

The boys jumped from the truck; Josh ready to defend himself. "You said you went to a meeting with Uncle Doug. I texted you and you said I could take the truck."

"I said *where* the fuck you been."

Josh narrowed the distance with Brett right behind him. "You always tell me to take care of things. Well, I was takin' care of some shit."

"Yeah?" Dan closed the last few feet and shoved his son's shoulders with both hands. "Well, the cops called while I was gone. Left a number with your mother for me to call." He shoved Josh again. "You'd better be straight up with me."

Josh stood his ground, a couple of inches taller than his dad, but down at least thirty pounds. A physical challenge was never in the cards. Brett, undaunted, stood next to his friend. "I sent a message to the little bitch who started that shit at school."

"What kinda message?"

"Nothing," he said with a sneer. "I sprayed something on the garage door to scare her."

"Listen to me," Dan demanded. "Anybody asks you, either of you," he said with a side-eye to Brett, "you tell 'em you brought the truck and my tools to me at Doug's. You got that?"

"Yes, sir," they replied in unison.

The exact response he expected. Anger was Dan Carter's go-to tool to get him what he wanted faster than anything else. Now that anger waned into his personal form of parental frustration. "Look," he said, with a visible frosty breath, "you got a future to take care of. You got a chance to be somebody, play football, and go pro. That's the plan. And you can't go acting like a third grader, dealing with some little bitch that doesn't even matter." Dan cupped the side of his son's face. "You understand me?" He acknowledged Josh's "yes, sir" with a gentle palm strike to his cheek. "Keep your grades up the best you can. Your ol' man'll take care of the other school shit."

Brett saw his opportunity and took advantage of it. "Then we got something you need to see." He fished his phone from his pocket and brought up the video. He handed it to Dan and hit play.

His brow pressed into deep furrows as Dan watched. "What the hell is this?"

Both boys began to answer at the same time, but Brett yielded. Josh kept his excitement in check and explained, "It's the little bitch's mother and one of the English teachers at school."

As Dan played it through again, Brett couldn't contain himself. "We're gonna put that shit out there everywhere!" When all he got was a blank look in return, he added, "TikTok, Instagram, YouTube, Facebook. Everywhere."

"You can't put that kinda stuff on TikTok," Josh warned.

"You're not going to put it anywhere," Dan ordered. He then directed his words at Josh. "You said someone has been hacking your accounts and sending out fake stuff that's supposed to be from you."

"Yeah. They're messin' with a lot of us."

He looked again at Brett. "They know your accounts, genius. They know who you are. How long do you think it'll take for that video to come back to bite you in the ass? You may not care about gettin' kicked out of school, but you'd better not do anything to put my boy at risk." He stepped to within inches of Brett's face. "You understand?"

Brett's eyes widened and he offered a weak nod. "Yes, sir," he replied. "Nobody's gonna mess with Josh." He reached out his hand for the phone. "I'll delete it."

"The hell you will," Dan replied. "Not until you send it to me. Then you can delete it."

Brett complied without hesitation, and Dan stared at his phone until the WhatsApp message came through. When it did, he nodded and added a crooked grin. "Okay, delete it," he directed. "This is way bigger than gettin' some laughs or showin' who the queers are. This is about who's teachin' our kids and what they're teachin' 'em. You leave *this* to your ole' man," he said, slapping his son's chest with the back of his hand.

Chapter 33

M A R C H   M A D N E S S

The signs in the school parking lot were no surprise. Different messages had been added from month to month, but the energy of the protesters remained the same, hostile and confrontational. Tonight, the message was clear.

"Teach— Don't Preach," "Educate not Indoctrinate," "We the Parents Stand Up," "Our Kids, Our Choice," "We Own this School—Not You!"

Miya and Chandra made their way to the entrance, through the shouting crowd and falling snow. The pressure and hostility had become an unhealthy normalization, expected—along with the police presence and personal security. The need for their presence was clear. The uneasiness was palpable.

They maneuvered the narrow path between thrusted signs and men with assault rifles strapped across their chests. So close, too close. *This shouldn't be*, Miya thought, this uncertainty, this fear. There should be no adapting to this, no allowing it to be. How did it all go so wrong?

The door closed behind them, muting the shouts and ushering them into the unusually quiet hallway. "How many of them are actually from here?" Miya asked, brushing snow from her hair.

"I recognize some of them," Chandra replied. "But we've identified quite a few outside agitators, too. I have to think that without outside money and influence, this would not be as well organized and attended."

"Agreed," Miya said as they entered the room, which was already beginning to fill. Blocks of teachers and administrators were forming. "How many do you think they will let talk tonight?"

"If it's anything like the last few meetings, this is going to be a long night. As hard as they've tried, they couldn't hold the limit to the speakers list or control how long each spoke. And after *that* —"

"It becomes the 'losing control' horror movie that no teacher wants to see."

"Yet," Chandra said, "here we are."

They claimed seats in the section including the English Department, and most of the Counseling and Media staff. Designated speakers from each department, as well as parents and students, were prepared to argue the case against banning books.

The noise level in the room, now filled to standing room only, dropped significantly as the last of the board members took their seats at the front of the room. Moments later, board President Bruce Taylor began the meeting with the standard call to business. Minutes were read, and financial and committee reports were given, followed by the expected seconds and approvals.

Chandra leaned closer to Miya to say, "This part used to fool me into assuming that the rest of the meeting would be as civil."

"I would be fine with bringing back boring."

Chandra's focus settled on two young men dressed in sharply creased, black uniforms standing near the door. She nodded in their direction and asked, "Are those the guys you told me about?"

"Yes, they're part of the private security company owned by Tee Charbonnet's brother."

"They're very professional looking."

"And armed and very well trained," Miya added. "Tyree vets all his applicants thoroughly. He doesn't allow attitudes or thugs."

"Board members having to hire personal security," Chandra said with a shake of her head. "I never would have imagined it."

"Here we go," Miya said, as President Taylor began announcing the complaint before them.

"As I indicated last month, we've received a list of books," he said, "five of them, that a group of parents want us to ban from our libraries and curriculum." He opened a folder in front of him. "I asked them to provide us with reasons for each book, which I see they've done—sort of." He spoke to the room in general. "I then turned the request over to our district committee, made up of administrators, teachers, and librarians. They have reviewed the list and recommended that none of the books on the list be banned." He scanned the faces of the three members on either side of him and added, "It's now up to us to either accept their decision or overturn it. We can also consider whether to single out individual books on the list rather than decide on the list as a whole, something the committee has already looked at and rejected. The discussion is now open to board members."

Doug Carter didn't wait to be recognized. "We need to listen to these parents. Not only is banning these books in our authority, but it is also our responsibility to the community. They elected us to this board to protect their children."

The voice of Jan Binder, one of two women on the Board, began, "I work in retail sales and have one year of Community College under my belt. I don't pretend to know what each of these books teaches our kids." She picked up the list of books.

"I've read three of the books on this list, and that was many years ago. I took some time to get a general idea of what the complaints were and to find and read those parts. And I have to say that I don't see the problems. Our teachers have studied and been trained to understand what should be taught and at what ages. They have been hired to educate our children, and I believe that they are the ones who should be making this decision."

"Amen, Sister," Chandra whispered amid spontaneous applause from the room.

The support, though, was short-lived. George Decker owned several restaurants in the area and sided way too often with Doug Carter. "Doug's right," he said, "the community put us on this board to listen to their concerns. And they have a lot of concerns about what's being taught and how it makes their kids feel. It's our job to listen and make those decisions."

"And if we don't?" Asked in frustration and a bit of anger by Les Andrews, one of three members who had to hire security after threats to them and their families.

"Well, of course, we're going to listen," President Taylor offered decisively, "and then we'll make our decision. It's clear to me, though, that the reasons given for each of these books are not adequate. "Inappropriate language," "sexual content," and "racism" can be interpreted in different ways. So, I hope that those speaking can explain them better. If we can stick to the speaking schedule, we will also be hearing from teacher and student representatives. And I'm hoping that will help settle some minds."

He scanned the board once again, then addressed the room in general. "So, you've heard from us, and now I'll open it up to those who wish to speak on the record."

It began in an orderly enough way, with spokespersons for the parent group demanding the banning of books that contained language or events that made students uncomfortable, and books that exposed them to inappropriate sexual content.

When pressed for details, they deemed *I Am Jazz,* a true story of transgendered identity, to be too sensitive, controversial, and politically charged. *Speak,* where a high school girl struggles to talk about being sexually assaulted, was challenged for being biased against males and for the inclusion of rape and profanity. And *Harriet Tubman: Conductor on the Underground Railroad* they claimed made white students feel uncomfortable. Pressed further, they explained that their children should not be made to feel responsible for something that they had nothing to do with.

Miya cringed at the implication. She took a deep breath and tightened the muscles of her jaw. *Out of ignorance grows hate* was the warning that pounded at her conscience.

Chandra sensed Miya's tension. "I know," she said quietly. "Bill and Lynda will counter. Logic is reassuring."

It *was* reassuring. History Department Head Bill Jenkins' message was both logical and concise and included, "As educators, it is our responsibility to teach an accurate history of our country—the good, the bad, and the ugly. We can't pick and choose only certain aspects of that history. Our students can't create a better future if they aren't given an accurate past to build on. I'm an avid sports fan, so I liken it to a team reviewing their game films so that they can learn not only what worked, but what didn't work and how they can adjust and correct. That's how they become a better team going forward."

Interesting analogy, Miya thought, watching an animated Dan Carter talking with people on either side of him near the front of the audience instead of listening. Too bad. It seemed like an example that would make sense to him. The concern, of course, held by many was that minds were already set and that no amount of reasoning would make a difference. Miya refocused as English Department Head Lynda Clayton reiterated Maya Angelou's message about "doing better when we know better."

"What good literature does," she continued, "is make us think about how what we read has, or will, affect us. Not just us individually, but us as a society. Good literature, including the books on that list, gives students the chance to learn about the world at large. They get to meet people and visit places beyond what is familiar to them."

Miya nodded. Yes, well said. What made her smile, though, came from Student Council President Carly Simmons.

She stepped to the microphone with an air of confidence and began, "Dictionary.com defines education as 'the act or process of imparting or acquiring general knowledge, developing the powers of judgment, and generally of preparing oneself or others intellectually for mature life.' That's what we're here for," she said, looking directly at the board members who she intended to impress. "Don't tell me what I already know or show me what I've already seen. Give me something that I don't understand so I have to ask a ton of questions and search for answers. I *want* you to make me uncomfortable so that I want to know why. That's how I'll grow and become the smartest, most compassionate, and most contributing member of society that I can be. Please do not ban these books."

Chandra leaned close and spoke amid an eruption of applause. "These are the moments that keep you teaching, aren't they?"

"Absolutely. It fills me with hope and makes my heart sing. Every teacher here is smiling huge right now."

The last person scheduled to speak was a woman familiar to many in the room. Renee Knowles was an outspoken, very involved parent and activist. And she used her time for a perfect, all-inclusive summation.

"I am not a poet, or an essayist, or an educator," she began. "I am a Black mother, and a necessary activist. On many occasions, you've listened to me speak my mind, and I appreciate that. Tonight, though, I'm going to let the words of Czech writer Milan Kundera speak for me, because I can't say it any better. 'The first step in liquidating a people is to erase its memory.

Destroy its books, its culture, its history. Then have somebody write new books, manufacture a new culture, invent a new history. Before long that nation will begin to forget what it is and what it was . . . The struggle of man against power is the struggle of memory against forgetting.' We must not be allowed to forget."

"Yes," Chandra said with a clench of her fist. "A perfect conclusion to a well-planned argument."

"I don't think it could have gone any better," Miya agreed.

The scheduled arguments had been made; the applause quieted. And the attention settled once again on the board and President Taylor.

"Thank you all for your input," he said. "Now, we've been asked to ban the books on this list. Is there any interest in voting on them individually, or shall we proceed with a vote on the whole?"

Again, Doug Carter spoke quickly. "There are valid reasons here," he tapped the list with his index finger, "things that parents don't want their kids exposed to. We should ban the whole list."

Jan Binder countered him again. "The one thing I agree with Doug on is voting on the list as a whole. For me, it comes down to who has the education and knowledge to best educate our children."

"Any objections then?" President Taylor asked. When no one objected, he called for the vote. "All those in favor of banning this list of books, raise your hand."

Doug Carter and two others quickly raised their hands, but four other members remained resolute. The ban failed and the reaction was immediate.

"No!" A woman shouted and moved with urgency to the microphone. "No. *I* decide what is best for my kids. You don't." Emotional and animated, she pressed her mouth close to the mic and pointed at the board. "You don't know them. You have no right to indoctrinate them and fill their heads with things we don't believe in."

She was only the beginning. Any thoughts of a peaceful, civil end to the evening vanished. The agitated protesters dominated the microphone, sometimes two at a time. Attempts by President Taylor to quiet the discourse were futile. The shouting became louder.

"Put your kids in a private school then," someone shouted.

"My taxes pay for this school."

"Why don't you worry as much about guns as you do books?"

But the parents and educators opposed to the ban were outshouted and outmuscled to the mic. Others decided that leaving after all reasonable discussion had deteriorated was smarter. Chandra and Miya were among them. They stood, gathering their coats. But as they moved into the aisle, Dan Carter's voice boomed above the throng.

"Oh, my God! You poison our kids with queer books and critical race theory, and we're just supposed to let it happen?" Then he turned to face the crowd, many now standing. "Did you know they have a lesbian English teacher influencing our kids?"

Miya grabbed Chandra's arm.

"I heard it," Chandra said. "Come on."

But Miya let go of Chandra's arm and squared her shoulders toward Dan Carter.

"It's only going to get uglier," Chandra warned. "Believe me."

And it did. Dan Carter wasn't through. "What's Miya James telling our kids?" he said, looking directly at her. "I wanna know. Don't you?"

"Yeah, I wanna know," someone shouted back.

"Put a camera on her in the classroom."

"She's not gonna teach *my* kid."

Lynda Clayton shouted for all the teachers. "We've been on camera for two years. Were you paying any attention?"

The room was in chaos, the board president unable to be heard until he stood and shouted into the microphone. "Clear the room!" He signaled to officers stationed around the perimeter. "Clear the room."

"Now," Chandra demanded, with a firm grip of Miya's arm.

She followed Chandra's lead, and they made their way out of the room and down the hall to the exit, her heart pounding with each step. Miya stopped at the door. "You know that fluffy cloud I had my head stuck in?" She asked. "Poof. Gone. Along with that little bit of hope you cling onto when you don't want to think how bad it could get."

They navigated a growing number of protesters outside and gratefully slid into Chandra's car. "Oh, much better." Chandra started the car, wasting no time heading for the parking lot exit.

"Thank you for getting us out of there. I had a strong urge to stand my ground."

"You had no chance. You would have been swallowed up by all that noise."

Yes, Chandra, measured and temperate, slicing through the 'noise' with surgical precision, laying bare an all-too-often uncomfortable truth. "You're right that tonight it would have been futile, but I'll find the right place and the right time," Miya promised. "I *will* stand my ground. I spent years whispering and running before I found my place, before I felt worthy of my place. And I'm not going to give it up now."

"And I would expect nothing less from you."

Chapter 34

FAST AND FURIOUS

The chaos of the school board meeting was nothing compared to the messages filling her phone.

"This is our school, and we won't have a lesbian influencing our kids."

"You're not teaching my kid, you fucking queer. Failin' the boys cuz they have dicks and kissin' the girls' pussies? Get the hell outta our school."

"You'd better resign now, or your life is gonna be hell."

Her stomach churned. Miya forced herself to stop listening. She paced a circle through her apartment—living room to dining area to kitchen to hallway and around again, phone in hand. Finally, she called Johanna's number and didn't stop or sit during the entire time she recounted the evening to her. Too much anxiety, too much nervous energy. Nervous energy that no amount of verbal camouflage could hide.

"Dropping out of the cloud my head was stuck in is one thing," Miya told her. "But I wasn't ready to be blindsided with an iron skillet."

"One thing I have learned raising a child is to have ice

packs on hand for lumps like that," Johanna replied. "Ready and waiting when you get here."

"I thought about this all the way home." Miya made another pass through the kitchen. "What if the message on your garage wasn't meant for Kayla? What if it was meant for me, and being in your house—"

"Kayla is sure that it was meant for her, and I think she's right. Everyone knows she organized the students against the bullies. Retaliation makes sense."

Miya finally dropped onto her couch. "It doesn't make me feel any less toxic. The phone I use for work is already blowing up with threats and demands for me to resign."

"Oh, no. Honey, I'm sorry. I'm so sorry. I guess I was hoping—I don't know where my head was."

"The same place mine was."

"Come over," Johanna said. "We'll figure this out."

"I can't chance bringing any more ugliness to your house. Remember how dangerous it has gotten for the school board. I need to think this through."

"You shouldn't be alone, Miya."

"I'll be fine, really. I'm on the second floor and the building has a secure entrance. I'm not worried. But what if someone knows that I've been at your house? I love you. I just want you and Kayla to be safe. Just let me think this through. I'll call you later."

Miya continued holding the phone in front of her as if the conversation hadn't ended. Frozen in the quiet, the solitude that normally buffers threats and fears felt strange now. Inadequate. Perimeters had always snugged their safety around her—the old musty wood of her garage hideaway, the flowered wallpaper walls of her room in her grandmother's house, and the walls of her own apartment. Walls that had always guarded her truth, protected who she was. Tonight, though, she struggled without relief, the words from the phone messages slicing their wounds.

How long she sat there, she couldn't say. She hadn't moved, physically. The lone light in the room glared over her shoulder. Her work phone taunted her from the coffee table with whistles of incoming emails and voice messages. She could check them in case there was something important, or she could shut it off. But she did neither, only stared, at space, at nothing. Her mind unable to focus. It wasn't as if she had to decide what to do. That much she knew. But her thoughts wouldn't settle into anything resembling order.

Phone calls, she needed to make phone calls. Chandra, she needed to let Chandra know what was happening. Would calling in sick calm the waters or make it worse? Her personal cell had slipped into the crevice between the cushion and the arm of the couch. Miya retrieved it, but then the door buzzer startled her. Reaching the door quickly, she heard Johanna's voice. Of course, she thought with a surprising sense of relief. Of course she would come here. Something about love and not needing to ask.

She opened the door to a determined Johanna, offering a slow, easy smile and pulling her into an embrace. "You didn't have to come here," she said. "I didn't expect—"

"I know," Johanna replied with a kiss, "because you are kind of slow catching on." She acknowledged the grin and added, "Come on and talk to me."

"This has gotten ugly really fast," Miya said as Johanna removed her jacket and pulled Miya onto the couch beside her.

Miya looked at Johanna and admitted, "I need to figure out how to deal with it."

The phone on the table whistled again. "Your work phone?" Johanna asked, picking it up.

Miya reached to take the phone from her. "Yes. Don't listen to it."

"I'm not going to. And neither are you." She kept the phone and shut it off. "And *you* don't have to figure it out—*we* do."

Miya stared for a long moment before saying, "I don't know what to do with you."

"Just keep loving me. And find a way to trust me . . . I know you haven't done a lot of trusting in your life."

Miya lifted the corners of her mouth in a weak attempt at a smile. "No. It didn't take me long to find the last line of defense."

"You."

"There have been smarter people in my life. Better educated, better traveled, more talented. And I've always respected that. I've watched them, listened to them, and learned from them. But I've never expected them to know what is best for me. They can't."

"But your grandmother knew, didn't she? You trusted that *she* knew."

"That was a long time ago. That kind of trust was gone when she was gone."

"What about Tee?"

Miya hesitated to reply, flashes of the professional hell Tee had dealt with tightening her throat. Tee'd have her back, cover her with whatever, however she could. There was no question. And that was the problem. "There is absolutely no way I'm going to put her in that position—ever."

"She's going to know about it tomorrow, so it's not going to be up to you."

"I'll convince her to stay out of it. It's bad enough that you and Kayla must go through this. You should go home and let me figure this out."

"Because that's what you've always done?"

"Yes."

"Alone," Johanna said, forcing directness from the grey-blue eyes. "Strapping on your armor and taking on the world."

The conviction of her tone surprised Miya. She stood in an attempt to match it. "Yes," she replied.

"Alone," Johanna said, standing sharply to face Miya.

"You need to go home. Please."

"That's not going to happen."

Miya turned away in frustration. "No. You don't understand." She held her hand up as if it would deter further insistence. "I don't know any other way to do this."

Johanna grasped the raised hand, turned Miya to face her, and replied, "But I *do*."

Miya was about to respond, to justify the long relied-on means of survival, but Johanna pulled her back down on the couch. There was intensity in her eyes and commitment in her voice.

"You are not facing this alone. It is no longer your choice. I am fighting this with you, for you. Me and Kayla and Kate and Brad and a family you should never underestimate. And don't count out Michael, and Chandra, and God only knows how many others. This is not something you're going to fight by yourself, not this time." She drew her fingers gently over Miya's cheek and brushed a kiss over her lips. "You got that, Ms. James?"

"I got that you love me. And that's all I'm counting on."

Chapter 35

FOREWARNED

Two days. Forty-eight hours that felt like she had fallen into a hole with no bottom. She was in free fall, not knowing when or if she would land. Exactly what she told Chandra. Exactly why they were huddled over Chandra's kitchen table.

"I know how unsettling this has been—the whispers, the questions, the looks with no words. But you can't let this chew you up, Miya. I really do think it was the right decision to go to work as usual. You have to be present, to be aware, as uncomfortable as it is. And I'm sure teaching hasn't been easy with everything swirling around in your head."

Miya's focus remained on the coffee mug wrapped in her hands. "I've been through worse."

"I'm not going to ask you to convince me of that. What did Carl tell you?"

"His office, like the rest of the district, is inundated with threats and complaints. Not unusual lately," she lifted her eyes to meet Chandra's, "but, now most of them are about me . . . If there's a formal complaint filed—"

"Contact your union rep." She acknowledged Miya's nod.

"In case you need him. Most complaints have traditionally been handled by Carl at the principal level, and he's always been fair and supportive of his teachers."

"But? I can hear it in your voice."

"A lot of them recently have gone directly to the Superintendent. Charles thinks that all the vitriol and threats to sue him and the school district are making him nervous. That's how the book ban complaint ended up with the school board."

Charles' distinctive voice preceded him into the kitchen. "Hey," he said, "I apologize for interrupting, but Ara here is registering her own complaint." The unusual long-haired tortie meowed loudly at his feet. "She's claiming cruel and unusual treatment since she hasn't eaten since this morning."

Chandra rolled her eyes and explained. "She's Papa's girl. And he believes everything she says."

"Oh, how can anyone resist such a beautiful girl?" Miya caressed the downy-soft head as Ara stretched her paws up to greet her. She pleaded her case with another loud meow. "I know, sweet girl, it's terrible how they treat you." But Ara abandoned her supporter at the sound of the refrigerator door.

Charles filled her dish and admitted, "You've made me guilty enough for mackerel."

Chandra dipped her head and raised her eyebrows at Miya.

"Uh-huh." Miya smiled at her. "Papa's girl."

He placed the dish on Ara's mat in the corner of the kitchen, then said, "So, what's the difference between a cat and a comma?"

The two women looked at each other. "He can't help himself," Chandra offered.

Charles continued undeterred. "One has claws at the end of its paws. The other has a pause at the end of a clause."

"See, that's why I'm here," Miya said at the end of a much-needed smile, "so that you can make me smile."

Charles offered a deep, throaty laugh in response. "Then my mission here," he said, folding his large frame onto a kitchen chair, "is almost done."

With a side-eye to Chandra, Miya asked, "Need I ask?"

"No."

"Facing two brilliant, accomplished women," he said, placing his palm over his heart, "I offer what I can."

And since what he was about to offer was born of experience, Miya was ready to hear it.

"Everyone in the district is trying to use reason and logic to negotiate the unreasonable. Some are more successful than others. These are decisions that should be easily resolved by normal policy and procedures."

Miya met his hesitation. "What exactly are you telling me?"

"To expect the unexpected. I've had to deal with complaints at Shepherd that normally would have been dismissed in a ten-minute discussion. But the pressure from outside groups and the news and social media forces us to try to find ways to de-escalate things."

"Yes," Chandra interjected, "the media picks up on hot-button issues and amplifies them. But spending more than ten minutes on most of them only adds legitimacy to lunacy."

"And you're right," he conceded. "But that's the quandary we're faced with. We're seeing more complaints moving up the chain, past principals, and threats that no one knows how to react to." He stopped and looked from Chandra to Miya. "I hadn't intended to sound so negative. I'm sorry."

Miya shook her head. "No, don't apologize, Charles. Forewarned is forearmed. I appreciate your candor. I really do."

"Well, I don't want to leave you with a head full of negatives," Chandra added. "We don't know that there *is* going to be a complaint. They got everyone all stirred up at the board meeting, but sexual discrimination is not only against policy, it's against the law. The district's not going to waste time and money defending an illegitimate charge."

"I appreciate what you're trying to do," Miya said. "But we

all know that we're always only one election away from reversal. And as for now, they'll just make the complaint about something else."

Chapter 36

INVOLUNTARY

She'd made it to Friday, three whole days past the accusations, but it had been a rare occasion that Miya entertained more than a glint of hope. The glint was still there when morning turned to afternoon with no notice from the administration, no indication of a complaint, but then gone the moment she was called to the superintendent's office.

Realistically, she knew it was coming. That amount of rage and agitation had so few places to go. Threats were everywhere, coming from every direction. They not only flooded *her* social media and *her* phone messages, or those belonging to board members and other staff, they had flooded Dr. Evans' email and phone as well as the district website. And the tipping point, no doubt, was the threat of a lawsuit, legally questionable, but which would have to be defended.

Dr. Evans hunched over his desk on folded arms and carefully explained the extent of the threats and the specifics of the complaint. Miya listened just as carefully. It felt as though she had been holding her breath, trying to maintain her focus and gird her wavering self-assurance. Gerald Levin, her union representative, sat next to her, her resource and witness. His counsel, in preparation for this probability, was for her to speak her defense clearly and succinctly while he remained silent.

Miya read the body of the complaint from the form Dr. Evans provided to both her and Representative Levin.

> Miya James has forced the students
> in her classes to read books that
> depict questionable and disturbing
> relationships and act them out in
> front of the class. For example,
> they have been forced to act like a
> slave and boys forced to act like a
> girl for a grade in her class. They
> were made to feel embarrassed and
> humiliated in front of their peers.
> They have suffered irreparable
> emotional harm. This woman
> should not be allowed to harm
> our children with her perversion
> and incompetence. If she is not
> fired, we will be forced to sue
> Superintendent Evans and the
> Emerson School District.

He waited as she read, the weight of his decision evident in the deeply furrowed brow and the heaviness below deep-set eyes. He waited—for a response, for a defense, for something that would lift the weight.

"Only one of these three parents, the complainants, has a student in my class, and he's a better than average student with no apparent issues that I'm aware of. Who are the other two?"

"One has a younger child. They're both part of the group that's been challenging—everything."

"Will I have an opportunity to meet with the student and parent?"

"They've made this complaint about more than can be resolved with one student. And there's the threat of a lawsuit."

Her words were definitive and more forceful than she intended. "Perversion," she began, a statement not a question. "No, there is no perversion. If they are referring to my sexuality, that's as much an inherent part of who I am as someone having red hair or being six-foot-two. It's not an issue. And as you know, discrimination is against policy and illegal."

His brow eased somewhat. A space of silence encouraged her to continue. "And incompetence," she said, "is obviously the only one of the I's in our contract that they think they can legally challenge. And I do understand that whether I've met the competency standard here will be based on my defense of my teaching method."

"You will need to make that defense to the school board. They will notify you of a date for a private interview. It will not be open to the public." With that formality out of the way, he added, "But I would like you to tell me about this particular method, and how long you have used it."

"One of the most effective teachers I had in my own education used a variation of it, so I was familiar with it when I began teaching. But what encouraged me to implement it myself was when I had a student in class with severe hearing loss. He wore hearing aids that helped some, and his parents wanted him to experience social inclusiveness. One of the ways that he endeared himself socially was to make others laugh by acting things out. He carried a bow tie in his pocket, and to depict authority, he would clip it to his shirt and twist an invisible mustache. Other times, he'd flip his hearing aids out and let them dangle like earrings, tie his jacket around his waist like a skirt, and wag his finger like a scolding mother. He approached me one day about doing an exercise in class where students could wear earplugs and learn more about his world. So, we put together a skit that the students could volunteer to participate in. It surprised me when every student wanted to participate. They really enjoyed it and learned more than I anticipated from the experience. Some of them began to learn sign language. That experience convinced me to develop the teaching method that I use now. It's simple. The class breaks into small groups. Each group chooses a scene from the book we're studying. Within their group, students volunteer to do one of four things—be the narrator who gives the lead up to the scene, be part of acting out the scene, present questions about the scene for the class to discuss, or they can choose to write about what they think about the scene. I have used this method for six years and, until now, have never known of any complaints."

"So, a student is not required to act out a character in the scene?"

"No, they can pick an option that they're comfortable with."

"And how are they graded?"

"They receive a flat credit for participation. I give a letter grade on the written test for each book."

"What is it," he said, straightening back into his chair, "that you think your students gain from your method that they don't get from a traditional method?"

"The same kind of understanding and sensitivity that the students gained from my hearing-impaired student. Instead of just reading the words, they hear the words. They hear inflections and see facial expressions and body language. They feel the words. It makes the written word human, personal." Evident in her voice now was her commitment and passion. "How does it feel to say the words, to feel them said to you? It's a more visceral way to walk in someone else's shoes."

He took a moment, eyes locked on Miya's. Was he questioning the path he'd chosen? But then, moving forward, "I'm sure that Mr. Levin has explained what you need to know for your written response." He noted a nod from the representative. "And I'd like to add a personal note. Do your best to have your words make the board members feel the same dedication and competence that you just showed me. I think that it's important that they know that before they interview you. It may help produce the kind of questions that you want and *need* to answer. I hope that will show them that you are the kind of teacher that this school needs. I will be recommending dismissing the complaint without action, but ultimately the decision is up to the board."

"I've been at the board meetings," she said, "so I do know what I'm facing."

"And because of that volatility, and until a decision is made, you will be taking a leave of absence starting tomorrow."

"I'd rather be in the classroom —"

"It's not only about your safety," he replied quickly, "I'm also concerned about the atmosphere that the students could face."

"How long?"

"Until a decision is made," he said with a look of resolve. "I'm sorry, Miya."

There was little else to do, or to think. Neither Miya nor Gerald said anything until they were nearly to the exit. Gerald broke the silence. "There is an advantage to Dr. Evans being a man of few words. He gave you a good amount of time to make your case to him."

"Yes. I didn't expect that. And thank you for prepping me for it."

"It's part of my job, a part that I wish I didn't have to do." He slowed his long strides and added, "You did a really good job of giving him what he needed. You defended against the specifics of the complaint and put it in both professional and personal context."

"It feels as if we're giving in to them, to their threats. They want me to be afraid, for the school to give up everything public education stands for. Sometimes, I believe they'd eliminate public education if they could."

"I *do* believe that. We're knee-deep in a war. One it feels like we're losing with all the teachers retiring and quitting. I can't think of anything more stupid than firing a good teacher right now. But all we can do is stay focused on the battle in front of us," he said, placing his hand on her shoulder. "You just do what you did in there today when you face the board."

As promised, Miya sent a quick text to Johanna, Chandra, and Tee before she left the parking lot. Of course, the message of "involuntary leave of absence" led to phone calls from each as she maneuvered across town. 'Yes', she would call Johanna back as soon as she got to the apartment. Chandra's invitation for an essential pub night was readily accepted. And Tee, well, Tee was still on the phone when Miya pulled into the apartment lot.

"Look," Tee was saying, "at least consider talking with an attorney, just in case."

"Seems like I'm making a lot of promises today. Hey, hold on a second," she said as she approached her parking spot. "There's a bunch of men hanging around the parking lot." She heard Tee say, "Don't hang up," as she started to turn into her space.

Startled by a loud bang against the back of her car, Miya stopped mid-turn. She turned her head as someone confirmed, "It's her." There was another bang, this one on the hood. Quickly, the parking spot was blocked by three men while others surrounded the car. Miya tried to inch the car back out, but the men wouldn't move.

Tee's voice called from the phone beside her, "What's going on? Miya, what's happening?"

The men were shouting at her, spitting on the windows and slamming their hands against the car. "Miya," Tee yelled.

"They're surrounding the car. I can't move it."

"Keep the doors locked and call the police—now!"

Her hand shook as she dialed. The quiver in her voice surprised her. A little bit of fear and a strong surge of anger. The officer's voice on the other end grounded it, overrode it. "We have a unit on the way," she said. "Stay on the phone with me. Do you know who they are?"

"I recognize a couple of them. Agitators from where I teach."

"What are they doing right now?"

"Shouting, spitting, shaking the car."

"Okay, stay put. Police are two blocks away."

"I hear the siren," she said, as had the men. They began dispersing. "I see the lights coming. Thank you."

The men were scrambling to their cars as the patrol car entered the lot and blocked one of the cars' exit route. One officer approached the blocked car and began to question the occupants. The other talked with Miya.

Maybe it was their commanding presence or the authoritative effect of the uniform, or just the relief that the situation had been neutralized, but there was that little glint of hope again. Right now, Miya decided to accept whatever it was. She stood beside her car and explained what had happened and who she recognized. The guy standing shoulder to shoulder with Dan Carter at the school board meeting was among the men tonight, and Josh Carter was one of the bullies that Kayla had stood up to. The connection was obvious. Hatred, the common denominator. It started like a spray of water from a pinhole in a pipe and, left unaddressed, soon burst into an uncontrollable spew.

She answered all the questions, then listened to a less than optimistic chance of any action being taken against the men. Once again, the glint slipped away. The best she had was a moment of relief as she pulled into the parking space, and the sound of a familiar and welcome voice from behind the car.

"Hey, are you okay?" Tee greeted Miya with a hug. "We just passed the cruiser leaving the lot."

"I'm fine," Miya replied, watching Tyree survey the area before approaching. "And I see that you brought the 'force' with you." He flashed a bright smile and squeezed her in a tight hug.

Tee walked around the car looking for damage as the parking lot lights flickered on. "So, what did the police say?"

Miya lifted an eyebrow and tilted her head. Tyree filled in the blank. "You aren't hurt, the car isn't damaged, and they swore that they just wanted to talk to you."

Miya nodded. "They told the police that they only wanted to ask me some questions. And crazy, paranoid me just freaked out."

"That's what they thrive on, instilling fear," Tyree added. "They want to see your eyes widen, hear your voice quiver. It makes them feel powerful and important when you shrink in front of them."

"And the police won't do anything unless it escalates. I know."

"Yeah, well," Tee began, "we're not waiting for someone to cross the line." She looked at Tyree. "Which place is best?"

"Single house in a residential neighborhood," he replied. "Much easier."

Miya looked from one to the other. "What?"

"Give Johanna a call," Tee directed. "Let her know that you're staying there. That way Tyree has you all covered."

"No, look, you don't have—"

"Not a choice," Tee said with a raise of her eyebrows.

"I don't seem to have any choices today."

"I know you, Babe. Make the call."

Funny how layers are peeled away—sometimes they fall away almost unnoticed in easy conversation or quiet observation, other times they're torched cruelly without warning.

Johanna and Tee watched Miya's expression, or more aptly, her lack of expression, as Tyree carefully and precisely explained what she wasn't ready to accept. He sat at the end of the couch—tall and severely fit, his black uniform military crisp. "It's what I do, Miya. I assess risks and mitigate them."

"I know you feel that your choice to stand and fight has been taken from you," Tee added, "And I—"

"It *has* been taken away," Miya snapped. She paced behind the couch, her hands on her hips. "I grew up with people trying to take away my choices. I won't do that again." Stripped away, the layers of control so carefully crafted and put in place over the years, gone.

"You haven't given up anything," Johanna began. "Protecting yourself, protecting those you love, is not giving in to the threats. You're not backing down—you're fortifying yourself."

Miya stopped mid-pace and turned to face the room. "I'm giving credence to hate speech and lies and behavior that we would never accept from our children. That's what it feels like I'm doing. Showing them that they can scare me out of the classroom. Showing them that they can scare me into hiding in my house with an armed bodyguard. Showing them that they have all the power. *That's,*" she said, slicing the air with her hands, "what it feels like."

They all heard the frustration, recognized the emerging anger. The silence that followed created a respectful pause and a moment to decide how to respond. Miya turned her back to the silence and opted for a distraction. "I'm getting drinks," she called from the kitchen. "Something I have control over. Coffee, beer, or tea."

"Coffee," Tee and her brother answered in unison.

Johanna rose to help with the drinks, and Tee took her arm as she passed by. "I think he should stay," she said, holding Johanna's gaze.

"Agreed."

Before letting go of her arm, Tee added, "And whatever you're doing—keep doing it."

An unexpected compliment, a reassurance that earned an appreciative nod.

Johanna delivered the coffee and then directed her attention to Miya, still lingering behind the couch. "Honey, please come and sit down. Let Tyree explain what he has in mind." Miya answered by moving as slowly as her resolve and settled in the chair at the end of the couch.

Tyree leaned forward over his knees, locked in, and spoke softly. "This is personal, Miya, you know that. You're family and I will never let family face the crazies out there alone."

"I know, Ty."

"Things have changed," he continued. "You're not dealing with the usual parent upset over a grade or their child being disciplined. These are loose cannons, set off by hate-filled ideology. You can't calm them with logic. They don't want to hear what you have to say. You're not going to change their agenda. The best you can do is protect yourself and those you love."

"That's why I didn't want to come here," she said, looking directly at Johanna. "Whatever danger there is, I'm bringing it right to your doorstep."

"They've already been here, Miya."

"Yes, when *I* was here."

"Alright," Tee interjected, "you need to let go, Miya. I know this is pushing you out of your comfort zone, but you need to let Ty do his thing."

Miya stared hard at the woman she'd sparred with so many times. No one said anything. They waited while reason made its case. Logically, it was the right thing to do. School board members were taking precautions and still standing their ground, at least for now. It *was* her decision. The silence in the room made that clear. Yes, she needed to let go, just as Tee said—let go of the emotional fortress that had served her since childhood. And trust outside the fortress. Miya looked from one to the other, each of them wanting to help, each wanting her trust. She knew now what her grandmother had meant, the words so much wiser now than she had known then—when the soft, gentle hands had held her own and said, "Now you trust the umbrella to protect you from the rain. Someday you'll trust someone else to hold the umbrella for you."

She directed her answer to Tyree. "What do we do now?"

"Get used to a shadow," he replied.

"A big one," Tee added.

Chapter 37

THE MENSAN & THE MAN

It was the Zack that Kayla hadn't seen in far too long—bounding down the steps of the bus, laughing and fist bumping with his friends. He'd persevered over the years, holding tight on the rollercoaster, breathing easy at the highs and holding his breath at the lows. And she'd been right there, concerned, trying her best to help, and relieved when things got better. This time, this dip, though, had scared her. Today, seeing his face, seeing him back at school, felt as though the universe had exhaled.

He raced up the steps and met her at the top with a hug that squeezed the breath from her. Friends and members of the Blue Crew burst through the door behind her and began to chant, "Zack is back! Zack is back!"

"Welcome back," Kayla said as he released her.

"Thanks," he replied. "Hey, do I get an armband?"

"Of course." Kayla pulled a blue band from her backpack. "You're going to see a lot of these today." Exactly why he was back. "Come on," she said, "the crew's waiting."

He was surrounded the second he entered the hallway. A village had marked its boundaries and was showing its strength.

For the first time in a long time, Kayla didn't worry about him. She was, though, about to have something else to worry about.

The text was from Elliott. She met him at their usual place near the freight elevator. The serious set of his brow caused Kayla concern. "Did the reminder text go out okay? Is the administration trying to stop us from walking?"

"Reminder went out early this morning," he said. "And objections or not, we're walking at ten o'clock tomorrow. But that's not what I wanted to talk with you about." He didn't waste words. "So, you haven't checked your social media this morning."

"No. Why?"

"A video of your mom and Ms. James is everywhere."

"What?" She retrieved her phone, watched the video, then looked sharply at Elliott. She searched his face for answers. How? When? Then looked again at the video—yes, it was there, in their own house.

"I know you're worried," he said, "and pissed right now. You have a right to be. But I'll do everything I can." He struggled to relieve her. "You know I'm here for you, and your mother. And I like Ms. James a lot." He leaned forward, waited for her to look up at him. "Trust me, Kayla, I'll do everything I can."

"Hasn't the damage been done? What can you do now?"

"Meet me back here after your last class. By then, I'll know who posted the video, and how successful we'll be at getting rid of it."

"You think you can erase it?"

"We're not dealing with Mensans," he said with a grin, "but *they* are. My tech partner and I have been tweaking the erasure bot that we used to search out some of the images of Zack."

"It didn't get rid of all of them, though."

"And we haven't used it on a video yet. But it's only one, and we're catching it right away. This technology is cutting-edge. I'm just learning what it's capable of, so I can't guarantee it'll work. But it has my full attention. I'm leaving right now to get whatever images of Ms. James the school has. We'll program them in, and I'll let you know."

"You do know that you're my favorite Mensan."

"Yeah," he said, offering a shy smile, "I know."

One class later, Kayla once again slipped through the heavy metal door to the maintenance area. Maybe she already saw the video, she thought, questioning whether to call her mother at work. Should she send a text instead? And what about Miya? If she didn't know, shouldn't her mother be the one to tell her? And if neither of them knew... *This shouldn't be this complicated. Just call. Just call.*

She stepped deeper into the room and the always-present aroma from a large old commercial coffee maker. Her mother answered with obvious concern on the third ring. "Kayla, are you okay?"

"I'm fine. I wasn't sure that I should bother you at work, but—"

"No, never worry about that. What is it?"

"It's about you and Miya," she began, then went right to the point. "There's a video out there, all over social media. Somebody took it right at our house."

"What?" Her pitch was tight and raised higher than usual. "What kind of video, Kayla?"

"You were dancing in the living room, and kissing. They must have been outside the side window. Elliott's trying to help—"

"It's too late."

"What do you mean?"

"The hearing," Johanna replied, "it's today. Now."

"She's there? Right now?" Silence on the other end. She could see her mother, forehead resting in the palm of her hand, worried that the worst was happening. "Mom, maybe they haven't seen it. Elliott said that it was posted this morning." She envisioned her mother's nod, nearly indiscernible. "*You* didn't see it, maybe they didn't. Try not to think the worst, Mom." Kayla turned at the sound of the door before adding, "Text me if you hear anything. Okay?"

Mr. Mangiaracino walked in and greeted her with a fist bump and a lift of his head, his 'what's up, is everything okay?'

"Mom," Kayla offered. "She's worried."

He continued to an old white refrigerator, retrieved two Cokes, and set one on the little table against the wall. With a groan, he eased into a chair and popped open his can. "What's she worried about?"

Kayla claimed the other chair, the decision to skip algebra class made. "Thanks," she said, accepting the Coke. "She said Ms. James is at the school board hearing."

He shook his head. "It's not right what they're doing to her."

"I was in her class first semester," she said, "none of the things that they're saying about her teaching are true. But they could fire her anyway."

"I've heard what they're sayin'. I just figure that if *my* personal life don't have anything to do with keepin' this school runnin', then hers shouldn't have anything to do with her teaching. If they asked me, which they won't, I could tell them what kind of person she is. Seems like they should know that about someone they're thinkin' of firing."

"If you could, what would you tell them?"

"First, I'd have to explain my method of judging people," he said. "It's simple, really. Might not pass muster with the school psychologist, but it works for me." He took a swallow of his drink, then hunched heavily over beefy dragon-tattooed arms. "The way I see it, there are three types of people. One will never come sit at this table. They function day by day on assumptions—heat, light, air, everything that keeps this building running will magically keep working. They don't need to know how or why.

Another type will sit at this table once, maybe twice. They want me to know who they are and that they know who I am. And they want to be at the top of the list when things need fixin'."

"And the third?" Kayla watched him finish off his drink and toss the can in the returnables box.

"The third sits at this table and talks about their day, asks me about *my* day. Some days they're tired or frustrated. Other days they share something that made them happy. They talk about ball games and school events, or their family. Sometimes they talk about politics, as long as they follow my rules." He hesitated for a moment, then made a gesture with his hand indicating the space over the table between them. "They share this space, and a little time, just because."

"Is that what Ms. James does?"

He nodded. "If they're payin' attention, she'll show them exactly who she is."

"I hope the school board pays as much attention as you do."

"Yeah, me too."

"Whatever happens today, though," Kayla said, "she'll know tomorrow how many *have* paid attention."

Chapter 38

HEAR ME ROAR

Miya sat with Gerald Levin next to her at a small table facing an intimidating line of board members. Either out of habit or a need to ease her anxiety, she watched their eyes and their body language as she spoke, looking for signals much as she did in her classroom. Were they taking notes, making eye contact? Or were they disengaged, eyes wandering? It's what she did every day—observe, adjust. But this wasn't the classroom, and these were not her students. Adjustment might not be possible.

She continued to watch them closely as she presented her statement orally, an opportunity she guessed was due to Dr. Evans' recommendation. As closely as she could, Miya matched the passion and clarity of the presentation that had impressed him. There were attentive eyes from some members, a nod here and there, and an understated smile. Positive, encouraging signs. But she hadn't missed other signs—the blank stares, the crossed arms, and the stiff push against the back of the chair. They came from the same board members who had voted to ban books. The same ones with a real possibility to influence others.

"Thank you, Ms. James." President Taylor offered a sincere

nod and added, "I admit to being one of those dinosaurs who thinks *hearing* what someone has to say is far more effective than reading it. So, thank you for explaining your methods so clearly." He turned his attention to the board members. "I know that we have questions for Ms. James, so let's start at the end of the table and go in order."

Jan Binder began. "Yes, I just have one question. You said that you've used this method for several years. Have you had complaints from parents of students before?"

"No, nothing that's ever been brought to my attention."

The questions continued, innocuous and easily answered. "Has there ever been an issue with the books that you have your classes read?"

"No, not until the recent attempt to ban books. Usually, I'll have a parent or two talk about their own experience reading the same book when they were in school. They share things that have stayed with them years later, sometimes funny things, sometimes things that they didn't realize the importance of at the time."

"But it seems like acting out parts of some of those books could make students very uncomfortable. Are you saying that that doesn't happen?"

"No, I'm not saying that at all. That *discomfort* is a natural result. It is expected. It stimulates questions and leads to discussions. What they become comfortable with is asking questions."

But in the space of a breath, the board's questions and their intent clearly changed. From Doug Carter's end of the table, "Do your students ask you about your personal life?"

"No," Miya replied, "they haven't gotten *that* comfortable." Her attempt to lighten and defuse received smiles from some, but not all.

"So, that kind of information you just give out anyway."

She matched the set of Doug Carter's stare, locked it in with the sharpness of her tone. "No, I do not." She offered no more, granted him no claim to intimidation. But he wasn't through.

"You're telling this board that you don't put your personal life out there where students and parents have access to it?"

"I do not," she replied firmly. But even as she outwardly held firm, the fear that things were turning south increased.

Gerald touched her arm, a silent acknowledgment that he thought the same thing—and a warning to remain composed.

Challenging that composure was an audible snort from George Decker, followed by, "Then what do you call the video you put all over social media?"

Miya's face smoothed to a blank, her focus narrowed onto her accuser. "What video?" she asked. "I don't know what you're talking about."

"Yes," President Taylor interjected. "I'd like to know what you're talking about, too."

"Lesbian porn," Doug Carter answered, "starring Ms. James here and the mother of one of her students. That's what we're talking about."

The stab Miya felt was quick, sharp. An old familiar pain, an old familiar threat. Always there, hiding under the comfort of acceptability, waiting to strike.

"Whoa," President Taylor warned. "Everything that's said here is on the record, so don't say anything that you can't prove."

"Oh, I can prove it," Doug countered. "I sent the link for it to all of you. Check it for yourself."

Miya turned at Gerald's question, reached for the old armor. Cinched it tight.

"Do you know anything about this?" asked Gerald.

"No. If there *is* a video of me out there, I have no idea how anyone could've gotten it."

"This link's no good, Doug." President Taylor slid his phone back onto the table. "Whatever you think you sent us is not available."

Doug Carter looked up from his own attempt to access it and shot a hard look at Miya. "You took it down just in time for the hearing, didn't you?" He turned his focus to the board. "She tried to take it down, but it's out there. I'll find it and send it to you."

"I saw it," George Decker confirmed. "It is out there. It's an embarrassment for the school system and nothing that our students, who are all over social media, should be seeing."

Clearly unsure of what to ask or how, President Taylor focused again on Miya and turned his hands palms up.

It was as if he had passed her the ball outside the three-point line for one last shot. One last shot, one last chance. If it were Tee with the ball, with the chance, she would take it. Without hesitation, without a doubt. Assess, decide, execute.

Admittedly, she wasn't Tee, but neither was she backing down. Assessed and decided. Miya stood up, despite a look of obvious concern from Gerald. She put her hand on his shoulder as reassurance and, armor securely in place, squared herself before the board. She'd been here before—standing on her truth, counting on its strength, trusting its path. Time to stand on it again.

"I don't have an explanation for a video that I know nothing about," she began. "I can only speak to who I am as a teacher, and to the method in question. And I believe I've done that. But this has gone beyond a complaint or a challenge to my teaching method. I am being challenged to defend myself, not as a teacher, but as a person. You're expecting me, through your accusations," she looked directly at Doug Carter and George Decker, "and your silence," her focus swept over the rest of the members, "to stand here and defend my personal rights—the same rights that each of you have. And I will not defend them anymore than you would be expected to. You're here to judge me as a teacher, and that's what I will defend."

Doug Carter threw his hands in the air and sat hard against

the back of his chair. Miya ignored him and continued.

"I worked minimum wage jobs for my living expenses, accrued a college debt that on a teacher's salary will take me well over twenty years to pay off, so that I can teach. So that I can help make sure that the future is in the hands of the most capable citizens possible. Our kids. From this school. Our smart, talented, curious, funny, sometimes rebellious and frustrating kids. I believe in them, in their potential, their curiosity, and their ingenuity. What I do every day, for more hours than I am paid for, is try to give them the tools to be the best adults they can be so that they can shape a future that is safe and just. They're our hope. But ..." she took a moment to look at each board member, "if you don't believe that I'm the kind of teacher that you want teaching your students, then you should fire me."

Miya turned to a clearly puzzled Gerald. "Let's go," was all she said. Without waiting for a response or a dismissal she met Ty at the doorway and left the room. The adrenaline that had steadied her legs and firmed her voice waned noticeably in the hallway. She fought the annoying quiver in her legs, striding longer and harder.

Gerald matched her stride. "I understand why you defended yourself the way you did," he said. "But please tell me why in the ... why did you tell them to fire you?"

"I guess I just needed to say the obvious."

There was a reason Ty insisted on driving. He'd been right about protesters being told about the hearing, and right about them following Miya from the parking lot. The goal was to lose them on the way across town and get tucked safely in the house before they found Miya again. And his method, remarkably successful, combined the driving skills of Ross Chastian and a Hollywood stunt driver. The car surged from zero to fifty on straight-away streets, squealed into sharp turns, and jetted through parking lot shortcuts and inconspicuous side streets.

"God," Miya exclaimed, adrenaline still coursing through her body as Ty backed into the driveway. "That was a ride that could challenge the Maverick coaster at Cedar Point."

He flashed a smile and replied, "Close the blinds and curtains and make sure that everyone stays inside. I've got it from here."

He stationed himself leaning against the front of his car, and Miya resolved herself to dealing with whatever was on its way.

Johanna greeted her at the door. "Ty had me pick Kayla up early and park the car in the garage, and your phone is still off, and where's your car—"

"I know," Miya replied, wrapping her arms around her. "I know. Just precautions. He's grateful that you have a garage that you can park a car in. And he wanted me to leave *my* car at the apartment. As far as the phone goes," she said, releasing her embrace, "the ride across town took both hands and the seatbelt to keep me seated."

Johanna's face was tight with concern. "And the hearing? What about the hearing?"

But before Miya had a chance to respond, Kayla burst into the room.

"Did you tell her yet?" Kayla directed at her mother. "About the video?"

"What *video?*" Miya replied. "*Is* there a video?"

"Yeah. Maybe. I mean, there was."

"Okay, sit down here," Miya directed. "One of you needs to *calmly* explain what this is all about."

"Go ahead," Johanna said, patting Kayla's knee.

"Somebody took a video of you and Mom right from that window," she began. "Dancing and . . . anyway, Elliott saw it early in the morning and he's been working all day to get rid of it. But there's no guarantee that he got it all, and no way to know who all saw it."

"Here? Through the window? How. Oh God . . ." Miya said, starting to understand what had happened. She stared for a moment while the dots lined up. "Does Elliott know who took the video?"

Kayla shook her head. "But he knows who posted it on social media."

"Doug Carter," Miya said with a nod. "He said as much at the hearing, but it sounded like only one other board member saw it. But once it's out there . . . So how did Elliott take it down? Wait, no," she raised her hand, "don't tell me. I don't want to know. It'll be enough to be eternally grateful if it works."

"This time," Johanna said. "But what's going to stop them from doing it again, or worse?"

The sound of car doors and loud voices sent Kayla to the front window. Cars lined both sides of the street, spilling their occupants across the pavement.

Kayla gave up her spot at the edge of the window to her mother.

The crowd covered the easement and sidewalk and was pushing onto the edge of the lawn and driveway. Arms spread wide, Ty shouted, "Back off! This is private property. I said, back off!"

They stopped, but held their ground, shouting threats and obscenities. Ty held his phone up above his head and shouted again. "Back off or I'll make the call."

One protester, savvy enough to understand the warning, stepped to the front and raised his arms. "Hold up, hold up," he said. "Nothin' the cops can do as long as we stay off their property. Hold the line right here." His arms indicated the line at the edge of the sidewalk. Then he turned to face Ty. "Now what you gonna do, Big Man?"

"I'm going to call in a disturbance of the peace complaint," he replied. "Got five hundred dollars you can spare? How about a ninety-day vacation from work?"

The man turned to address the shouts behind him. "Shut up for a minute," he said, then turned back to Ty. "You're forgettin' one thing there, Big Man. We got rights, and one of 'em's free speech."

"Not here you don't. You're disturbing the peace. Pack it up."

Hands on his hips, the man leaned heavily into his bluster. "Is that a threat?"

Ty stepped forward, resolute steel. "It's a promise."

Johanna watched from the edge of the window as Ty stared down the leaders of the crowd. "What's wrong with these people? What makes them so hateful?"

Miya dropped onto the couch. "I ask that every time we have to maneuver our way through them—in the parking lot, outside the school, outside the hearing—through their signs, through their insanity."

"You shouldn't have to go through this, no one should," Johanna said as the shouting outside grew louder. "And I don't like that Ty is out there by himself."

"I've seen him in action," Miya replied. "Believe me, they do not want to mess with him. He's locked and loaded, military-trained, and smart. If it gets beyond him, he won't hesitate to call the police in." All true, she thought, he'll handle the situation. This one, and probably the next. But he couldn't make the hate go away or make everything normal again. No one could.

"They're getting back in their cars," Kayla reported.

"I told you, he's very good at what he does," Miya said. "But I'm so sorry I brought this mess into your lives."

"No, no, no," Johanna said, joining Miya on the couch. "That's not even logical. You alone can't solve it from your classroom, or with a lesson plan, or by convincing a school board that you're one hell of a teacher. It's not just *your* responsibility to fight it, it's *ours* as well, and the school's and the parents' and the community's. We will not be an obstacle or an excuse for you not giving it everything you've got."

The tension-tightened lines on Miya's face softened. She held Johanna's gaze in amazement. "God, I love you."

Chapter 39

IMAGINE

The next morning, Johanna met Chandra and Jim Aggar inside the front entrance of the school.

"Well done," Jim greeted, exchanging a high five with both women. "I think it's safe to say that anti-bullying isn't the only thing this team's capable of. Sharon and John have the Jefferson and Shepherd staff on board; they're walking with their students."

"As expected, the administration is noncommittal," Chandra said, "so we're good."

"And if everyone who signed up shows," Johanna added, "we should have a good turnout of parents at each school. Our little online group started working the day Miya was suspended and it has amazed me how much we've been able to organize."

Chandra checked her watch. "Our student team is amazing, too, but I'm not surprised. I've never seen a more committed group of kids."

"Okay," Jim said as the hallway began to fill with students. "Time to walk the walk."

It was an orderly exodus, a continuous wave of students and staff flowing through the hallways and out through the exits.

Premade signs supporting Miya James, demanding her return, were stacked and available outside each exit.

Amazing. The word had taken on a whole new dimension. Johanna stood next to Chandra in the shadow of the bronze falcon perched over the school's red brick sign. Johanna looked out over the sea of people covering the last bit of green lawn. Until now, until this, she had no idea of the extent of the support. Even as she had talked with other parents, even as their online group had expanded and grown in number, she hadn't expected this. All three high schools walking out, news cameras filming, parents and supporters filling the parking lot. No, she hadn't imagined it, even while she tried to convince Miya of support she could count on. If only Miya could be standing here in the moment and feel it for herself.

They stood together amid the sounds of young energy and untested power until Chandra, her gaze taking it all in, asked, "How's our girl doing?"

Our girl, Johanna thought. Indeed, she was. "I'm hoping she's not doing what she's done all her life, hitting her forehead against brick walls and trying to pretend the lumps don't hurt."

"And if she is, how are we going to minimize those lumps?"

"Short of knocking down brick walls," Johanna replied, "I don't know."

It was true, grading tests untouched since her suspension might be moot. That she could be fired was real, Miya knew. But she read the answers as if the tests mattered. Because they needed to be finished. Because grading them was one of the few things that still made sense. Because she needed to.

She huddled over the papers on the coffee table until Ty returned from his security round. "All clear," he announced, shutting and locking the door behind him.

"You know," she said, sinking back against the couch cushions, "it's true that waiting is the worst part. You get to a point where you just want to know, good news or bad, you just need to know."

Ty settled into the chair at the end of the couch. "Yeah, either way it gets you out of limbo."

"It's an awful place, not knowing." Resting her head on the back of the couch, she added, "You think of the worst and hope for the best. But you have no control over either."

"Find something good out of it," he said. "Imagine a positive, either way it goes."

She rolled her head to look at him, comfortable in his chair, comfortable in his thoughts on life. "Will it keep me sane?" she asked with a smile.

He offered a soft rumble of a laugh. "Hey, I'm good for suggestions—the rest is on you."

"Okay, looking for a positive—or a lesson." It didn't take long. "There is a lesson here. I see how important it is for me to apologize to Johanna for leaving *her* in limbo. It may take a bit longer, though, to find—" The musical tone of her cell interrupted her search. "Yes, we're fine . . . What channel? . . . Okay, yes," she said, reaching for the remote. "You can't tell me that enough. I love you, too."

The screen lit up with masses of students covering Jefferson High's football field, then switched to the athletic fields at Shepherd High as the reporter explained, "the student body, teachers and staff walking together in protest at all three city high schools." And then the L.J. Patterson Falcon glided across the screen. The camera scanned the crowd of so many familiar faces, stopping at signs that read "Bring Her Back" and "Ms. James Is Patterson's Best."

Ongoing coverage of the other high schools played at the top of the screen while the camera followed the reporter as she interviewed a variety of students and parents.

"This is just so wrong," said a male student. "We deserve good teachers. We should have a say in this."

"Ms. James is my daughter's favorite teacher," said a parent. "I don't understand this."

Another parent added, "We can't afford to lose good teachers over someone's personal or political agenda."

Miya watched the faces, intent and committed, and listened to the chants of support, the calls to bring her back. It took her to a place she never thought she'd be—outside herself, past the expected support of friends and even possible support of a newfound family. It made her breath catch and hold for a moment of disbelief.

And now as she sat staring, Student Council President Carly Simmons spoke to all who were listening. "We're here, marching and making our voices heard, because this is about our education. We want to leave this school with the knowledge and ability to think for ourselves and to be able to make good decisions for our future. To do that, we need good teachers. Teachers like Miya James, who gives her best to her students every day. If this school really cares about us, they'll put Ms. James back in the classroom. And we'll keep walking out until they do."

Ty placed his hands on Miya's shoulders from behind the couch. "There's your positive," he said.

Excited voices, happy voices burst through the door and took over the room. Welcome energy that Miya had missed.

"If you can't be at school," Johanna called out, "then school has come to you—at least part of it."

Miya sprang from her seat on the couch and welcomed the invasion as each of them in turn: Chandra and Charles, Jim, and Tee, greeted her with exuberant hugs.

His excitement clear, Jim asked, "Did you see the coverage?"

"I . . ." Miya looked from one to another, their smiles wide with pride. "I don't know what to say. Yes, I saw it. I . . . never expected that."

"You've underestimated people," Chandra said with a hand on Miya's shoulder, "because you underestimate yourself."

"Uh-*huh*," came Charles' distinctive voice behind her. "You need to stop doing that."

"I *do* know how amazing you all are, believe me. I don't know how to thank you. Whatever the board's decision is, I want you to know how much I appreciate all that you've done." She motioned for them to sit. "And I'm really glad you're here."

On his way to the door, Ty stopped next to Johanna to say quietly, "I expect we're about to get unwanted company. Where's Kayla?"

"Safely at her aunt's. What do you need us to do?"

"Stay inside. I have reinforcements coming. This is typically when things escalate."

"Maybe this wasn't a good idea tonight."

He shook his head. "The crazies have already taken a lot from Miya. Let's not let them take this, too."

"You got it," she returned with a nod, then addressed the group as they settled in the living room. "Don't be surprised if the crazies show up. Ty just asks that we stay inside and let him handle it."

Charles replied, "That's something we're unfortunately getting too used to."

"Carl said that they've ramped up terrorizing the board members," Chandra added.

Jim leaned into the corner of the couch. "Let me guess which ones."

"Ty's entire security company is contracted out," Tee said. "He's been recommending a company in Detroit to help. This is out of control."

Miya, sitting in a chair at the end of the couch, was unusually quiet. Johanna pulled a chair in from the kitchen and sat next to her. "After such an uplifting day," she began, "I hate to ask this, but . . . how much do you think the threats and harassment will affect the board's decision?"

That exact concern had haunted Miya day and night since the complaint was made. A private haunt that evidently wasn't so private. She scanned their faces as they contemplated an answer. She stopped at Tee and tried to read the familiar eyes.

Chandra's voice interrupted her read. "Oh, it will affect it," she began. "They'll either buckle at the knees to make it stop, or it'll make them so angry that they stand on integrity and do what's right for the students and the school system."

"Well, if anger doesn't do it," Tee said, directing her words to Miya, "the outpouring of support today should make that decision a whole lot easier."

Her sincerity was an easy read. She wanted this outcome to be different than her own years ago. She wanted things to be better. But wanting didn't make it so. And the shouts and voices coming from outside were proof of it.

Jim beat everyone to the window, and Charles started toward the door. Johanna took his arm. "Ty told us to stay inside. He's got this."

"It's okay, Charles," Miya added. "I know you want to help, but this is what Ty's trained for."

The voices outside grew louder and more agitated. Chandra stayed at the window with Jim. "This is getting uglier," she said. "No one should have to fear this or put up with it. It's just ugly."

"There's more of them each time," Miya said, joining the others. "I—"

"No," the voice of a coach commanding attention, "there's no 'I.' Get your head where it belongs." Tee stepped closer. "Look at them out there—angry, hateful, screaming in their echo chamber. *They* brought this. *They're* responsible. And if it weren't you, it could be any of us—for whatever insanity they're pushing."

"Amen!" Chandra replied. "You said it before I could. And with wonderful authority, I might add."

Charles stopped his restless pacing at the back of the couch. "What's going on out there, Jim?"

"Ty's men are holding a line, but they're starting to throw things. We should move away from the window."

Johanna's phone pinged. "Ty," she reported. "Yes, stay away from the windows. Police on their way."

Seconds later, shattering glass sent everyone ducking for safety. The blinds pushed inward, containing most of the glass and breaking the flight of the brick that landed on the floor. Both men started for the door.

"No, no," Johanna said, standing her ground in front of the door. "No heroes here."

Even as Miya also moved to guard the door, Charles insisted. "Look, this is getting dangerous."

"Exactly," Miya agreed.

"Some of them are armed, Charles," Johanna added. "Let security and the police handle it."

He placed his hand on Jim's shoulder. "God, I hate this."

Jim stepped back.

The sound of sirens sent both men back to the window. "Yeah, they're scramblin'," Jim reported.

"Not all of them," Charles said. "They're still challenging Ty's men." He shook his head. "But they're getting their asses kicked and eatin' dirt."

"Miya, are you seeing this?" Jim asked, as Miya peered through the sidelight next to Johanna. His voice lifted. "Handcuffs and arrests."

"I am indeed."

Johanna turned from the excitement outside to look at Miya. "And if I had known that this would have brought the first smile that I've seen in a week, I'd have made popcorn."

Smiles and laughter ushered in much-needed relief, and diffused, at least temporarily, the anxiety and anger that had dominated for too long. It allowed leaving the comfort of each other's support easier, and the house unusually still. The broken window had been boarded with plywood, and Ty's security remained in place.

"I don't know about you," Johanna called from the kitchen, "but I could use a drink."

"Make it stronger than a beer and smooth enough to let me sleep tonight, and I'll join you."

"You got it."

Miya turned down the lights, then checked the boarded window and the sidelight to ensure all was quiet outside. Things she already knew, but necessary, nonetheless. The blinds, too, and the curtains over the previously breached window warranted scrutiny.

"Is it possible," she said, as Johanna delivered their drinks to the coffee table and circled an arm around her waist, "that just peeping through the gap in someone's curtains could change the whole course of a life?"

Johanna pressed her lips against Miya's ear and whispered, "Do you hear that? Nothing. Only stillness and the sound of my voice." She drew her fingers gently over Miya's cheek and looked into reflective eyes. "Just us. Isn't that where it started? Where it should be?"

She took Miya's hand. "Come here," she said, lacing their fingers together and leading her to the couch. Johanna eased down onto the pillows and pulled Miya alongside her. "I just want to hold you," she said, closing her arms around her.

The initial tension eased as Miya's body softened. She

snugged into their embrace and breathed a slow, deep breath. *Yes, this is where it should be, where it will be.*

"There's something you don't need to say, because I know," Johanna said against soft, dark curls. "You *are* going to teach, whether it's here or somewhere else. And that's exactly as it should be." Miya shifted to look into her eyes. "I just want you to know that *wherever* that is, we'll be there with you. No matter how long it takes or how far you have to go, we're going with you."

Eerily familiar. The few words from Miya's teenage religious indoctrination that had stayed with her, embedding themselves for unforeseen relevance: "Said Ruth to Naomi, 'Where you go, I will go, and where you stay, I will stay.'" She pressed a kiss to Johanna's cheek and added, 'Where you die, I will die, and there I will be buried.'"

"Yes," Johanna whispered, "like Idgie and Ruth in *Fried Green Tomatoes.*"

Chapter 40

RUN, KATE, RUN

The moment he walked through the door, Kayla knew that Kate was going to like him. Not because Elliott Dean was a genius, which he was, but because he entered her home with homemade banana bread and a half-moon smile that traveled to his eyes.

Kate placed a plate of warm banana bread slices on the dining table and eased into her chair. "So, Kayla tells me that you worked some kind of miracle with Zack's photos and the video."

"I guess it looks miraculous in a way," he replied. "Improbable, unexplainable. But it's real technology, and when it's perfected, it will be one of the most important tools against social media abuse."

"Well, this family is extremely grateful for you and all that you've done to help," Kate said. "To be honest, I didn't think anything could be done. I see our local problems as a microcosm of what's happening nationally, globally. And it doesn't seem like anyone is having much success."

He nodded in agreement. "But all things transformative start in a single place—one person with one idea in a little office or classroom, or someone's basement or dining room," he replied, adding a raise of his eyebrows.

"Yeah, *this* dining room," Kayla said, "is where a lot of problems have been solved—big ones and small ones."

"Then I am in the right dining room," he said.

Kate shot a quick look at Kayla. "Well, we'll see," she said, "since Kayla's been spilling my thoughts 'out of school.'"

"They're good thoughts," he replied. "Les Andrews *is* resigning before his term on the school board is up, so they have thirty days to select someone to finish his term. Then you'd have two months before the election for the new term."

Kate nodded. "I got all the information from their website."

"They didn't put a reason on the school system's website," he continued, "but the school asked me to clean the threats and disgusting comments off the website and trace down who sent them. From what I saw, I don't doubt that he is leaving because of threats to his family. Many of the board members have hired security, and you would probably be dealing with the same kinds of threats and harassment."

"Did Kayla enlist you as the voice of reason?"

"No," Kayla replied quickly. "If everyone is afraid to run, the crazies will just get another seat. And if they gain a majority, they can do a lot of damage. The reason why people like Doug Carter are on the board is because people didn't take school board elections seriously enough."

"If you could, *you'd* run, wouldn't you?" Kate asked.

"I would," she said without hesitation.

"Yep," Elliott said with a grin. "I've seen her in action."

"Then you should know something about your Great-aunt Kate," she said. "I've marched and protested more times than I can remember. I've been tear-gassed, burning my eyes and throat and lungs, just for executing my First Amendment right. I escorted women into abortion clinics through lines of threats. They screamed just inches from our faces that we were murderers, spit on us, and promised that they would make us pay. I fought for women's rights and equality, and it mattered. And now I see an empowered small minority trying to take away what so many fought hard for. Rights that I believe in. So, I've been there before. It doesn't scare me; it makes me angry. The only thing worse than not having those rights, is losing them."

Kayla clenched and pumped her fist, and Elliott's face lit with excitement. "That's a 'yes,'" exclaimed Kayla.

"If it *is* a 'yes,'" Elliott said, "then you're going to need a media manager."

Kate glanced across the table at Kayla and back to Elliott. "And someone convinced you to offer your services?"

He shook his head. "No convincing involved. All I needed to hear was that you were thinking about running. I'll give you the best online presence the school system, heck, this city has ever seen."

"First, I must submit a letter of intent, make it through an interview, and see if the board votes me into that empty seat. *Then* I run."

Elliott tilted his head. "Then let's get to it."

Chapter 41

THE LETTER

"Does Kayla mind staying at Kate's?" Miya asked across the breakfast table.

"Are you kidding? She's loving it," Johnna replied. "She's excited that Kate's going to run for the school board seat. And Kate's taking her for another driving lesson around the neighborhood today."

"Oh, I'm sure she's excited, but are *you* ready for her to drive?"

"Hmm, one minute I'm counting the advantages of her being able to do things on her own, and the next I'm doing the mommy worry."

It was a conversation to start the day, a level just above small talk, filling the space, avoiding until they couldn't. "You really don't need to take the day off work," Miya said, clearing their dishes from the table. "I'll call you right after the meeting."

She felt Johanna press against her back, her arms circle her waist, and her face snuggle into the tender skin of her neck. And softly, the words, "I know."

"But, the smart woman that I am," Miya replied, "I know better than to argue with you." She felt the smile against her neck and turned into an embrace. "However, the decision goes, I'll be fine."

Johanna brushed her lips over Miya's. "I know that, too. But you will *not* come home to an empty house."

"Do you have any idea how much I love you?"

"Mmm," Johanna replied, "I believe I do."

"Hold that thought," she said, returning a kiss. "Ty's waiting for me."

Gerald met her in the parking lot. "The board made their decision yesterday," he began, "but Dr. Evans was smart enough to call your meeting this morning. He didn't tell the board when he was going to meet with you, so," he motioned across the lot free of protesters.

"I can at least appreciate that," she said.

As they made their way to the superintendent's office, Gerald used the time to re-prep her. "Of course, hopefully, the decision is for reinstatement," he said. "But, as I was explaining last week, if the decision goes the other way, we'll have their written response and more than enough reason to take it to court on wrongful termination."

Miya stopped outside the office door and turned to look at him. "Have you seen one go through court before?"

He met her eyes directly. "No, not personally. But the attorney I recommended has been very successful with these cases." He smiled at the mix of relief on Miya's face. "I sat in for a colleague one day," he continued, "and she is a joy to watch."

"Well, that's a joy I am hoping to avoid." She offered her hand and shook his. "Thank you for being here and on the other end of the phone for me."

"I take this responsibility seriously."

"You do indeed," she said, releasing his hand. "Let's get this over with."

Another handshake and a cordial greeting from Dr. Evans did nothing to calm jittery nerves or slow a racing heartbeat. Whatever the decision, there was one thing she knew for sure. It would depend on which they were more willing to deal with—continuing harassment and threats, or a court case.

His eye contact was brief, spotty. Not good, she thought, not good. He tried at a smile. *Is he nervous, uncomfortable? Or is it me?*

"Well," he started, before clearing his throat, "it looks like meeting this morning turned out to be good timing, no protesters."

Yes, yes, I know. Her body tensed, prepared. She stared hard at him; he looked down at the desk. *Just tell me.* He handed her an envelope. Her heart beat hard in her throat. *He won't say it, can't say it. He's making me read it.*

But before she could open it, he said, "Your father brought this to my office and asked me to give it to the board."

"My father?" *What? No, no, no, no. Again. Still.* She dropped the letter, a contaminate, talons that had never let her go. Her breath caught in her throat.

"I read it," he admitted, "and decided not to send it on to the board."

She let go of the breath she'd held, but not the anger. She watched him drop his eyes again. He had done what he could, she decided. *Just tell me you're sorry, tell me you hope the best for me, tell me. It's okay.*

She was about to tell him so when he picked up a second envelope and said, "I'm really pleased that the board found no merit to the complaint."

It took a few seconds for the words to register. And when they did, the relief softened her body against the back of her chair.

"You're the kind of teacher we need in the classroom," he added. "Public education shapes the future of this country, and it's under attack in more ways than ever before." The tenor of his words was resolute. "I've committed myself to public education because I believe in it. Without it, and without committed teachers of whom we ask way too much, we cease to be a nation of the people. We need people who believe it's worth fighting for."

Miya nodded. "Something that this school system and community has shown it's willing to do."

"I admit that I'm surprised," Gerald added, "which goes to show how much *my* faith in humanity has been damaged."

"And you?" Dr. Evans directed to Miya. "How are you doing through all this?"

"Beyond relief? To be honest, I'm tired." She hesitated momentarily, accepted the sincerity in the waiting eyes, and continued. "I'm tired of the hate and the lies. I'm tired of intolerance and unabated anger, and bigotry. Not just here, not just now. I'm tired of the length of it, the depth of it." She shoved the letter into her pocket. "I thought education could change it . . . I hope I still do."

The look on Dr. Evans' face changed, as if the story unfolded before him. He stood and offered his hand across the desk. "I do, too."

Miya shook his hand. "I hope you're not sorry for asking."

"No," he replied. "I'm not sorry at all. I want you in the classroom confirming that we do make a difference."

Johanna wrapped Miya in a full embrace the moment she came

through the door. "*Finally*, oh my God," she exclaimed while Miya swung them in a tight circle. "It's over. That must feel good."

"Yes, it does," Miya replied, and kissed her firmly. "Like a car has been lifted off my chest."

"That good, huh?" She grabbed Miya's arm and pulled her into the room. "Come on, tell me everything."

Miya shed her jacket, dropped onto the couch, and sunk into the pillows. She laid her head back and closed her eyes as Johanna settled next to her. After a long moment, she met the attentive eyes and relayed the entire tension-filled meeting.

"You really misread things that badly?"

Miya nodded. "I did. I was way off."

"Maybe you were overcompensating, overpreparing for the worst. I'm just glad you were wrong." She leaned over into Miya's arms.

"Chandra already has a celebration planned at Thayer's Pub Saturday night," Miya said. "*That* doesn't surprise me. If the decision had gone the other way, she would have changed it into a strategy session."

"There's going to be more than one celebration."

Miya snugged her arms around her. "I'm counting on it." Counting on it, she thought, to nullify for at least a little while what even the decision couldn't change, the old painful dig of her father's talons.

Johanna traced her fingers with feather-like touches over Miya's cheek in the following silence and asked, "What are you thinking about?"

"Oh," she replied softly, "adding this to my list of blessings. It's quite a list when I think of it, with you at the top."

Johanna sat up, offered a tilt of her head, and asked, "*And?*"

She wasn't being contrary or questioning the sincerity; Miya knew her well enough to know that. And she knew what Johanna was asking. "The board's decision allows me to teach, here," Miya replied, "but it doesn't change the intolerance and ignorance that forced it. That's not going away tomorrow. It may never go away."

"Like the letter?"

Miya rose from the pillows. "Yes, like the letter," she said. "Like a judgment with a never-ending sentence. A reminder that trying to be the best person, or friend, or teacher that you can be will never be enough."

"You shouldn't have to feel like that."

Miya rested forward on her knees and nodded. "No one should."

"I know this has taken an emotional toll," Johanna added. "But these people don't know who you are, they don't really care. You were convenient. They used you to further their crazy cause. That's all it was."

Miya ripped the letter from the pocket of her jacket. "This *is* personal," she said, throwing the letter on the coffee table. "This is not letting go of something that you can't change. It's an attempt, even now, to control my life, to force his beliefs on others." After a deep breath and audible exhale, she added, "I'm grateful that Dr. Evans had the consideration not to pass it on to the board. It makes my stomach roil, though, that he read it."

"Do you think it would have made a difference in the board's decision?"

"*He* must have thought so." The nod from Johanna was so slow it was unconvincing. "He didn't say anything more about it, and I didn't ask. And no, I didn't read it—I didn't want to ruin something good."

Johanna reached for the envelope. "Can *I* read it?"

"Why would you want to?"

"To learn more about what has haunted you for so long."

"I won't stop you," Miya said with a wave of her hand. "But it'll only ruin a nice evening, and you'll need a bottle of Tums."

Despite the warning, Johanna opened the letter and began reading.

"I'm going to get a drink," Miya said, rising and heading to the kitchen.

When she returned with a drink in her hand and placed one on the coffee table, Johanna reached for her hand. "You need to sit down here and listen," she said.

Miya sat reluctantly. "You may be a glutton, but I don't want to hear it."

Undeterred, Johanna began:

> Dear L.J. Patterson School Board,
>
> I'm writing you today regarding teacher Miya James. You are about to make a decision that will affect her career and her life. It is a very important decision. I know that because I made decisions that affected her life years ago. As her father and a Christian man, I have been seeking atonement for those decisions ever since.

Miya held her glass in both hands, leaned forward over her knees, bowed her head, and listened.

> I never questioned the Church doctrine that I was raised under. I accepted its definition of good and evil and the right to judge. It wasn't until I lost the love and respect of my daughter and nearly ruined my marriage that I understood that I

wasn't following the teachings of
Jesus. I thought love was discipline,
strictly adhering to Church doctrine,
guiding my family on a Godly path.
I was wrong. Yet, despite my failings
as a father, Miya has grown into a
loving, caring woman and a teacher
dedicated to the education and
welfare of her students.

Please don't allow the power of
ignorance and intolerance to hurt
her again. I pray that your integrity
and sense of justice will do for Miya
what I failed to do.

Sincerely,

Donald James

The silence that followed felt as though the wind had
stopped. The rush of it, always there, sometimes blowing,
sometimes swirling, always surrounding it all. Gone now, a hush
in its place. She pressed her forehead against Johanna's and held
her there, in the silence. "Thank you," she whispered.

Johanna lifted her head, brushed a tender kiss over Miya's
lips and asked, "A phone call might be in order? It's up to you
now."

The knowing, the love in Johanna's eyes held her safely in
the moment. New words, new thoughts, unexpected, untested,
and needing time. "But this is not for tonight," she said, running
fingertips through the soft brown hair over Johanna's ear.
"Tonight is for us."

Acknowledgments

I have understood it for as long as I can remember, and I've said it many times over the years—writing is my therapy.

For me I attempt to grasp what seems uncontrollable, to solve the unsolvable. Writing is my attempt to take events and situations that are too large, narrow them down, make them personal, and place them in the purview of my characters. Through them, I have hope, encouragement, and the strength to get through what at times seems impossible.

There are times, though, when the world around us is so unsettling and emotionally fraught that writing is difficult at best. Solidary, concentrated time to write is a struggle, both physically and mentally, and the need for positivity, the safety of structure, and for hopeful perspective, is undeniable. Yet, that is the time that I feel most blessed—with people who unselfishly make my world better and make writing possible. Enter Kelly Smith. Sometimes words are inadequate to thank her for being there when she is most needed, as a friend and as an editor. Thank you for bringing me through.

And I must give special thanks all around to my Bywater Books family for all they do, and did, to make this book possible. Our calm Zen, Salem West, magically makes the schedule work.

Ann McMan, cover artist extraordinaire, makes us beautiful. Editors Fay Jacobs and Nancy Squires gently suggest, correct, and make our stories better. Then, after all the eyes have scrutinized, edited, and rewritten, Carleen Spry finds the mistakes we all missed. And Christel Cogneau, the newest member of our family, finds ways every day to make us smarter, stronger, and more efficient. Thank you all so very much!

About the Author

Marianne K. Martin is the author of thirteen novels. She is a five-time Lambda Literary Award finalist and has taken home one Goldie and two Independent Publisher (IPPY) Awards. She has been honored with the GCLS Trailblazer Award and the Alice B. Medal, and she has been inducted into the Saints & Sinners Literary Festival Hall of Fame. Marianne is a retired teacher and coach and is a founding partner of Bywater Books. Her latest project is the documentary, *In Her Words: 20th Century Lesbian Fiction*, chronicling the impact of lesbian fiction from the 1920s to 2000—the film was awarded the Publishing Triangle Leadership Award in 2020.

Bywater Books believes that all people have the right to read or not read what they want—and that we are all entitled to make those choices ourselves. But to ensure these freedoms, books and information must remain accessible. Any effort to eliminate or restrict these rights stands in opposition to freedom of choice.

Please join us by opposing book bans and censorship of the LGBTQ+ and BIPOC communities.

At Bywater Books, we are all stories.

For more information about Bywater Books, our authors, and our titles, please visit our website.

https://bywaterbooks.com

www.ingramcontent.com/pod-product-compliance
Lightning Source LLC
Chambersburg PA
CBHW020352110726
47899CB00006B/1699